SINS OF THE MIND

Red River Series

L.J. GARLAND

and

DEBBIE GOULD

℃ℬ

Decadent Publishing Company
www.decadentpublishing.com

This book is a work of fiction. Names, characters, places, and incidents are the products of the author's imagination or used fictitiously. Any resemblance to actual events, locales or persons, living or dead, is entirely coincidental.

Published by Decadent Publishing Company
www.decadentpublishing.com

Printed in the United States of America

Also by L.J. Garland

Dead or Alive
A 1Night Stand Story

Also by Debbie Gould

Second Chance
A 1Night Stand Story

"I have loved to the point of madness;
that which is called madness,
that which to me, is the only sensible way to love."
— Francois Sagan

~DEDICATION~

To the girl across the pond,
Who read our story and never yawned.
One talented chick,
Who told us real quick,
Twas a tale of which she was fond.

Chapter One

*D*etective Ethan Parker stepped from his Chevy Tahoe, ice-cold air biting every inch of unprotected skin. He jammed his hands into the pockets of his police jacket and glanced around, a familiar trepidation heavy in his gut. Inside the ordinary, ranch-style house, a brutal murder had been committed.

"You're not going to believe this one, Parker." Steve Gordon, the Crime Scene Unit's photographer, scurried across the yard. The wiry guy jerked his thumb over his shoulder, indicating the residence behind him. "Whoever did this is one sick puppy."

Ethan scanned the yard and the dense woods encroaching on the property. Red River was a quiet town, only four houses out this way. The likelihood of any witnesses was slim, but hey, they might get lucky. He made a mental note to have the officers make a door-to-door sweep, questioning the neighbors.

The photographer met him halfway to the concrete walkway leading to the porch and turned to walk with him, matching his stride. "I mean, I've seen a lot of sick shit, but this—"

"Montgomery here yet?" he cut in, not wanting to endure Steve's typical blow-by-blow commentary.

"Yeah. Already inside. Got here about five minutes ago," Steve said. They paused on the porch, and he gestured toward the door. "He's in the bedroom assessing the carnage. Down the hall and to the left. I'm gonna grab some stuff from the van. I'll be right back in."

The photographer's feet pounded down the wooden steps, and Ethan shook his head. Steve was all right, at least as far as he was concerned. The guy just didn't know when to shut his mouth. Took damn detailed pictures, though.

Donning protective covering for his shoes, Ethan entered the house. Warmth enveloped him, taking the numbing sting where the cold had bitten his nose. He scanned the living room on his way to the hallway. The place looked lived-in but clean—a couch, matching love seat, recliner, two end tables, and against the wall of windows, a huge flat-panel TV.

Against an adjacent wall sat an entertainment center with a good-sized stereo system. DVDs and CDs neatly lined the shelves. The entire room was crisp, efficient, and nothing appeared to be out of place, which ruled out robbery as a motive.

As he headed down the hallway, his new partner—of three whole weeks—exited the bedroom, his face a little pale. Grant Montgomery had just earned his detective shield one month earlier, and Ethan was the lucky sonofabitch who got to break him in.

Having been a detective for ten years, he, for one reason or another, had been without a partner for the last two. But though he'd much rather have remained on his own, change had been inevitable.

The new guy paused in the doorway and swiped a bead of sweat from his forehead. Ethan sighed. For now, Montgomery was all his.

"Hey. So, who do we have?" he asked Montgomery before entering the bedroom. *Might as well let the kid strut his stuff.*

Glancing up, recognition flashed in Montgomery's eyes, and he straightened, clearing his throat. "Thirty-five-year-old white male by the name of Judson Roberts. Employed by Southern Vermont Tech as a math professor. Only child, parents both deceased. No next of kin really but does have a fiancée by the name of Karen Talbert. Said fiancée found him this morning when she showed up for their daily run."

"Well, shit. I'm impressed. You've been here five minutes and got all that?"

"Not quite. Mr. Roberts was a friend of the family. Seven years ago he was engaged to my sister." He pointed into the bedroom. "He was a good guy, Ethan. Sure as hell didn't deserve that."

"Shit, man. I'm sorry." Ethan shook his head. "You gonna be okay?"

"Yeah. I just need a minute of fresh air."

"Sure. I'll meet you back outside in a few. Why don't you get a couple officers started on interviewing the neighbors?"

"Sure." Montgomery skirted past him in the narrow hallway.

"Hey, by the way, where is the fiancée now?"

"In Officer Moore's squad car. She phoned 911. Officers Moore and Hanson were first on the scene. Apparently Ms. Talbert was near hysteria, and Officer Moore had her sit in the squad car. She's with her, waiting for orders, but thinks the woman may need a trip to the Emergency Department. She's pretty out of it." With a nod, he turned to walk out of the house.

He shook his head again. Not for the first time, he told himself he was in the wrong damn business. No matter how hard he tried, things always had a way of turning personal. Not every case, but enough so that a tiny part of him died every damned day.

He snorted. The shrinks would have a field day with him, but he just couldn't seem to compartmentalize everything. Couldn't keep his personal life and job separate. Which might be the reason he didn't have a personal life.

Taking a deep breath, he walked into the bedroom and froze. The amount of blood in the room staggered him. It covered the two closest walls so thick it appeared painted on. Drenched the carpet in sticky pools. Streaked the lamp and nightstand. God, he couldn't even make out the pattern on the bedspread beneath the victim who lay spread-eagled, his arms and legs tied to the four bed posts.

The CSU's forensic investigator, Gary Black, looked up from

the body. "Hey, Ethan. Sorry to see you pulled this case. It's one of the nastiest I've ever documented."

Ethan stepped further into the room and swallowed the lump in his throat. Damn. He'd never seen anything like what lay before him now, not even in his worst nightmares.

This poor man had died a traumatic, humiliating death. Good Christ. What kind of psycho were they searching for?

"Can't say I'm too thrilled with being here either, Gary. Anything you can tell yet?"

The forensic investigator paused while Ethan's new partner and the CSU photographer entered the room. Though his face remained waxy, it seemed Montgomery had recovered enough to return. He positioned himself near the back wall, a respectful distance from the victim. In contrast, Steve yanked out his digital 35mm camera and started snapping pictures.

"Well, let's see," Gary said. "I can't say anything for sure till I get him back to the lab, but my best guess is he bled out. Both femoral arteries have been cut as well as the left carotid artery. But most of the injuries occurred before those cuts were made." He shook his head as he studied the body.

"Across his chest, you can see something was carved into his skin. I'll be able to tell you what it says after I get him cleaned up. Right now, there's just too much blood." Gary indicated the victim's head. "Both eyes were removed from their sockets—I'd say by a small surgical blade that was probably used to carve the vic's chest as well. There's not a lot of damage, so the killer must have known what he was doing. However," he said, and gestured lower on the body, "the most disturbing injury is to the penis. Two incisions were made down the length—one on top, one on the bottom—effectively slicing it in half."

Ethan's stomach rolled, and bile rose in his throat. Unfucking-believable. "Are you telling me all this happened while this man was still alive?"

"Yeah." Gary motioned toward the walls and bed. "There's too much blood for it to have happened post mortem."

Holy shit! The guy had been tortured. What transpired here

made water-boarding look like a day at the park. "Had to be a lot of hate on the killer's part. What the hell kind of animal do we have out there?"

"One that you two detectives need to get off the street before he decides to have another play date," Gary murmured as he collected evidence. "Now, if you ladies don't mind leaving me and this poor guy alone, I'll get to work helping you with that."

"Have at it. Get me the reports on any preliminaries ASAP." He glanced around at the carnage. "I hope I'm wrong, but something tells me we haven't heard the last from this guy."

"Don't get pushy, Ethan. You know this stuff takes time to process." Gary swiped the blood spray on the walls with cotton tipped applicators. "DNA alone will take weeks."

"It's not my first day on the job, Gary. I know this. Just get me what you can."

He and Gary had been friends for years, but the guy got touchy if he thought you were telling him how to do his job.

Ethan left the room and exited the house with Grant on his heels. Outside, he found the patrol car holding Karen Talbert. Time to talk to her.

He turned to Grant. "So how long were these two engaged?"

"They'd been dating about three years. I don't know how long they'd been engaged, though. Jud was closer to my sister than me. I didn't keep up much with him after they split."

"Okay. Well, why don't I do the questioning? If there's anything that doesn't sound right, go ahead and jump in."

At the patrol car, Officer Hanson leaned against the back fender in a spotlight of sunshine, his hands jammed into the pockets of his winter-weight police jacket. His partner, Officer Moore, sat cozy in the backseat of the idling vehicle, consoling the woman. As Ethan and Grant approached, Hanson pushed off the car and trudged toward them.

"Man, I thought you guys would never get out here. Hysterical females make me crazy. You'd think she was the one in there all cut to pieces." Smoky puffs of air emanated from his mouth with each word. He nodded toward the car and said with a sneer, "I tell ya, it's the first damn time I've ever been glad to have a woman for a partner. They're not good for too much, but they're great dealing with the waterworks."

Ethan bristled at the officer's words. The old school mentality that women didn't belong on the job was intolerable, and if anyone fell into the old school category, it was Hanson. The guy had been reprimanded on more than one occasion for improper conduct toward female officers. In Ethan's opinion, Hanson's macho attitude and degradation of females in general explained why he'd never advanced in rank. Thank God he was nearing retirement.

He hardened his gaze on the older cop and got up in his face. "Sorry to have inconvenienced you, Officer Hanson. You know how these pesky little murder investigations can go. Are we keeping you from the fucking donut shop? Can you get any further out of line than you already have?" He stood toe-to-toe with the now wide-eyed officer. "Just what is your problem with women, Officer Hanson? Because if you have a problem with your partner, you can be sure I will mention your attitude to the captain. He'd be happy to have your ass reassigned."

Grant placed his hand on Ethan's arm. Reluctantly, he backed off and gave Hanson one last glare then continued on to the patrol car. Damned decrepit sonofabitch.

When they approached the car, Officer Moore slid out, blocking the door, and spoke quietly. "She's a real mess. She's been alternating between crying and staring blankly at the house. The shaking hasn't stopped either. I think when you're done with her here, she needs to go to the hospital and be treated for shock."

"That's fine. Why don't you call the squad while we talk to her?" He looked around the slim officer, catching a glimpse at the fiancée. "Has she said anything?"

"No, not really." Officer Moore shoved her hands into her jacket pockets and moved away from the car door. Brows knitted, she met his gaze. "She just keeps repeating the vic's name and looking at the house like she expects him to walk out the front door at any moment."

"Okay, thanks for sitting with her. In her condition, I doubt this will take long." He paused then turned back to the young officer. "Meant to ask, how you're coming along for the detective's exam?"

She nodded. "Studying hard, sir."

"Good." He reached for the car's rear door handle. "When's the big day?"

"March, sir."

"That soon? You going to ace it?"

"Going to do my best." She met his gaze. "You've been an inspiration, Detective Parker." Cheeks flushing, she looked away and took several steps backward. "Thanks for asking, sir."

Officer Moore turned and strode toward the house. He stared after her. An inspiration, huh? With a shake of his head, he opened the door and folded himself into the back of the patrol car.

Pulling out his small note pad, he angled toward the grief-stricken woman. Shoulder-length blonde hair hung loose around her pale face, framing her glazed eyes, red and swollen from crying. She rocked back and forth.

"Ms. Talbert, I'm Detective Parker." He paused until she turned her head toward him. "I'm sorry for your loss, but I need to ask you a few questions."

She stared at him, a lost look in her eyes. "He's dead, isn't he?"

That she could ask such a question after seeing him proved to Ethan she was in shock.

"Yes, ma'am, he is." He waited for another round of sobs to subside and then continued. "What time did you find him?"

"I...I always get here at six a.m. We run five miles every morning before work."

"And what happened when you got here this morning?"

She twisted her hands in her lap and shook her head. "I let myself in as I normally do and called out to him. Usually, he's in the kitchen getting our coffee ready, but he didn't answer. So I thought maybe he was in the bathroom. I...I smelled it before I saw him. Oh, God, that *smell*." She covered her mouth, and her whole body shook.

Ethan gave her a moment. "Was the door always unlocked for you, or do you have a key?"

"I have a key, but he always unlocks it for me when he gets up in the morning."

"Was it unlocked this morning?"

She nodded, and a sigh shuddered through her. "Yes."

"Did you see anything out of the ordinary, anything out of place?"

"No, nothing."

"Had he been worried about anything lately? Anyone threatening him?"

"Oh, God, no. Everyone loved him. He got along with everyone." She looked at him, her gaze wide and glassy. "Who would do such a horrible thing to him? Why, why did this happen?"

"That's what we're going to find out." Ethan glanced down at his notepad then back at the distraught woman next to him. He ground his molars and ignored the sympathetic feelings pushing around in his gut. Judson Roberts' murder had been bloody and personal. That made Karen Talbert a suspect in an ongoing investigation. Until her alibi checked out, he needed to remain focused. Otherwise, he might miss something. "Can you tell me where you were last night until you got here this morning?"

"Here. We had dinner here and watched a movie. I left about ten and went home to bed." She raised her eyebrows and tilted her head. "You can't think I did...that to him?"

"I'm sorry. It's just a question we need to ask. The quicker we can rule you out, the closer we get to finding the person who did this. Can anyone verify you were home?"

"Yes, my roommate." She twisted her diamond engagement ring around her finger while she spoke. "We sat up for half an hour talking about the wedding then I went to bed. She works as a nurse eleven-to-seven but had last night off, so she was up all night. You can check with her."

"Again, Karen, I apologize. It's all part of the process. That's all I need for now." He pulled his card out of his pocket and handed it to her. "If you can think of anything else, anything at all, please call me." He glanced out the window. "The rescue squad is here. You've had an awful shock and need to go to the Emergency Department. Is there someone you can call from the hospital to pick you up?"

"Yes, my roommate."

Ethan moved to get out of the car, but Karen grabbed his arm. "You will find the person that did this. Won't you?"

"I'm going to do everything in my power, ma'am."

She nodded, and he slid out of the car.

Motioning for Officer Moore, Ethan turned to Grant. "Okay, let's head back to the station. We need to start researching the victim and his last movements."

"Do you mind if I go home first? I need to tell my sister about Jud before she hears it somewhere else." He glanced at the house. "Even though they broke off their engagement years ago, they remained good friends. This will upset Abby a lot, and I'd like to be there for her."

"Yeah sure. Just meet up with me when you're done." He shifted his gaze to Officer Moore. "She's ready to go. Call her roommate to pick her up at the hospital. Also, please let Ms. Talbert know she needs to come down to the station tomorrow and sign a formal statement."

"Yes, sir."

He gave her a curt nod. She'd done a damn fine job handling the witness. Shifting his gaze to Officer Hanson, he said, "Oh, and Hanson, come see me at the end of your shift, please."

Chapter Two

*A*bigail Montgomery's stomach knotted tighter. She busied herself in the kitchen, drying dishes, wiping down counters. Earlier this morning, her brother Grant had called and said there was something he needed to tell her. Whatever he had to say, it probably wasn't good.

At the sound of the front door opening, Abigail tensed. She laid the dishtowel on the counter. Without looking at her, her brother shuffled into the kitchen, scraping the wrought iron chair over the tiled floor as he sat at the small dinette table. The late morning sun streamed through the window, illuminating the cozy breakfast nook, creating the illusion of comfort. Still wearing his shoulder holster, his posture stiff, and his large hands folded atop the petite tiled table, he appeared anything but comfortable.

Abigail took a deep breath and plastered a cheerful expression on her face. She would smile while she could because his drawn brows and grim mouth told her there would be no laughter tonight. Maybe not even for days.

"I made a fresh pot of coffee." She crossed to the counter, placing her palm on the cool granite. "I could get you some if you'd like."

"That would be nice, Abby." He stared at his hands, and the muscle in his jaw twitched while he ground his teeth.

Dread bloomed deep in her chest. She swallowed and focused on getting the coffee. Retrieving two mugs from the cabinet, she filled each close to the rim. After returning the pot to the coffeemaker, she turned to cross to the table with a steaming cup in each hand. As she neared, Grant looked up, his brown eyes dark with worry and grief.

"He's dead, Abby."

She paused mid-stride, and her fingers tightened around the thin handles on the mugs. "Who?"

"Jud." He swallowed, looked away. "Jud Roberts is dead."

"Oh, my God." She'd expected bad news—something sad or appalling—but the death of the man she'd once been engaged to had never entered her thoughts. The dread already swimming within her took hold and morphed into an awful beast that ate her from the inside out. Tendrils of ice snaked through her body, wrapped around her bones, squeezed her lungs.

She trembled, and one cup slipped from her grasp, crashing to the floor. Ceramic and hot coffee exploded in all directions. Abby jolted, and steaming liquid sloshed over her other hand. The second mug plummeted to the tile, impacting with a sharp crack.

Staggering back, she glanced down. The coffee had stained her shoes, splashed against her pants. Broken stoneware littered a muddled pool of brown liquid that reflected the sun streaming through the window. Raising her head, she gazed at her brother, who stared with wide eyes at the disaster she'd created.

"I'll get a broom." Without waiting for his reply, she spun and fled to the garage. Broom and dustpan in hand, she hurried back to the kitchen and swept up the broken mugs.

"Abby." Grant came to her side, took the broom from her hands, and pulled her into his arms. "I am so sorry. I know how much he meant to you."

"Oh, God." Sobs wracked her body, and hot tears poured down her checks. Jud was dead. Oh, my God. Dead. How could that be?

Jesus, just yesterday they'd met for lunch, talked about his upcoming wedding this spring. He'd been nervous about the big day but excited about getting married. He'd asked her about her plans for the future, to which she'd admitted being ready to move forward with her life. He'd smiled, warm and sweet.

Her best friend. Gone forever.

Her brother arms tightened around her while she wept against his shoulder. "I am just so sorry, Abs."

"W-what happened?"

"He was murdered." He swallowed. "I can't go into the details."

She pushed back from him, swiping a hand over her damp cheek. "I just...I just can't believe...."

He nodded then gestured to the table. "Here, sit down."

Circumventing the worst of the broken cups and coffee, she eased down into a chair in the sunny little nook. Grant grabbed the broom, swept up the remaining debris, and dumped it into the garbage. A few minutes later, he sat opposite her and pushed a glass of water across the table.

She sighed, fresh tears threatening behind her lids. She wrapped her fingers around the glass and drank the cool water. Just a couple of sips to appease him. Any more and she worried she might hurl.

"What about Karen?" A tremor ran through her hand, and when she set her drink down, the glass clinked against the tiled tabletop. "Does she know yet?"

His lips thinned. "She found him."

"Oh, God." Abby closed her eyes and tried not to imagine what Karen had unknowingly walked in on. And when she realized how thankful she was that her own memories of Jud would remain untarnished, guilt shrouded her heart. "How horrible that must have been for her."

"For you, too, Abs." He balled his hands into fists on top of the table. "You and Jud were engaged. I know it was years ago, but he meant a lot to you, too."

Her heart ached, as though an ice-cold knife had plunged into her chest. "That was a long time ago. Before."

"I know." He stared at his hands. "Before the incident."

The mention of what happened seven years ago triggered the sensation of a million ants crawling over every inch of her skin and the overwhelming need to take a shower and scrub them off. "Jud deserved better."

Grant shifted in his chair, his shoulder holster creaking with the movement. A shrill beeping erupted from his cell phone, and Abby jumped, nearly knocking her water over.

He punched a button, and held the phone to his ear. "Montgomery." He bounced his knee while he listened, his gaze on the puddle of coffee waiting to be mopped up. "Right. I'll be there in ten." Ending the call, he shoved the cell in the holster at his waist and rose from the chair. "I have to go."

"Everything okay?" She followed him to the door.

"Ethan needs me back at the station house." He shrugged on his jacket and glanced at her. "Parker questioned Karen Talbert at the scene, so it's probably just more paperwork."

"Karen's been questioned already?" Anger tore through her. "Hasn't she been through enough? She just found her fiancé murdered, and your partner felt the need to grill her?"

Grant retrieved his keys from a rack next to the door, and they jingled against his palm. "You know the drill." He gave her a meaningful look. "Everyone's a suspect."

She snorted. "You mean everyone close to the deceased is a suspect." She folded her arms over her chest, a mixture of anger and grief swirling through her. "I pray she has a solid alibi like we did when Uncle Marty was murdered. All those questions...right after. It was horrible."

He squeezed her shoulder, and she looked up at him.

"She didn't do it." Abby shook her head. "She loved Jud."

"We'll see." He strode out onto the porch. "Lock up. I'll call you later."

He climbed into his black Ford F-150 and, with a final wave, drove away.

Abby closed the door and grabbed the mop from the garage. Returning to the kitchen, she began the mundane task of sopping up the coffee. Halfway through she paused and stared out the picture window in the breakfast nook. So much tragedy in her life. Her parents. Her uncle. Herself. A shiver coursed through her, and tears sprang unbidden to her eyes. And now, Jud. Sweet, easy-going Jud.

Who would want to kill him?

Ê

Ethan hung up the phone and glanced back at the computer. He'd have to tell the chief what he'd dug up, and that was one conversation he was not looking forward to. He pushed his chair back from the desk and strode to Chief Hague's office while dread tied knots the size of baseballs in his gut.

At his knock, the chief looked up from his paperwork and motioned him in.

He took a seat in one of the beat-up, brown leather chairs. "Just need to update you on the murder case from this morning."

"Damn, you're quick if you've got an update for me already." Chief Hague shuffled his papers to the side and gave Ethan his full attention. His graying hair and craggy face made him appear much older than his fifty-one years.

"Not so much an update in the investigation, but more of what might be considered a conflict of interest." He clenched his jaw and glanced out the window. Shit. He didn't want to open this can of worms.

The chief cocked an eyebrow. "Go on."

"You remember all the bullshit with my brother, right? I'd just tested for detective when he was arrested."

"I remember." Hague rubbed a hand over his jaw. "He's your half-brother, right?"

"Yeah. Different fathers." He cringed inwardly. Michael's actions had been horrendous. His arrest and subsequent conviction had torn their family apart, not to mention almost ruined his career.

"What's he got to do with this? He's still in jail, right?"

"Yeah, he's still there. But you've partnered me with Grant

Montgomery," he said. "Did you realize that his sister was the woman my brother raped?"

"Hell, no." The man sat up straight, eyes wide. "I didn't know that. Montgomery never said a word."

"Well, he may not know. Michael and I have different last names. And if he doesn't know, I'm sure as hell not going to tell him." Ethan had never given his new partner's last name a second thought. Montgomery was a common name. But then Grant had said his sister's name—Abigail Montgomery—and something in the deep recesses of his brain had clicked. Sixty seconds on the computer and the truth had stared him in the face. The one thing he wished he'd been able to bury forever. Damn, but karma was a bitch. "The problem is, Montgomery's sister used to be engaged to this morning's victim. And was still a very good friend. I'm going to have to question her."

The chief stood and rounded his desk. He leaned against the corner and stared at Ethan, his weathered brow creasing with concern. "You do realize the fine line you're walking here. Damn it, you're my best detective. I need you on this one."

"I don't think it has to be a problem. If neither Grant nor his sister know who I am, what's the big deal?" He needed to question Abby. "This is just an informal interview to get some background info on the victim and make sure she has an alibi. If all goes well and she has nothing to do with it, there is no conflict. I don't see any need to recuse myself at this point. If that changes, you'll be the first to know."

"Fine. Record the session." The chief gave him a stern look. "If at any point in the questioning it looks like she has no alibi and has means and motive, you end the interview and report back to me immediately." He moved back behind his desk and dropped into his chair. Straightening some paperwork, he said, "I also assume you've considered the fact that Montgomery cannot do any of the questioning."

"I have." Now, if he could only make that point clear to Grant. Ethan rose to leave. "I'll keep you up to date."

"Don't fuck this up, Parker."

Chapter Three

*E*than returned to his desk and found his partner leaning against the wall, waiting for him. Hague's words rung in his ears. *Don't fuck this up, Parker.* Yeah, no pressure.

"Hey." He shoved his hands into his pockets, tried to appear relaxed and not like he'd just discussed his half-brother's attack on his new partner's sister with the chief. Hell. Could things get more screwed up? "How'd things go with your sister?"

Grant shrugged. "She was pretty upset."

"That sucks for her. I'm sorry she had to go through that." He glanced at his desk, took a breath, then looked back at his partner and said the crappy words his job required him to say. "Unfortunately, she's going to have to go through a little more before she can put this behind her."

Grant furrowed his brow and shifted from one leg to the other. "What are you talking about?"

"She knew the victim, she was close to him." He shrugged, tried not to make it a big deal. "I need to question her."

"You can't think she's a suspect." Grant's volume increased a notch, and his tone became edgy. "My sister could never do something like that to someone. Besides, did you see what that guy went through? It was brutal. No woman did that."

Ethan walked around to his desk, slipped some reports into

a manila folder then glanced at Montgomery. The guy wasn't thinking like a detective at the moment, but like a brother. "Basic Investigation 101. Everyone is a suspect until we can rule them out. Whether I think she's a suspect or not makes no difference. She can give us invaluable information this case needs. You know that."

"Doesn't mean I have to like it." He pushed away from the wall. "I'm going with you."

"That's fine." He pointed his finger at Grant, gave him a firm stare. "But you cannot be part of this interview. You can be present only as a family member, there to add your support. But in no way can you question her or prompt her. Is that going to be a problem for you?" Giving his partner a moment to mull over his limitations, Ethan picked up his notepad and grabbed his jacket off the back of his chair. Facing Grant, he lifted his brows, awaiting his answer.

His jaw clenched. "No, it won't be a problem," he said in a calm voice. "Just don't do your bad cop act. She's been through a lot."

"I'm not a complete ass. Let's go."

℞

Ethan drove over the slush-filled roads while Grant sat stiff and silent in the passenger seat, staring out the window. No easy conversation, no speculations about their current case. The tension inside the police-issued Chevy lay thick like early spring molasses.

He ground his molars. What past indiscretion had he committed for fate to partner him with this man? Yeah, maybe he'd raised a little hell over the years, no doubt broken a few hearts, and home and hearth wasn't in his vocabulary. But this seemed more like some kind of cosmic punishment.

Then there was his half-brother, Michael. Trouble followed that guy like a puppy dog. He was steeped in shit. Constantly. While they were growing up, Ethan had gotten him out of more jams than he cared to remember.

And then there'd been that final call.

"E, man I need your help." Michael's voice had wavered over the line, indicating how worried he was about his current dilemma.

He'd sighed. "What is it this time, Mikey?"

"They got me on some kinda trumped-up charges." He snorted. "Said I attacked some girl."

"Oh, my God!" His stomach churned. "What did you do?"

"Nothing, E. I swear." He inhaled then coughed. "It's all lies. I didn't do it."

Then Michael had gotten quiet, and Ethan had known it was bad.

"What else, Mikey? That can't be it." He ran a hand through his hair.

"Nothing."

"Tell me."

The silence on the phone had stretched out for over thirty seconds, and he'd wondered if their connection had ended.

"Rape."

Bile had risen in Ethan's throat. He couldn't speak.

"E. You still there?"

"Yeah."

"You gotta help me." He'd cleared his throat. "I didn't do it."

Except he had done it. The evidence had been so incontrovertible that he hadn't been able to save Michael from jail. Hadn't wanted to. Didn't even attend a single day of the trial.

He shook his head as he turned the Tahoe onto the snow-packed driveway. Guilt pushed down on his shoulders, weighing heavier the closer they drew to the large, older white farmhouse. His half-brother's transgressions had reared their godforsaken head in Ethan's life once again.

He stopped the SUV, slung the strap of the bag with the recording equipment over his shoulder, and stepped out into the cold, mid-morning air. Turning up his coat collar, he surveyed the area. Snow skirted robust elms and maples, their naked, craggy branches reaching toward the icy blue sky. Horses roamed in a field to their left, and several white barns stood sentry beyond the house. The scene appeared warm and comforting, straight out of a Norman Rockwell painting.

"So you live here with your sister?"

"Yeah." Grant shoved his hands in his jacket pockets, stared out over the field. "Our parents died years ago, and the house was left to both of us. Since neither of us had a significant other at the time, we decided to share the place. It's where we grew up, what we consider home. Till one of us decides to get married anyway."

"Looks like a really nice place."

"Thanks."

He followed his partner through dapples of sunlight as they trudged up the slate walk. Grant unlocked the door and let them both in. The aroma of a roast hit Ethan the moment he entered the foyer. He inhaled the heavenly scents and regretted his confirmed bachelorhood included very few home-cooked meals. Walking through the door after a long day to smells like this could almost change a man's mind about things.

Almost.

Grant led him into a cozy living room and gestured toward the couch that faced an open fireplace. Flames crackled, and soothing warmth radiated from the fire. A homemade meal, a well-stacked fire in the hearth? Oh, yeah. He could get used to this. All he'd add was a tumbler of brandy and a gorgeous woman.

"I'll go find my sister."

After shrugging off his jacket, Ethan busied himself setting up the recording equipment. Simplistic in design, it only took a few minutes to position the camera. He sank into the immense pillows situated on the couch and waited for the siblings to return.

In all honesty, he believed Grant was right. The murder of Judson Roberts had been committed by a male, not a female.

But experience had taught him that just because something seemed out of the realm of possibility didn't mean it couldn't happen.

"Detective Parker?"

He pulled himself from the couch and turned toward the doorway. Good Lord. Now all he needed was that tumbler of brandy. Before him stood one of the most beautiful women he'd had the fortune to lay his eyes upon. His gaze swept over the jeans and teal T-shirt that snugged over her lean curves. Long waves of thick, dark blonde hair graced her head and flowed over her shoulders, framing crystal ice-blue eyes. *Wow!*

He tripped over the coffee table, caught himself, and stumbled over to greet her. Great professional first impression. Embarrassed by his unexpected ineptness, he grimaced while his face burned. "Just call me Detective Klutz. You must be Abigail."

"It's Abby." Expressionless and distant, she motioned to the couch. "Please have a seat."

Okay, that went well. "Thank you." Ethan situated himself on the edge of the plush sofa. Leaning forward, he propped his forearms on his knees and clasped his hands. He stared into her captivating eyes for a long moment then took a breath. "I assume your brother told you why I'm here."

"Yes, he did." She lowered into the rocker next to the couch, her narrowed gaze entrancing him. "I must say, you don't waste any time. Do you, Detective? First, you interrogate poor Karen at the scene, and now, not even a day later, you're here in my home." She jabbed a long finger toward the picture window behind him. "Why aren't you out there, finding the person who killed Jud?"

"That's a bit easier said than done. Unless you've got the guy holding the smoking gun over the victim, there's a lot of work to be done. That includes interviewing friends and acquaintances. I realize this may not be the best time for you, but the sooner we get going on this investigation while the evidence is still fresh, the sooner we get some leads."

She folded her arms across her chest and rocked the chair

back and forth. "What is it you need from me?"

"I need to ask you some questions." He waved his hand toward the camcorder. "For documentation purposes, I need to record this."

Her gaze flicked to the camera, and she gave a slight nod.

Ethan tapped the record button and looked over at Abby. Smudges beneath her eyes spoke of sleepless nights, and her thinned lips told him she was losing patience with his approach to locating Judson's killer.

"For the record, please state your name."

She glared at the camera. "Abigail Peyton Montgomery."

Easing onto the couch, he took out his note pad. "Is your brother joining us?"

She stopped rocking, but her arms remained folded. "He'll be here in a few minutes. I'm a big girl, Detective. I can manage just fine without him."

He clamped his teeth. Belligerent didn't begin to describe her. The girl had an attitude a mile wide. Then again, could he blame her? "How well did you know Mr. Roberts?"

"Very well." She pulled one leg beneath her then tucked the other to sit cross-legged in the rocking chair.

He noted that the corner of her mouth twitched, indicating she had strong positive feelings for the deceased.

"We met in college and got engaged our senior year."

"Who broke off the engagement and why?" He braced himself for her answer, guilt creating a ball of ice in his stomach.

She stiffened, displeasure morphing her features. "What has that got to do with Jud's death?"

"Gives me background and insight into who he was."

Grant entered the room and stood behind his sister, his hands on her shoulders. Ethan gave him a pointed look.

"I broke it off for personal reasons that had nothing to do with him. Jud was a caring, giving, gentle man." Tears threatened to spill over her cheeks. Abby swallowed and looked at Ethan, despair clear in her eyes. "He didn't deserve this."

It tore at him to see the anguish his questions caused her, so he didn't push it. It wasn't necessary at this point. He glanced down at his notes and composed himself before looking back at her. "When was the last time you saw or talked to Mr. Roberts?"

"Yesterday. We met for lunch. We usually meet at least once a month to catch up on everything going on in our lives. He talked about his upcoming wedding, and how he was...he was...." The tears she'd fought to hold back began to fall, and she pulled a tissue from her pocket and dabbed her eyes. "He said he was actually having fun helping Karen with all the arrangements."

Ethan gritted his teeth, gave her a moment. Damn, he hated this part of the job, but he needed the complete picture if he was going to have any chance of catching this guy, and that meant asking the tough questions. In this case, it really sucked being the interrogator.

"Did he mention having any problems with anyone, or that anyone might want to hurt him?"

"No." She sniffed and glanced up at him. "I don't know of a single soul who would want to harm Jud."

"Where were you last night, Ms. Montgomery?" This was the question he had dreaded most. He half expected her brother to jump down his throat. But he didn't. He stood behind his sister and remained calm and supportive.

"I was at work until eight and then came home. Grant and I watched an old movie on TV, then I went to bed."

"Where do you work?"

"St. Vincent Hospital in the Radiology Department. I'm an Ultrasound Technician."

He made a note. Depending on the timeline he got from the ME, a quick call to St. Vincent along with her brother's verification should put her in the clear. "Is there anything else you can think of that might have something to do with the investigation?"

"No." Abby glanced out the window behind him. "I wish I did."

"Okay then. I guess that's it for now."

Ethan rose and shut off the camera. After packing the

equipment away, he pulled on his jacket and slung the camera bag's strap over his shoulder. Abby rose and escorted him and her brother to the door.

Pausing on the porch, he scanned the surroundings one last time, his gaze settling on her. "I'll be in touch if anything else comes up."

"Don't worry. I won't leave town." She closed the door, and a distinctive click reverberated through the cold air as she locked the deadbolt.

Ethan glanced over at his partner. "Guess she doesn't like me too much."

Grant shook his head and headed toward the Tahoe. "Damn, you *are* a good detective, aren't you?"

Chapter Four

*A*bby sat in one of the eleven padded chairs arranged in a circle, each filled with the victim of a horrible assault of one kind or another. She tried to focus on what the next group member had to say, but her mind kept drifting back to the day before.

She'd worried about the questions her brother's new partner, Detective Parker, might ask. Memories of how she'd been grilled for over two hours by the detective investigating Uncle Marty's murder seventeen years ago had overwhelmed her. The ordeal had been horrific—even with Grant shielding her from the details. Back then, she and her brother had been hauled down to the station and interrogated for hours. She'd been forced to sit in a small room and repeat her alibi over and over, every word scrutinized. She'd been prepared for the same treatment by the detective investigating Jud's murder.

But it hadn't been like her previous experience. Nothing at all, in fact.

Detective Parker had acted professionally and shown respect for the loss of her best friend. He'd asked about her relationship with Jud and the last time she'd seen him. He hadn't spent hours drilling down on every detail and nuance of her answers, probably because her brother had been with her.

That didn't mean he wouldn't grill her later when Grant

wasn't around to watch over her.

With a sigh, Abby turned her attention back to the group meeting.

"Normally, I'm locked in my apartment by sunset." The woman speaking looked down at hands where she wrung a tissue in her lap. "But last Friday, I went out to dinner with my parents."

"That's very good, Carol." Joann, the leader of the therapy group, scribbled something in her notebook then looked up and smiled. "How did that go?"

Abby held her breath. Carol had been raped a year ago and, shortly after the attack, had become nyctophobic. She slept with every light in her apartment on in order to keep the darkness at bay.

"Dinner went okay. We went to a brightly lit restaurant, so no problems there." A nervous giggle escaped the woman's lips. She glanced around the group. "But I have to be honest. My parents picked me up and took me home afterward. I was never truly alone."

"But you still went out." Joann made another note in her book. "The point is you took a chance and you made it through. You took a big step, Carol, and that's great."

Carol nodded and dabbed the corner of her eye.

Abby blew out the breath she'd been holding and clapped along with the rest of the members, acknowledging Carol's accomplishment. Everyone at group aired the internal battles they fought on a day-to-day basis, and each story reminded her of just how far she'd come from that horrible rape she'd suffered seven years ago. The physical pain, the humiliation, the nightmares, the constant worry that it would happen again. To this day, she still looked over her shoulder, and the sweet smell of peppermint made her physically ill.

Joann glanced at her watch. "Well, I guess that's as good a note as any to end our session. This week I want you all to write in your journals. Dreams, random thoughts, fears, or a note of how your day went. I don't care if it's your grocery list. Write it down."

One by one, members rose from their chairs. Some stretched, others broke off in pairs to discuss the meeting. Several drifted by Carol and patted her shoulder, offering their congratulations and further encouragement.

Abby beelined for the coffee urn at the snack table.

"Hey." Joann touched her shoulder. "You really didn't have to come today."

"I know." She snatched a cup, shoved it in place, and depressed the nozzle on the urn. "I just needed the contact."

Joann nodded. "Well, we're always glad to have you here." She tilted her head, scanning her face. "How'd you sleep last night?"

She shook her head. "Not so great. Jud was my best friend. His funeral will be sometime next week."

Joann patted Abby's arm, a sympathetic smile on her lips. "Don't feel like you have to come to group if you're too tired. Just write in your journal, and we'll catch up the following week."

"I will."

With a final squeeze of her forearm, the meeting leader turned away.

Abby sighed and drank the pungent liquid. The hot coffee snaked down her throat and warmed her from the inside out.

Jud was dead. Gone forever.

Blinking rapidly, she fought back the ever-present tears that welled in her eyes. His death had created an unexpected hole in her life that could never be filled or repaired.

"So, are you ready?"

She turned. "Cal."

Green eyes sparkled over the rim of a white paper cup. "Elliot said he's still interested in meeting you for dinner tomorrow night if you're up to it."

"Well...."Abby swallowed and blinked back tears.

"Hey, it's okay." He held up a hand. "We can put it off another week if you're not ready. Heck, we can put it off indefinitely. Of course, Elliot will be crushed."

She spotted Carol near the snack table, talking with another member, her face beaming with pride. She'd taken a huge step. Wasn't that what therapy was all about? Overcoming fears and taking risks in order to regain a sense of normalcy was part of the healing process.

The last time she'd seen Jud, she'd told him she was ready to get on with her life, to go on a date. He wouldn't want her to stop moving forward. She would go to his funeral, grieve the loss of his friendship, but she would also continue working toward becoming the confident woman he'd known and fallen in love with. An image of the handsome Detective Parker entered her mind.

"No." She shook her head. "I mean, yes. I'll go to dinner with Elliot tomorrow night. Is it okay if I meet him at the restaurant?"

"Absolutely." Cal patted her shoulder. "And good for you. It's your first date in how long?"

She lifted her cup and drank, muffling her answer. "Seven years."

"Damn." He laughed, and she raised a brow. "Sorry. But wow. That's a long time. I can't imagine how someone who looks like you has stayed off the market. If I wasn't already engaged, I'd be asking you out."

"Yeah." She rolled her eyes and grinned. "But you already found the love of your life."

"I did." An almost imperceptible shudder coursed through him. "And if she hadn't run for help after I'd been...after he'd...."

Her heart ached for him, and she touched his arm. She understood his pain. Too well.

"Bastard," he growled. His whole body jerked as though the knife that had originally plunged between his ribs and sliced his lung had happened all over again. His free hand came up, shook violently, and covered what Abby believed to be the location of his injury. Coffee sloshed over the edge of the cup in his other hand. "Damn it."

"It's okay, Cal." She grabbed a handful of napkins and handed several to him while she used the rest to dab the carpet.

He inhaled sharply. Relief flashed in his eyes, but then his brows drew together, and he frowned. "God. You'd think six months would be long enough to get past this."

She tossed the damp napkins in the wastebasket. "Joann says it'll take time, that everyone will work through their problems at their own pace and regain control over their lives."

"Or they won't." Cal glanced at her from the corner of his eye, his mouth a thin line. "Damn. Sorry."

"You will get through this." She retrieved her coffee cup from the table. "Kelly saved your life. You owe her to try."

"I know I do. And look at you." Though he remained slightly hunched over, his hand over his scar, he gestured toward her. "Going on your first date."

"Yeah."

"You're making progress. Though I hope it isn't seven years before I take Kelly dancing again." The glint in his eyes told her he wasn't serious.

"It better not be."

Cal laughed. "Well, at least I won't have to pick up the pieces of Elliot's broken heart. That would've been...awkward."

She giggled.

"So, how will he know it's you at the restaurant?" He grinned. "You gonna wear a name tag or something?"

"No." The nerves in her stomach bunched, started conspiring with her legs to run and get her the heck out of there. But the memory of Jud rooted her to the floor and steeled her resolve. "I'll be wearing a dark blue sweater and gold hoop earrings."

Good Lord, tomorrow night she was going out on a date.

03

"Here you go, Parker." Steve Gordon tossed a manila envelope on Ethan's desk. "The Judson Roberts crime scene photos. Got some good ones. Close up. I know how you like to study the details."

"Thanks." Ethan opened the envelope, slid the pictures out.

The top photo was of the sliced penis. "Jesus!"

Steve moved around the desk to stand next to Ethan's chair. He leaned over and studied his handiwork.

"Ouch," he said, and followed with a laugh that sounded like a giggling dolphin.

Ethan's stomach flipped and his lunch threatened to come back up. He glanced up at the photographer, whose gaze remained pinned on the photo. The guy always went for the shock factor. And boy, he'd nailed it this time.

"Sorry about that. Here, you can just put it on the bottom." Steve grabbed the stack and shuffled the pictures, leaving a headshot of Judson Roberts on top. "I sent another set to the coroner. But this one's yours. Thought you might not want to wait while Gary pokes, prods, and sews buttons on the body."

"Thanks." Ethan laid the pictures on his desk.

"Hey, New Guy." Steve glanced over at Grant, who sat studying a file. He pointed at him, snapped his fingers twice. "Um, Montgomery. Man, you need to come see these shots."

Grant looked up. "Saw it at the scene."

"Yeah. But you might've missed something." He pointed to the stack of photos. "These are up close, detailed. I don't remember you getting that close to anything."

"I'm good." Grant tilted his head, stared at Ethan. He arched a brow, silently requesting backup.

Ethan rose from his chair. Steve was taunting the new guy, attempting to get a rise out of Grant, and while he found the new detective's discomfort amusing, he needed to curtail the ribbing quickly. If he didn't, the situation would end with Steve shoving those horrific genital photos in Grant's face, which would probably be followed by his partner puking in the wastebasket. And as entertaining as that might be, the smell of vomit wouldn't mix well with the bean burrito he'd eaten for lunch.

"Don't worry, Steve." Ethan laid a hand on the wiry guy's shoulder, and urged him toward the door. "I'll make sure he sees them."

"You will?"

"Absolutely. It's part of his job."

"Well, make sure he studies that last one." The photographer ambled across the room. "Okay?"

"Will do. And Steve?"

The guy spun around, his eyes wide. "Yeah?"

"Great job as always." He nodded. "Thanks."

"Just doing my job." The guy grinned, raised two fingers to the edge of his brow, and saluted. "Just doing my job."

Ethan dropped into his chair and swiveled toward his partner.

"Thanks." Grant eyed the empty doorway.

"No problem." He peered down at the photos still stacked on his desk, Judson's pallid face staring up at him. "Of course, now you owe me."

"What?"

He looked up from the photo. "I saved your ass. Now you owe me."

Grant's lips twisted into an uneasy smile. "What do you want?"

He fought not to laugh while his partner wondered whether he'd jumped from the frying pan into the fire or not. "Coffee."

"Coffee?" The relief on the guy's face was priceless.

"Yep. Two sugars."

Grant rose and grabbed his jacket. "I can do that. Back in ten."

He snickered. Montgomery might turn out okay after all. With a shake of his head, he picked up the photos and walked to the dry erase board. Taking the top picture, he attached a magnetic clip to it and posted the headshot. On a nearby table, he laid the rest of the pictures out one by one.

As he placed the final photo, the phone rang. He grabbed the handset and jabbed the button for his phone line. Studying the horrific menagerie on the table, he spoke absentmindedly into the phone. "Parker."

"Well, hey there, big brother."

The familiar voice flowed over him, as thick and dirty as old motor oil. Ethan's jaw tightened, and he found himself holding the phone in a death grip.

"Michael."

"Thought you'd forgotten who I was, seeing as you hadn't come to visit me in quite awhile."

He glanced at the photos then at the notebook on the edge of the table. He'd flipped it open to the last page he'd written on. The page with Abby's interview notes.

Damn. Karma hated his guts.

"I told you when Mom died two years ago." He rubbed his jaw. "Came and told you in person."

"Yeah, you did. So, what, that makes you brother of the century?"

Ethan sighed. How could two people so completely different come from the same mother? "What do you want, Michael?"

He chuckled. "See? Still the same old E. Always straight to the point."

He checked his watch. Only five minutes or so since Grant had left. How long did it really take to get two cups of coffee?

He took a step to the side and peered around the dry erase board. Chief Hague sat hunched over his keyboard, typing information into the computer. Ethan leaned against the table. It appeared that for the moment he could talk without being interrupted.

"Out with it, Mikey." He cringed at using the boyhood nickname and falling into old habits. His gut twisted with disgust.

The distinctive click of a piece of hard candy hitting against a molar sounded over the line. *Peppermint.* Even in prison, Michael Greene continued sucking on those damned peppermints.

"Nothing big, really. I'm just getting outta this hellhole in a week." Michael paused, took a breath. "Thought we might talk."

"So, it's been seven years already?"

"My, my. How time flies." Michael grunted.

His sarcasm dripped over the line and left Ethan wanting to

slam down the phone. But he couldn't. If he did, Mikey would take revenge in one form or another. And the bastard was getting out in a week. Damn it.

"Look, I really don't have anything to say."

"Oh, E." He sighed. "We have so much to talk about. Like the little lying slut who put me in here."

"You put yourself in there." He gripped the phone. "The evidence was overwhelming. The woman you assaulted described you to a T, right down to those damn peppermints that you had in your mouth when you ra—"

A noise came from the other side of the dry erase board. He peeked around the corner to find his partner setting two large coffee cups on his desk. Damn, the kid was fast.

"Montgomery," Hague yelled from his office doorway and waved him over.

"Look," Ethan said, his tone firm. His time on the phone had become limited to whatever questions the chief had for the kid. "You get out in a week. Great. My advice? Start a new life."

Grant left the chief's office, spotted Ethan on the phone, and waved. Ethan waved back, his stomach churning up acid into his esophagus.

"Okay, E. I can do that." Mikey laughed. "Easy-peasy."

"Good." He turned his back to his partner's approach. "You do that."

He hung up the phone and inhaled deeply. Damn. He didn't need all this shit getting dragged up now. Hell, *ever*.

"Here's your coffee."

Ethan turned and took the large cup Grant held out to him. He tugged the plastic lid off. The rich, aromatic scent swirled beneath his nose. Ambrosia. The dark, steamy liquid flowed down his throat as he took two large gulps. "Thanks."

"My debt's paid in full."

"Yep." He took another gulp. Could he trust that his half-brother would do as he said and start a new life? Hell no, probably not. He leaned against the table with the crime scene photos spread out on it, knowing he'd have to make the trip to the state prison and follow up on his half-brother.

"I see you've started laying out the investigation." Grant pivoted toward the dry erase board and stared at Jud Roberts's picture.

Ethan noticed his partner kept his gaze averted from the crime scene photos. If the guy wanted to make it as a detective, he would need to toughen up. "Yep."

Montgomery twisted around toward him. "So, who was that on the phone?"

"No one." The lie came smooth as butter. The less Grant knew about Mikey, the better off everyone would be. Besides, nowhere was it written that partners had to share everything. "Grab me the reports from the patrol officers."

And Michael Greene's name was better left unspoken.

Chapter Five

The one-hour drive to Pine Valley State Prison was almost long enough to make Ethan turn around. Giving in to his brother ate at him, but after the phone call the day before, there'd been no way around it. He had to make the journey. Mikey wanted to talk, and it was a heck of a lot better to chat in a controlled environment than run into him somewhere unexpected.

So this afternoon, after coming up with a lame excuse to get rid of Grant by sending him to the morgue, he'd called Warden Murphy and set up a meeting with his half-brother. Childhood experience had taught Ethan that if he didn't give him his fifteen minutes, he would come looking for him. Or worse yet, do something extremely stupid like try to find Abby Montgomery. And that was unacceptable.

His half-brother had been angry on the phone. Ethan needed to convince him to leave the area, put this all behind him, and start over. No easy task, that.

Gray clouds covered the sky and warned of an impending storm. Parking his truck in the visitor lot, he secured his sidearm in the lockbox of his console, pulled the collar of his jacket up around his neck, and trudged through the heaps of icy slush into the building.

When he opened the door, a wave of heat hit him. Stepping

inside, he signed in with the guard at the front desk. "Got an appointment with the warden."

The guard glanced at the sheet and picked up the phone. He gestured with the handset toward a row of well-worn, dirt brown vinyl chairs. "Have a seat. Shouldn't take long."

The heat that had been a wonderful respite from the frigid outdoors became stifling, and he shed his coat then sat on the closest chair. He glanced at the door leading into the jail, thankful he was in law enforcement and not a regular visitor, otherwise there would have been a bunch of hoops he would've had to jump through to visit a prisoner. While he still had to log in, he didn't have to go through the holding room and be subjected to a search with a metal detector. Or worse.

A grating buzzer sounded, and an officer opened the waiting room door. He led Ethan down a long hall to Warden Murphy's office, where the older gentleman motioned for him to have a seat.

"Detective Parker, nice to see you again. Your brother is waiting in one of the private interview rooms."

He nodded. "Thanks for setting this up. When I realized he was getting out, I figured this talk would go better in here than out there. The guy's been a thorn in my side for as long as I can remember. I just want him to get on with his life and stay on the right side of the law this time."

"Did you know he got his bachelor's degree while he was in here?" The elderly warden shook his head, his bright blue eyes remaining keen on Ethan. "In criminology of all things. He's passed all his psych evals, and on the cover, everything points to a rehabilitated man."

He ran a hand over his jaw and nodded—he'd heard what Warden Murphy *wasn't* saying. "But you have your concerns?"

"No, nothing I can put a finger on. He says all the right things, does all the right stuff, model prisoner. But I've seen guys come through here for twenty-five years." His thin shoulders rose and fell. "You just get a feeling about the ones that are going to make it and the ones you're going to see back again. Michael

Greene may talk the talk, but...." He stared at Ethan, his eyes telling the truth of what was on his mind. "Well, let's just say I wouldn't bet my pension on that rehabilitation of his. For your sake, though, I hope I'm wrong."

"Yeah, so do I. Seems like I've spent my life picking up the pieces after him. Thanks for the heads up." He shook the warden's gnarled hand then gestured toward the door. "Guess I better get this over with."

Warden Murphy strode across his office and opened the door. The officer who'd led Ethan from the waiting room leaned against the opposite wall, his arms folded across his chest.

"Thanks again, Warden." He stepped out into the hallway.

"Good luck, son." Murphy nodded toward the officer.

"This way, Detective," the officer said. He pushed himself from the wall and sauntered down the hallway.

Ethan trailed behind his escort, unsurprised by the officer's leisurely gate. The temperature in this part of the prison neared the sultry heat of July. They came to another checkpoint, and he signed a second log.

Another discordant buzzer sounded, and a heavy clank filled the air as the metal bars unlatched. The door ground along a thick track, the bearings growling as though they hadn't been greased in decades. He stepped through the opening, his escort on his heels. They walked down the narrow hallway shoulder-to-shoulder. The gated door slid shut behind them, the bulky lock slamming home, ringing of finality. No one got in or out unless approved.

"In here," the officer said and thumbed toward a sterile white door. He marched to the opposite wall and took up his residential lean.

Ethan nodded and put his hand on the doorknob to the room that held his brother. Taking a deep breath, he pushed the heavy metal door open.

A table and two chairs sat in the middle of an otherwise barren room. Mikey glanced up, and a smirk tugged one corner of his mouth. He shifted slightly, allowing the distinctive clatter of chains to reverberate off the stark walls—his subtle way of ensuring Ethan knew his older brother had been shackled to the floor and cuffs remained locked on his wrists.

Letting the door close behind him, he gave his half-brother a quick once over. Nothing had changed about the man. He still had the straggly, dirty blond hair, scruffy facial hair—couldn't really be called a beard—and that soulless hazel gaze. Mikey's eyes had always bothered Ethan the most. They were dead. For all the years growing up together, he'd never found a spark of life in them unless he'd been in some kind of trouble.

"Bro. After our conversation I didn't think I'd be seein' ya. Least not till I got out of this hellhole. Can't say I'm disappointed, though." Michael tilted his head and looked up at him. "Well, you're looking pretty good, spit-shined suit and all. Have a seat. Sorry I can't offer you a beverage. My hosting abilities are kinda limited in here."

He tried to quell the nausea and took a seat opposite his brother, the chair scraping over the concrete floor. "Let's cut the crap, Mikey. What is it you wanted to talk about?"

"Same old, Ethan. Always so serious. Can't a guy want to reconnect with family? You and Ever are the only family I got left, I might add. And that prissy little snip of a sister done took off. So, that leaves you, E." He pinned him with a flat stare. "I thought you'd want to help me out when they release me, seeing as you didn't lift a finger to keep me from landing in here."

The mention of their sister burned in Ethan's gut. "I couldn't fight the facts." He met his half-brother's gaze and tapped his index finger on the table to accentuate his points. "This was *your* screw-up. I couldn't have gotten you out, even if I'd wanted to— which I didn't. And if you think I'm going to pick the pieces up for you when you get out, you're dead wrong. You went too far, Mikey. Even I can't get past what you did."

Michael lunged toward Ethan, but his shackles stopped him. "She's a lying bitch, E. I didn't do anything she didn't beg me to do."

His stomach rolled, and he fought to keep his breakfast

burrito where it belonged. His brother had that effect on him. And for some macabre reason, he'd felt the need to go over the investigative reports from Mikey's case before he came to see him.

Including the hospital photos of Abby.

He wished he hadn't. The guilt of keeping the truth from her and her brother had increased ten-fold. Karma truly was a bitch.

Ethan shot to his feet and slammed his hands on the table, his gaze hard on his half-brother. "The only thing she asked was for you to stop. You brutalized her, Michael. You beat her, you tortured her, and you raped her. No woman asks for that. Not Abby, not anyone."

Mikey wiped his hand over his mouth, a shit-grin peeking out between his fingers. "Abby, is it? Don't tell me, dear brother, we have the same taste in women." He looked away, his hazel eyes glittering. A coarse laugh erupted from some deep, dark place inside him and set Ethan's teeth on edge. "Aw, E. This could turn out to be very fun."

Ethan dove across the table and grabbed his half-brother around the throat. "You stay the fuck away from her, Mikey. You understand me? You come within a thousand yards of her, and I'll kill you myself."

The door opened, and the guard stepped in. His gaze shifted from one man to the other, assessing the situation. "Is there a problem here?"

"No, Officer." He released his half-brother and dropped back into his seat. "I'll only be a few more minutes."

With a nod, the guard left and closed the door.

He tried to calm his pounding heart without success. His brother was scum, and he needed to make sure he left Abigail Montgomery alone. But instead of appearing rattled, Michael still wore that slimy smile.

"Seems like I hit a nerve, E. Tell ya what." He ran his hand over the scraggly hair on his chin. He glanced at the ceiling for a moment then turned a serious gaze on Ethan. "I'll leave Little Miss Priss alone on one condition. You get me fifty thousand dollars when I get out of here, and I'll leave town. Never darken your door again."

He choked. The guy was seriously touched. "I don't think so. You'll stay away. The order of protection, her brother, and my Glock will make sure of that." He stood and moved to where his sorry excuse for a brother sat. "Do yourself a favor. Get as far away from here as possible. Use the degree you got yourself and turn your life around."

He pivoted toward the door.

"Don't know if I can do that, E. She was one mighty fine piece of ass."

With a growl, he turned and leapt, slamming full force into Mikey. The chair toppled over backward and crashed to the floor. Ethan landed on top. Every punch connected to his half-brother's face or ribs, his restraints holding him captive, making retaliation all but impossible. Two guards scrambled into the room and manhandled Ethan off their prisoner. He shook free.

"Just couldn't leave it. Could you?" Ethan spat. He pointed a finger at him, all the rage boiling inside him trained on the piece of shit that had made his life a living hell for as long as he could remember. "A thousand yards. You remember that."

A guard held the door and gestured for him to leave. With a final meaningful glare at his half-brother, he stalked out of the room, Mikey's laughter following after him.

"Damn it." He cursed all the way out of the building and to his car. Once again, he'd let the son of a bitch get the best of him. The sorry bastard had manipulated him, discovered he had some kind of personal attachment to Abby—which he didn't. Not really. Good Lord, he barely knew her, but he wanted to protect her. And in his half-brother's eyes, that made him weak.

Ethan unlocked the truck and slid into the seat. Retrieving his gun, he snugged it back into the holster under his jacket and started the Tahoe. In a renewed burst of fury, he slammed his fist against the steering wheel. Hurt like a bitch, but the pain damped the rage inside him.

"Damn it to hell." He'd handled the meeting with Mikey all

wrong.

His cell rang. Jerking it from its holster, he jabbed the answer key and barked into the phone. "Parker."

"Whoa," Chief Hague said. "Catch you at a bad time?"

Shit. He ran a hand through his hair, took a breath. "No. Sorry, sir. What's up?"

"There's been another murder. The condo on Flower Street." Hague paused and swallowed. "Looks like the same M.O. as Jud."

"Fuck! I'll be there in an hour." He flipped off his phone, shifted the Tahoe in gear, and stomped on the gas pedal. Trying to gain traction, the tires spun through the icy slush, and the heavy SUV fishtailed as he tore out of the parking lot.

Chapter Six

 *A*bby stared at the plate in front of her. The half-eaten piece of chicken, the roasted vegetables, the mound of rice pilaf. She pushed the broccoli and cauliflower with her fork, creating a ring around the chicken.

She glanced up at her date. With his muscular build, jet-black hair, and tanned skin, Elliot was nice enough in the looks department, but from the moment they'd shook hands, he'd talked about nothing but himself. Work, sports, beer, the gym. God, it was driving her nuts. But what had she expected on her first date in seven years? And a blind date at that.

When she'd told her brother the night before about her impending dinner date, he'd cringed and told her good luck. He'd offered to call her after the first thirty minutes in case she'd wanted an easy out, and now she wished she'd taken him up on it.

"So, I told her if she brought me another beer, I'd trade her my top fantasy football pick." He laughed and cut his steak. The meat was so rare his plate swam in blood.

Abby's stomach churned. After a sip of wine, she forced a smile at the joke she didn't understand. A surreptitious glance at her watch told her she'd been sitting across from him for an hour and thirty-seven minutes. Taking a gulp of wine, she leaned back in her chair and let the restaurant's mood music drown out Elliot's constant litany.

The music, however, didn't distract from the massive slice of cow he folded into his mouth. She'd never considered herself a vegetarian, but after watching her date cram a chunk of beef the size of his fist into his maw, she seriously started mulling it over. She'd never actually tasted tofu, but how bad could it be?

"You done eating?" The corners of his mouth pulled into a grin while his teeth ground the meat. "'Cause if you are, it's not a big deal. This place is only moderately priced, so don't worry about my not being able to cover it on my salary. As a defense attorney, Elliot Swanson rakes it in."

She glanced down, her appetite gone. "Um, yes. I think I'm finished."

Elliot leaned across the table and stabbed her chicken with his fork. "You mind?"

She shook her head, too mortified to speak. God, had he been raised in a barn?

He yanked the chicken back to his plate and sliced what remained into healthy chunks. "Waste not, want not." He glanced up and smiled. "I come from a big family. Two brothers, three sisters. 'Grab it and growl' as my dad always said."

Goodness. A family of six? Well, that sure explained a lot. All during dinner, she'd thought him rude and self-centered, but that bit of information said a lot. Of course, it didn't trigger the desire to put his name on speed dial either.

The waitress came by, a perky young girl who fawned on Elliot. She looked at him with her huge doe eyes. "Can I get you some dessert, sir?"

Elliot glanced at Abby, licked his lips, and turned back to the waitress. "No. Ice cream and cakes? Nothing but fat."

"I know. But they make me ask." The waitress rolled her eyes and nodded, her finger twirling a long golden ponytail. "Isn't it disgusting?"

A loud snort erupted from Elliot. "Yeah, it is."

The waitress leaned forward, her overly endowed bosom

about to pop the top buttons of her extra small uniform. "They make me ask the fat people, too. It's really sad."

"That's terrible." Elliot furrowed his brow in sympathy, placed his elbow on the table, and flexed his arm. The muscle his bicep produced pressed against the sleeve of his oxford button-down shirt.

The waitress's gaze cut toward his display, and her lips rounded into a bright pink circle. "Well," she said, then giggled. "Gotta make a living."

Elliot snapped a business card from his breast pocket and pushed it toward her. "You ever need a lawyer, darlin', you be sure and call me."

She glanced at the card then tucked it in her bra. "Oh, I sure will."

With a satisfied grin, he looked at Abby. "We'll have two coffees."

"Yes, sir." The waitress twirled away, her green-eyed glare raking Abby's face. She swished across the dining area, her butt swinging like a pendulum.

Abby shifted her attention back to her blind date, who turned out not to be so blind after all. "You gave her your card?"

"Absolutely." He stuffed a chunk of chicken into his mouth, the piece so large he had to chew with his mouth open. "I can always use the business."

"You're a defense attorney." She drank her wine. "You think that girl is going to rob a bank or hijack a plane?"

His laugh caused him to choke on the beer he swilled. "Doubt it. She looks like a sweet girl. But she might know someone who could partake of my services."

"Yeah, well." She peered over her shoulder in the direction the waitress had sashayed. "If looks could kill, she'd be calling for your help with murder charges."

"What?"

"Never mind." She sighed. For a first date after nearly a decade, this one wouldn't go down in the memory books. Would anyone ever measure up to Jud? An image of his smiling face came to mind, and her breath caught.

Jud was gone. Forever. She'd settled with the loss of their intimate relationship years ago. But the loss of his friendship? That would be tough. She touched the inner corner of her eye with her napkin, drying the tear that had formed there.

The flirty waitress returned and set a cup of steaming coffee in front of each of them. In a bold move, she laid a hand on Elliot's shoulder and smiled. "Anything else I can get you?"

Abby gritted her teeth. The girl's obvious come-on dripped with adolescent skank. How old was she, sixteen, seventeen?

"Just the check, darlin'." He swiped the last bite of chicken through the bloody steak remains on his plate and packed it into his mouth along with the previous bite.

Abby thought she might lose her moderately priced meal all over the floor. She swallowed hard to keep it down. Wrapping her hands around her coffee cup, she soaked in the soothing warmth.

After the waitress pranced off again, she eyed Elliot over the rim of her cup. "Make sure you check her age before you go out with her."

Elliot's tanned brow furrowed. "What?"

She drank the steamy, aromatic beverage. "I'd do a background check. Make sure she's over eighteen."

The corners of his mouth quirked. "Jealous?"

"No." She returned the cup to the table, the white linen tablecloth smooth beneath her hands. "Just trying to make sure you don't end up needing a lawyer yourself."

"Elliot Swanson doesn't need a lawyer." He downed the rest of his beer, set it on the table with a muffled clack. "Elliot Swanson is the lawyer."

"Fine." She waved her hand, letting the matter drop. He'd do whatever he wanted. And she was so going to kick Cal's ass at the next meeting. What the heck had he been thinking, setting her up with this fool?

The perky jailbait dressed in a waitress' uniform returned. With great fanfare and very little grace, she leaned over and set the check in front of Elliot. On top of the crisp green bill sat two tightly wrapped peppermints.

Abby's gaze locked onto the round candy. The bright red and white stripes glowed cheerfully beneath the cellophane. Air rushed from her lungs. Her throat tightened. She touched a hand to her cheek, the restaurant suddenly unbearably hot.

"Abby?" Elliot looked at her, mild concern showing in his eyes. "Are you all right, darlin'?"

"P-peppermint." She pointed a shaky finger at the offensive objects. Even wrapped, the distinctive scent wafted across the table and filled her nose. A shiver rippled down her spine, and she started to shake.

That animal, the one who attacked her seven years ago. Oh, God. He'd crunched the candy between his teeth as he...he.... Peppermint on his breath as he heaved and shoved and hurt and...he'd whispered in her ear. Said she was sweet...as candy.

She sucked in a breath. Then another. And another. The room tilted. She pushed up from her chair. On stiff, numbed legs, she backed away from the table.

Elliot stood and grabbed her arm. "Where are you going?"

Abby jerked at his touch, fear pumping through her veins. "I can't...."

"What?" He ran a calming hand up and down her arm. "Are you allergic or something?"

"N-no. More of a phobia." Her head bobbed. It was close enough to the truth and not nearly as embarrassing.

"I'm sorry." He rubbed both her arms. "Cal told me about you not having sex for a decade, to treat you nice. But he never mentioned this. Jeez. What an idiot."

Tremors ran through her body. Images of the sadistic bastard who'd raped her flooded her brain. So long ago, yet the memories remained sharp as ever.

"I mean, that's not the kind of thing you just forget." Elliot leaned over the table and swiped the mints. Crinkling cellophane filled the air. Holding an unwrapped red and white candy between his thumb and forefinger, he said, "Look. They're just mints. It's not like they're going to bite you." He popped it in his mouth and grinned.

A terrified scream pushed from her throat, and she stumbled backward. When a set of arms wrapped around her from behind, she jolted and screamed again. With all her strength, she lashed out at her attacker.

"Abby," a calm and familiar voice said. "Abs. It's me."

"No!" She shoved against his weight, clawed him.

"Abs, it's me, Grant." He released her, and she spun around. "It's okay. I'm here."

Relief flooded her. Her brother had come to save her. The restaurant floor shifted beneath her feet, and she stumbled again. With a deep breath, she stared up into her brother's face and threw her arms around him.

"Grant."

Elliot stalked over, his brawny shoulders thrown back. "Who are you?"

Releasing her, he leveled his gaze on her date. "I'm Detective Montgomery, and I'm her brother. Who the hell are you?"

"Elliot Swanson, attorney at law." He popped out a card, held it in Grant's face so he could read it. "I took your sister out on a date, and everything was going fine until she freaked out over a simple piece of candy."

Abby jerked at the sight of the peppermint dangling from his fingers. A couple of sidesteps and she used her brother as a shield against the atrocious mint.

"Well, Elliot Swanson, attorney at law," he said, fisting his hands on his hips, "your date with my sister is over."

Elliot's gaze flitted to Abby, and she cringed. He pursed his lips, snickered air through his teeth. "I suppose you're right."

With the peppermint safely ensconced in Elliot's hand, she skittered to the table and snatched up her purse and coat. A furtive glimpse at the prissy waitress revealed a triumphant smirk pasted across her painted lips. Had she left the peppermints intentionally? Had she known the reaction they would elicit? No, she couldn't have; that was just paranoia talking.

She returned to the two men who continued to glare at one another.

"Sorry, Elliot," she mumbled as she passed by him.

The moment the words came from her mouth, it brought her teeth to grinding. Why had she apologized? She'd done nothing wrong. But to be fair, he hadn't known about her all-consuming terror of peppermint either.

He had flirted with the waitress—she'd freaked over the peppermints. He paid for dinner—she apologized for the freak-out. In her book, that made them even.

Buttoning her coat against the cold outside, she trailed after her brother, never so thankful as she was at that very moment to see his immense black truck sitting in the parking lot.

"Need a ride home?" he said over his shoulder.

"Yes." She scurried around the rear of the pickup to the passenger side. "I'll come back for my car tomorrow."

He unlocked the doors with the remote, and she scrambled inside. A moment later, the engine roared to life, and she sat shivering while the vehicle warmed up.

"That was your date, Abby?" His voice was quiet, filled with concern.

"Yes." She burrowed into her coat, slouched in the seat. "I thought a seven year hiatus was long enough. That guy makes me want to change my mind about dating again. Almost."

He nodded. "I suppose."

"What were you doing there anyway? I thought you had to work late."

"Got done early." He shrugged, his coat rustling against the seat. "Stopped for dinner. The bar makes a mean fish and chips."

"Really?" It was nice to think about something other than her reaction to peppermint.

"Actually, I eat there a lot." He grinned, reached over and flicked the defroster on. "So, how was your date? Or dare I ask?"

She huffed out a breath. "Total dud. Actually, I should really be thankful for what happened. Otherwise, I would still be sitting at that table, bored to tears." She shook her head. "I tell you, if I had to listen to one more sports story or how great an attorney he is, I would've stabbed myself with my bread knife."

Grant laughed. "That bad, huh?"

"Yeah." She shrugged her coat up around her ears and gave a derisive laugh. "He flirted with an underage waitress, and then offered me a night filled with pity sex. Good times."

"So, you going out again?"

"Not with him."

He snorted. "Don't see why not." He reached over, slid the switch over to the heater.

Warm air blew against her feet, curled around her calves, and she sighed. But would she ever be rid of the persistent chill that had plagued her every day for the past seven years?

He shifted the truck into reverse and looked over his shoulder. "Ready to go home?"

Before she could answer, his cell phone rang. Pulling it from the holster at his waist, he checked the screen.

"Work." He tapped the answer button and held it to his ear. "Montgomery."

She waited in silence while her brother listened to whoever had called. He leaned against his door and lowered his forehead to his hand. His mouth pulled into a thin line.

"Yes, sir. I'm on my way."

"What is it?" she asked once he'd hit the disconnect button on his cell.

"Damn it!" He slammed his palm against the steering wheel and looked out the driver's-side window.

"What's wrong?" She straightened in her seat. "Who was that?"

"Chief Hague," he said, still staring out the window. "There's been another murder."

"Oh, my God. How horrible."

Movement outside the truck caught her eye, and she spotted Elliot and the young waitress strolling arm in arm across the parking lot. That certainly didn't take long.

Grant eased the truck out of the parking place. "I've got to take you home then head to the crime scene."

The thought of sitting at home alone after smelling those peppermints brought a chill of dread hammering down her spine. She tapped her toes against the floorboard and rubbed her arms. She looked at her brother, his face solemn.

"Do you think I could tag along?" Her timid voice filled the cab.

"I don't know, Abs." He stopped at a red light. "I don't know how long I'll be."

"That's okay. If I get tired, I can just sleep in the truck till you're through." She rubbed her arms again. "I just don't want to be alone after what happened at the restaurant."

"Yeah, I get it." The light changed, and he turned onto Main Street. "Sure. You can come."

"Thanks." She sighed and slouched down in the seat again. It might be a long night, but better than being at home unable to sleep and jumping at shadows.

Grant glanced down at her, his mouth pulled into a teasing smile. "Sorry your date was such a dud. Guess those mints really topped your night off."

She reached over and smacked his shoulder. "Jerk."

❧

Ethan arrived at the crime scene address in time to find Grant racing around the front of his truck in an attempt to block what looked like his sister from running into the crime scene. He snagged her, but when she broke free from his grasp, Ethan jumped out of his SUV and ran toward the hysterical woman to cut her off.

"Whoa there, Ms. Montgomery. Slow down. Where do you think you're going?" He held tight as she struggled against his arms. He tightened his grip and pulled her against him. Damn, she was strong but pretty darn soft at the same time.

"Abby, it's me, Detective Parker," he said. Silky blonde tresses brushed against his cheek, the scent of lilacs and vanilla filling his nose. God, she smelled good. "Calm down and tell me what's got you so worked up."

She looked up at him, panic clear in her wide eyes. "Cal! This is Cal's address. I have to make sure he's okay."

He loosened his hold on her, immediately missing the warmth of her body crushed against him. He opened his mouth to ask her more questions, but Grant rushed to her side.

"Thanks for the catch." He took his sister by the shoulder and attempted to pry her away from him. "I can take over here."

A little put off by his partner's tone, Ethan did not release his hold. Just the opposite. He drew her to him again, and she buried her face in his neck. Nothing about the way she felt in his arms was appropriate, and in a minute he would have to let her go. But for now, he savored the warm, sweet-scented woman clinging to him.

Grant gave him a cold stare, but didn't force the issue. Moments later, he called Officer Moore over to them. "Could you please stay with Ms. Montgomery? She's Detective Montgomery's sister and had the misfortune of coming to the scene with him. She can sit in her brother's truck, but please stay with her. She believes she may know the victim."

"Sure, Detective Parker." She leaned toward him, lowered her voice so only he could hear. "By the way, I wanted to thank you for talking to Officer Hanson. I don't know what you said, but he's been much easier to work with. I'm glad I didn't take you up on the offer of a partner change. Your words were enough."

Ethan nodded at her. "I didn't do a thing but put a bug in someone's ear. Glad it's working out for you."

With regret, he released his hold on her, and she stepped away, her warmth going with her. He met her gaze. "I realize you think you may know the victim, but right now, this is a crime scene. I can't let you anywhere near that house. I'd appreciate it if you'd stay in your brother's truck with Officer Moore here, though. If it turns out you're right, we'll need to talk again."

Abby peered at the house, her brows knitted with concern. Returning her gaze to Ethan, she bit her lip and nodded. Without another word, she pivoted and trudged back to the truck with Moore trailing behind her.

He rounded on Grant. "Just what the hell were you thinking bringing your sister to a fucking crime scene?" he blasted. "Oh wait, you couldn't have been thinking. Either that or you don't have the brains God gave a gnat. Especially if she knows the victim. Do you realize the implications? Shit, even a rookie wouldn't pull a stunt like this. She almost made it to the house. Then what?"

Ethan glared, and the guy had the decency to appear apologetic. Stupid, stupid, stupid!

"I know this is bad." He shoved his hands into his jacket pockets. "But I had no idea she would know this address."

"That doesn't matter." He waved his arms. "She shouldn't have been here in the first place."

"Look, she'd been on a blind date that ended really badly. I just happened to be at the same restaurant having dinner when I heard the commotion. She was so shaken she couldn't drive home, so I offered her a ride." He glanced over his shoulder toward his truck. "We were just about to head home when the chief called. She begged me to come, promised she'd stay in the truck, but she really couldn't be alone." He shrugged. "I never told her the address. How the hell was I supposed to know it might be familiar to her? Once we pulled up, she freaked, yelled out a name, and took off like a crazy woman."

Ethan shook his head. Talk about a totally screwed-up situation. What was done was done. Not much sense in yelling at the kid anymore.

"Whatever. Let's just get in there and get this scene moving." They started toward the house that had been surrounded by yellow tape. "So, what about the date had your sister so spooked?"

"Long story best left in the past, but she has an aversion to peppermints. More like a phobia, really. Bad one. And the waitress brought a couple over to the table with the bill. The stupid guy she was with saw her reaction and kept waving them in her face. What a jerk, huh?"

His step faltered. Dear Lord, what had Mikey done to her?

Chapter Seven

*E*than tried to shrug off the guilt of his brother's actions. He couldn't think about Abby or Mikey right now. He had a crime scene to process. Nodding to the patrolman at the door, he donned his booties, signed himself and his partner on the log, and entered the two-level ranch with Grant on his heels. He found Gary, who had set up his CSU forensic equipment in the hallway. "Been here long?"

"Only long enough to do a cursory look." Gray glanced down the hall. "This looks remarkably similar to the Roberts scene. I'm more than a little worried."

He frowned. "How so?"

Gary tossed him and Grant each a pair of gloves. "Follow me."

They trailed him down the sparse hallway, turning into the first doorway on their right. The tangy, metallic smell of blood and death assaulted Ethan's senses. For a moment, nobody spoke, and only the distinctive sound of liquid dripping onto a hard surface filled the room. *Splat...splat...splat....*

He forced his mind to focus on the horrific scene in front of him and, flipping a mental switch, he took it all in with detached coldness. On the bed, a male subject in his mid-thirties lay supine. Hands and feet bound to the headboard and footboard respectively, he was spread-eagled, naked, and drenched in blood.

Red spatter streaked the walls and ceiling. The bedspread, saturated beyond its limit, released thick, crimson droplets of life onto the hardwood floor. The stillness only amplified the sound.

Ethan glanced over to Gary. "So, what have you got so far?"

"Well, like before, both femoral arteries have been cut, as well as the carotid. And, like before, the injuries, such as the carving in the victim's chest and the damage to his eyes and penis, were done prior to death."

"Shit!" The word, a breathy whisper on Grant's lips, stabbed the air.

"Did you find out what was carved into Roberts' chest yet?" He knew what they had on their hands but wasn't about to say the words out loud. Not yet anyway.

Gary turned away from the body and scowled at Ethan. "Yeah, finished the autopsy this afternoon. The report is probably on your desk as we speak." The forensic investigator swallowed but didn't avert his gaze. "It was the word YOU. And, before you ask, I found no trace evidence. No DNA, no fingerprints, no foreign fibers that didn't belong. Nothing."

"Well, that just makes my night. CSU found nothing at the scene either. I have absolutely nothing to go on." He worked his jaw and swept his gaze over the carnage. The killer had left no clues to his identity at either scene, which meant he was either lucky or damn smart. "This guy isn't going to make it easy for me, is he?"

"Why should he? He sure as heck hasn't made it easy for the men he's killing." The medical examiner stared at the man swathed in blood and shook his head.

"Yeah, I guess not. Any idea as to time of death?"

"Won't know for sure till I get him back to the shop, but with the level of rigamortis and lividity of the body, I'd say it's been less than five hours."

"Five hours. That brings it to somewhere around three or four p.m. Broad daylight." He scanned the room again. There was no sign of a struggle. Did the vic know his killer and just open the door to him? "Okay, I'm going to turn the scene over to you and your guys, see if we got lucky with any witnesses. I know better than to ask, but could you put a rush on this? I don't think this guy is anywhere near done."

The examiner's lips thinned, but he gave a curt nod. "I'll do the best I can."

"Thanks, Gary. I appreciate it." Ethan nudged Grant, who'd said next to nothing the entire time. "C'mon, we need to interview the responding officer and find out who called this in."

They made their way back down the hallway, and he paused in the living room, giving it a once-over. Nothing appeared out of place. The house was well kept yet lived in. A throw blanket lay crumpled on the couch, and on the side table, a half-empty coffee mug and an open book waited for the reader to return.

He exited the house and zipped his jacket against the cold air that rushed to devour his body heat. With Grant at his side, he turned to the bundled officer standing watch at the door. Glancing at his nameplate, Ethan addressed him, "So, Officer Miller, what can you tell me?"

"The gentleman in there is Cal Gibson. The call came in from his fiancée, Kelly Lowell. She'd come home from a day out with friends and found the deceased." He gestured toward the ambulance parked in the yard. "She's in the back. Been throwing up all over the place, so we called the shiny white bus for her. EMTs are treating her now for shock."

"Don't suppose there are any witnesses?"

A young officer walked up the steps balancing a cardboard carrier holding four cups of coffee. Thin trails of steam curled through the tiny holes in the white plastic lids, and the distinct aroma of freshly brewed caffeine filled Ethan's nostrils.

"Thanks," Miller said and took a cup. Wrapping both hands around the container, he turned back to Ethan. "No witnesses I'm aware of, sir. Gibson's closest neighbor is half a mile down the road."

An icy wind blew across the porch, and Ethan burrowed

deeper into his jacket. This had certainly turned out to be one hell of a night, and there didn't appear to be any improvement in sight. He stared at the cars parked in the driveway and yard. Had the killer driven here or arrived on foot? Did he break into the house or boldly ring the bell?

"Were the doors and windows intact?"

"Yes, sir. Ms. Lowell was waiting outside for us. There was no sign of forced entry."

"Okay." He glanced at Grant, who had his pad out, taking notes. Ethan heaved an internal sigh. This was basic information—vic's name, fiancée—no more than a line or two. Montgomery had scribbled so much it looked as if he were writing a book. *Rookie.* He turned back to the officer. "Anything else you can think of?"

"Just the fiancée. She said, 'He was always so afraid this would happen. He knew this would happen.' Kept repeating it over and over. We asked her what she meant, but she just said it again. That's when we called for the squad to come help her."

"All right, thanks." He elbowed his partner, who'd continued to remain silent, and motioned toward the ambulance. "Let's go talk to the fiancée."

Once in the yard, he spoke directly to Grant. "Hold up a second. How come you were so quiet back there?"

The guy looked up at him wide-eyed. "Uh, I'm still learning here. There wasn't anything I wanted to ask that you didn't. Besides, that was an ugly scene in there. I'm still trying to wrap my brain around these two murders." His gaze darted toward the house. "What makes someone do something like that?"

"I don't know." He studied the man. Sure, his partner had been quiet. A little too quiet. Maybe there was more going on in that rookie brain of his than he wanted to admit. "Are you sure the real reason why you haven't said anything all night is because you've been trying to wrap your brain around the idea that your sister is somehow involved in all this shit?"

Grant straightened and squared his shoulders, growing an extra few inches. "Positive. I know my sister. She has nothing to do with what happened in there."

"Oh, she's involved somehow. I don't know yet to what extent, but you can bet your next year's salary she's connected."

"You're wrong."

Ethan gave his partner a hard stare. "I am going to have to question her, because she obviously knew this guy well, and because she was pretty upset when she found out the address. That gives her intimate knowledge of both victims, and if you're going to try to tell me you don't think these two cases are connected, then you don't deserve that detective shield."

His jaw tightened, telling Ethan he'd hit a nerve. "How do you get intimate knowledge? Maybe it's the fiancée she knows."

He held up a finger. "Number one, I get intimate knowledge because she said our vic's name, this was his address." He added the next finger. "And number two, there is no such thing as coincidence."

Grant's nostrils flared, and he leaned toward him, his voice hard but low so no one could overhear him. "I have no doubts whatsoever that if my sister knew this guy, it's just coincidental." He made a short slashing motion with his hand. "She's not involved."

Ethan leaned forward as well, looked him in the eyes and said, "Are we going to have a problem here?"

"No." Grant straightened, and turned up his collar against cold. His gaze flitted to the house and back again. "We're not going to have a problem."

Ethan shoved his hands into his pockets, giving his partner a moment to cool off, and then said, "C'mon, let's go interview the fiancée. After that, I'll talk with Abby."

Moments later, they found Kelly Lowell sitting on a gurney in the back of the ambulance, her tear-streaked face pale and contorted with grief. He asked the attendants to give them a moment of privacy. When they complied, he and Grant stepped up into the back and sat down.

"Miss Lowell, I'm Detective Parker, and this is my partner, Detective Montgomery." He spoke in a quiet, respectful voice.

"We need to ask you a few questions if that's okay."

She nodded her acceptance but didn't speak, just continued to stare out the side window of the rig.

"So, tell me from the beginning what you did today," Ethan prodded.

"Cal had a meeting yesterday, so we had a late dinner and rented a couple movies. We didn't get to bed until three, so we slept late and got up around nine-thirty this morning."

"Meeting?"

"Yes, he attends a support group."

"Really? Did you or Cal know Abby Montgomery?"

"Yes, she's a...*was* a good friend of Cal's. They met at the meeting when he joined six months ago and hit it off immediately."

"I'm sorry," he said, interrupting her. "What kind of support group was this?"

"It's a survivors group. Cal was mugged." She swallowed and blinked away fresh tears. "Stabbed. Abby was a rape victim. The group meets every Thursday over at the rec center."

He made notes while guilt clamored onto his shoulders again. Miss Lowell sighed, a tremulous smile on her lips. "She seemed to understand the pain and fear Cal was going through in a way I couldn't. He relied on her a lot, and in the beginning, he'd call her daily, sometimes more." She looked at him. "And before you ask, no I wasn't jealous. I was with him almost every time he called her. They were just very good friends who bonded because of their tragedies."

"Okay, so what did you do after you woke?"

She turned to stare out the window again. "Like I said, we got up around nine-thirty and had breakfast together. I left at eleven to meet two girlfriends at the mall. We went shopping for my wedding dress...oh, God...." She bowed her head for a moment and pinched the bridge of her nose. After wiping the tears away, she looked back up and cleared her throat. "After that, we spent a couple hours at the spa getting facials and manicures. Around five, we left the spa and grabbed some dinner and then an early movie."

Ethan stopped jotting the particulars in his notebook to hand her a tissue. Interviewing the family was always difficult, but eight times out of ten the vic was murdered by someone they knew, so family members had to be questioned and ruled out first in order to move on to other suspects. "I'll need your friends' names, so we can verify you were with them all day. What were Cal's plans for the day?"

Kelly accepted the tissue and dabbed her eyes. "He went to the gym."

"How do you know?"

"He called me on his way home."

"What time was that?" He asked and jotted down the information on his pad.

Kelly pulled out her cell phone and retrieved the history. "One p.m. He told me he planned to work on his thesis. He was working on his doctorate in psychology and told me not to worry about being late, that he would be able to get lots of work done with a quiet house."

"What time did you get home?"

"Somewhere around nine-thirty." She swallowed, and murmured, "About two minutes before I dialed 911."

"Did anything look out of place?"

Kelly shook her head. "No, not at all. The door was locked, but he always kept it locked, even when he was home—especially after the mugging."

He nodded. "Can you tell me about the mugging?"

"He was attacked and robbed at knifepoint eight months ago. We'd been out dancing and had walked halfway to the car before I realized I'd forgotten my scarf and hurried back for it. I guess the guy had been waiting in the parking lot." She shivered and hugged herself. "After taking his watch and wallet, I don't know why, but the guy stabbed him in the side. Punctured his lung. I came back with the scarf and found Cal lying on the ground. Blood...." She squeezed her eyes closed for a moment then opened them. "I yelled for help, dialed 911. It was only by the grace of God he survived."

Ethan ran a hand through his hair. So, Cal had been slashed before and survived. Could it be the same perp had come back to finish the job? And if so, what was the connection between Cal and Judson Roberts, the first vic, other than Abigail Montgomery? He looked up from his notebook. "Did you talk to Cal at all after he called you the first time?"

Kelly's eyes filled with tears again. "No. I tried calling around five, but when he didn't answer, I just assumed he was absorbed in his work. I should have been here. I should have known something was wrong when he didn't answer."

"I don't think there's a thing you could've done to stop this from happening. If anything, it might've been worse."

Kelly met his gaze. "How could anything be worse than what happened in that bedroom?"

"Believe it or not, lots of things." He stared at her, wondering whether the realization she could've been tortured and mutilated like her fiancé had entered her mind yet. "The officer said when he got here, you were saying 'he knew this would happen.' What did you mean by that?"

"Ever since he was attacked, Cal worried it would happen again. He was so scared he would be attacked and killed that he became obsessed with locking doors, checking windows, and he hardly went out after dark. Getting cut like that changed him." She stared at Ethan, grief weaving across her features. "He went to weekly meetings, that survivors group I told you about. He wanted to be whole again, to start our life together without that horrible night hanging over our marriage. But his fears came true, and it happened anyway, didn't it?"

He clenched his jaw, her words clawing at his sense of justice. Kelly Lowell didn't deserve this any more than the victim did. "Do you have somewhere to stay for the night?"

She nodded. "My mother is on her way."

"Good. As soon as CSU gives the okay, I will have one of them escort you in to get some of your things."

Kelly stiffened, and words tumbled from her lips. "I can't go in there. I don't need anything right now."

"Okay, I'll let you know when the house has been released. Please leave your mother's name and a number where we can contact you with the officer waiting outside." Ethan placed his hand on her shoulder and wished he could say something to take away her pain. "I'm very sorry for your loss."

She looked up at him, her bottom lip trembling. "Do you have any idea who did this?"

"Not yet, ma'am, but were working hard to find out."

Outside the ambulance, Grant stalked up to him. "Why did you question her about Abby?"

"You knew I was going to." He stared at him. "You don't see a theme here? Your sister was good friends with both victims."

"I see another theme as well. Both victims were only months away from marriage."

"Excellent point, Detective." He eyed his partner. He couldn't blame him for wanting to protect his sister, but all leads needed to be followed if they were going to catch whoever did this—and the rookie just presented a new one. "First thing tomorrow, I want you to start working that angle. Find out if the victims had anything in common, such as tailors, wedding planners or maybe the same venue. See if their paths crossed anywhere."

"What about Abby?"

"What about her? Just because we have another lead doesn't mean all others are ruled out. We work every one."

Ethan met Grant's gaze. The guy was a hothead where his sister was concerned, and he supposed he couldn't blame him. Abby had been through a lot.

An image of the sultry blonde bloomed in his mind. He just hadn't been prepared for her to be so...enticing. Hell, a guy would have to be dead not to notice.

But a lead was a lead. He donned what previous partners had termed his "pissed-off face" and glowered at Grant. "Are you going to question me about this throughout the entire investigation? Because that's going to get old real quick. We're a small office, and I need you on this. If you can't handle it, tell me now."

The guy took a step back. "I can handle it. But I'm not going to let you railroad my sister."

"I have no intention of doing that, although I can't ignore the connection until it proves to be a dead end. Like I said earlier, there is no such thing as coincidence. Now, do you want to come with me while I question her?"

"You know I do." He looked toward his truck parked on the snow-covered grass at the end of the driveway. Puffs of white smoke trailed from the tailpipe while the F-150's engine purred along, allowing the heater inside to keep Abby and Officer Moore warm. "If we're done here, why don't I take her home and meet you there?"

"We're going to be here a while longer." Ethan ambled across the yard in the direction of Grant's truck. In the driver's seat, Abby sat talking with Moore. "Let's see if she's okay to drive herself, and I'll give you a ride home when we're finished. We still need to go through the house and talk to the nearest neighbor. I can speak to your sister later."

Chapter Eight

*H*alf an hour shy of midnight, Ethan pulled into Grant's driveway. They hadn't spoken on the ride home, both deep in thought about the case—well, at least he was. He really couldn't say what his partner might have been chewing on, but he was fairly sure it included his sister. He was also sure his and Grant's thoughts in regards to Abby were worlds apart.

Deep sapphire eyes and long, honey-blonde hair dominated his dreams, night and day. He found himself wondering how she would feel in his arms, or underneath him with her legs wrapped around his waist and that beautiful blue-eyed gaze staring up at him.

Damn! He needed to stop this. He'd known her all of what, three going on four days? She was a suspect in a murder investigation. To say his thoughts were unprofessional was beyond an understatement—especially given his brother's role in her past. Any thoughts he might have about getting closer to her would be blown out of the water the moment she discovered his relationship to the man who'd assaulted her.

Ethan shut the engine off and zipped his jacket. "Ready?"

"Sure."

The word came on a burst of breath and carried a healthy dose of sarcasm along with it. But before he could respond,

Grant shoved the passenger door open and exited the truck.

He clenched his jaw. It seemed his partner continued to believe in a department-wide conspiracy, hell-bent on implicating his sister for the murders of two men. Or maybe the guy just thought he was a lazy bastard who'd decided to chuck his moral sense of justice and convict Abby for murder because it was easier than tracking down the real culprit. Who the hell knew?

With an irritated sigh, Ethan slammed the Chevy's door closed. He strode around the truck, bitter cold enveloping him with each step, while the icy northeastern winds nipped at his hands and face. He hunkered down in his coat and cast his gaze skyward. Low cloud cover obscured the jewel-encrusted, black velvet sky that typically swathed the crisp winter heavens over Red River. Instead of the fathomless depths of space above, the oppressive clouds gave a heavy, muffled feel to the night that left his nerves more than a little jangled.

Stuffing his hands into his jacket pockets, he followed Grant up the slate walkway while fluffy, wafer-sized snowflakes danced through the air and landed with a hushed sigh on everything around them. The muted sound of the falling snow, the encroaching clouds, and the indelible memory of the mutilated body from earlier that evening set Ethan's teeth on edge. He imagined it was how a claustrophobic might feel—boxed in, confined, trapped. Fortunately for him, it was nothing a roaring fire and a stiff drink couldn't fix. Or the molten heat created from rubbing his body against a certain blonde.

His gaze shifted to his partner as they mounted the porch steps. The problem with living and working in such a rural area was the lack of manpower. By all rights, the guy should not be working this case with him, but the only other Red River detective had been loaned to a neighboring county to work on a spree of home invasions where two people had been killed. But with Montgomery already deep into the investigation, Ethan knew it would be detrimental to pull him now.

He'd let Grant be present during any interviews with his

sister, but he couldn't let him take part or have a voice in any investigation of her. A good defense lawyer would be all over that. The lead that the two deceased men were about to get married was a good one, and one the guy could sink his teeth into. Although, in his gut, Ethan didn't believe it would pan out. No, this case revolved around Abby.

While he wasn't about to let her whiny-ass brother know, his instincts told him she was the reason these two men had been killed, but not through any fault of her own. Some whack job out there had fixated on her and had decided to kill off the men in her life. Which, if he was right, put both her and her brother in danger. But before he could tackle that problem, he had to question her and officially rule her out.

"Hold up a minute." He waited until Grant took his hand off the door handle and turned toward him before he continued. "Look, I know I gave you a hard time back there about your sister, and you may not believe it, but I do know what I'm doing. I can't have you second-guessing my every move. If you're going to be my partner, you're going to have to trust me."

"Easier said than done. She is the only family I have left. I know you're the best, but you're focusing on my sister, when I know she had nothing to do with this. That gets my back up." He glared at Ethan. "I will protect her till the day I die."

"I have a sister of my own, so I get you." He pulled his hand from his pocket, pointed his finger at his partner, and stared him square in the eye to ensure the man understood he wasn't the least bit intimidated. "But don't make the mistake of interfering with this part of the investigation. Understood?"

Grant folded. His gaze flitted to the porch floor, his shoulders slumped, and his brows unfurled. "Understood. And whether you believe it or not, I do know my job."

"Good." He hoped he'd gotten through to the rookie, and if this interview went the way he expected it to, he could clear Abby tonight, and his partner could focus his attention on the case.

Grant turned to unlock the front door, but it flew open

before he could insert the key into the lock. Abby stood in the doorway, her arms wrapped around herself in an attempt to ward off the frigid air, her hair pulled back in a ponytail, her feet bare. He stared, the sight giving the impression of a lost little waif.

"Abby, you'll catch your death out here. I had my keys." Grant ushered her inside.

Ethan had an overwhelming urge to grab her and envelop her in his arms. The need to comfort her, keep her warm and safe from harm, compelled him over the threshold. He also craved the taste of her lips, to experience the rush of her long hair as it brushed across his chest in a whisper touch, and those cute little toes curling into his thighs as she came.

He shook his head and tried to climb his way out of the fantasy. When he realized they'd gone inside while he remained standing in the doorway, he clenched his jaw and cursed himself. What the hell was wrong with him? Closing the front door, he followed the voices to the kitchen where he found them getting cups of what smelled like hot chocolate.

"I'm sorry it's so late, but I wanted to talk with you tonight." Ethan stood at the edge of the tiled floor and gazed at Abby, memorizing the color of her hair, the narrowness of her waist, the swell of her hips. When she turned to face him, dread pervaded her face, and he gritted his teeth. She was a suspect who needed to be questioned, and he was acting like a love-struck schoolboy. Get it together, Parker!

"It was Cal, wasn't it?" She looked at him, searching for answers. "He's dead."

"Yes. I apologize for not being able to tell you earlier at the scene. Procedure and all." He unzipped his jacket. His explanation sounded good. But what he'd really wanted was to see her reaction to the news.

She moved to the small round table in the breakfast nook and sank into a chair as tears streamed down her face. Clutching her hands to her chest, she rocked back and forth.

"What happened to him?" she asked, her voice barely

audible.

He wished there was an easier way to break the news, but experience told him what people really wanted was the truth. Not the glossed-over version to make it more palatable.

"He was murdered, the exact same way your ex-fiancé was."

Abby leapt from her chair and bolted down the hall. The distinct sound of her retching the contents of her stomach echoed from the bathroom. Grabbing a dishtowel, her brother charged after her, and Ethan waited in the hallway for the siblings to come out.

She appeared first, her face pale and forehead dotted with beads of sweat, followed by her scowling brother. She motioned for Ethan to follow her to the living room while Grant stormed off in the opposite direction, the dishtowel clutched in a chokehold.

"I apologize for that," she said after her brother disappeared into the kitchen. "I'm not usually one of those melodramatic females who freaks out at the faintest suggestion of bad news, but I just...I don't know. I hoped somehow he'd be all right. I don't understand what's happening."

He had to hand it to her, she was one tough lady. She'd pulled herself together well, though her eyes still held a line of fresh tears that threatened to fall. Even with her face as pale as paste, she managed to hold her own for the moment.

Unable to resist, Ethan moved toward her, closing the distance between them. He was too close. He knew it, but he couldn't stop until only inches separated them.

He stared into her eyes and found a swirling sea of grief and worry that elicited a depth of longing he never knew existed. His breath stuck in his throat with the overwhelming need to touch her, to feel the warmth of her skin beneath his fingers. With a tentative hand, he reached out to clasp her arm.

Wrong. So wrong. Touching her brought a wave of need crashing through him with such intensity he struggled to keep control.

He studied her face, searched for any hint of reproach. Her

gaze flitted to where his hand lay on her arm then back to his face. When she didn't flinch or pull away, he drew her closer, gathering her into his arms, and coaxed her head to rest on his chest. After a moment of stiffness, her shoulders relaxed, and she leaned into him.

Soft, full breasts crushed against him. Holding her was better than he had ever imagined. It felt right. He rubbed his hand over her back in a gentle circular motion and whispered soothing words in her ear. The rest of the world slipped away, leaving just the two of them.

At least until the sound of shattering glass broke the magic of it all.

Abby jerked away from him, her face flushed, and ran to her brother's side where he'd dropped the tray of hot cocoa. Ethan jolted back to reality. Here he stood in his partner's home, holding his partner's sister, who also was a suspect in a murder investigation. He shook his head to clear it. What the hell had he been thinking?

He strode over to where the two knelt, picking up pieces of ceramic mugs and mopping up cocoa. "You okay, partner?"

Grant looked up, his face red. "Yeah, just feel like I'm sleepwalking. Apparently I'm too exhausted to pick up my feet. I tripped over the throw rug."

"I'll go grab the mop," she offered.

"No, you stay here, so Ethan can question you and be going. He's got to be as tired as I am and wanting to go home and get some shut-eye."

Abby stood, her gaze on Ethan. "Question me?"

"Yeah," Grant said amid the piercing clinks of broken pieces of ceramic banging against one another as he dropped them onto the tray. "He still considers you a suspect in the murders."

"A suspect? Is that right, Detective?" Chin held high, she marched across the room and perched on the edge of the couch.

"I just have a few questions, that's all."

"By all means, Detective, let's get this started so you can leave."

The thick sarcasm and hurt in her voice hit him like a swift punch to the gut. He sat on the couch opposite her and dug out his pen and pad from his coat pocket. He tried to look at her, to meet her gaze, but couldn't. God, he had to be the biggest jackass known to man.

"How did you and Cal meet?"

"I met him about six months ago after he joined the support group." Her clipped words stung him like birdshot from a twelve-gauge shotgun.

He cleared his throat. "What was your relationship to him?"

"We were friends, good friends. He was mugged—the guy stabbed him for a wallet that had all of forty dollars in it. He had a hard time dealing with his inability to stop the attack and the powerless feeling it left behind. I was able to help him through that."

"How?" The word came out harsher than he'd intended. He glanced up, saw her wince.

"By talking with him. If you're trying to insinuate we were anything other than friends, Detective, you're way off base. He loved Kelly with all his heart. As a matter of fact, I went on a blind date earlier tonight with someone he set me up with."

He remembered Grant mentioning she'd been on a date the night before, but hearing the fact from her lips triggered a surprising shock of jealousy to sucker-punch him in the chest. He tried to feign passivity, but his heart raced at the thought of her with another man. "Really, and how did that work out?"

"It didn't."

Relief coursed through him only to be replaced by a wave of guilt. Damn it. He shouldn't be thinking this way about her. "Are you aware of whether he knew your ex-fiancé, or if they had any connection at all?"

"No, not that I know of."

"Where were you today between two and six p.m.?"

If possible, her voice grew even colder. "At work. I usually have the weekends off, but one of the girls asked me to cover for her. I got off at seven p.m. after a twelve-hour shift, changed my clothes at work, and arrived at The Bistro at seven forty-five for the date."

He stared at her, wishing he could find the words to erase the distress so vivid in her eyes. But there was nothing he could do. "I guess that's all I need."

"I'll see you to the door."

Ethan followed her, each of her steps rigid, determined. He'd blown it with her, he knew that, and he damn well deserved to have his ass kicked for it.

Abby yanked the door open and stood aside to let him pass.

He dragged his feet over the threshold and, once on the porch, turned back to her. "I was just doing my job."

"Really?" Her eyes widened, and her face darkened. "Your job? It's your *job* to embrace the suspect, to make them feel safe in your arms, wanted? That's an ingenious interrogation system you've got worked out for yourself. Make the suspect let their guard down and move in for the attack." Shaking with rage, she glared at him. "Well, let me just say, you are very good at your job."

"Abby, that's not what I meant—"

"Goodnight, Detective." She reared back, slamming the door in his face.

Dismissed. Ethan stomped through the newly fallen snow to his truck and wrenched the door open. After climbing in and jerking the door closed, he punched the steering wheel.

"Shit!"

Chapter Nine

*E*than stood next to a well-kempt cedar tree, its boughs laden with the previous night's snow. With his jacket collar turned up and his hands shoved deep in the pockets, he stared across the Red River cemetery at the freshly turned grave for Judson Roberts. The harsh winter sun glared down on the piles of snow workers had pushed aside for the graveside service, and the little that remained on the ground had turned to slush beneath the soles of the mourners who had long since gone.

Only Abby remained.

Her thin, stark figure contrasted to the heaps of snow behind her as she stood beside the grave, head bowed with her arms wrapped around herself—whether in self-comfort or to ward off the cold, Ethan didn't know. In one hand, she held a single, long-stemmed red rose. An ache seared through his chest at the sight of her, and he longed to gather her in his arms and console her and protect her from the evils of the world.

Her lips moved, starting and stopping, trembling between one sentence and the next. A final prayer for the departed? Professions of undying love for her lost former fiancé? At the distance he stood from her, he couldn't hear her words, but he understood the grief slashed across her face and what Jud must have meant to her.

She reached out, her hand trembling, and dropped the rose into the gaping rectangular hole—a hole that reminded him more of a deep, dark freezer than a final resting place. He shivered. The weatherman had predicted more snow and plunging temperatures over the next few days, which meant Jud was probably the last to be buried, and then the gravediggers would go on hiatus until spring.

He stepped away from the tree, treading across the frozen ground that separated Abby and him. Stopping at a respectful distance, he waited for her to finish her goodbyes.

When she turned away from the grave and found him, her eyes widened in surprise. "Detective." She hugged herself again—although this time he suspected it was to ward him off more than the cold. "You look tired."

"I went back to the station last night. Needed to finish some paperwork, answer emails. I caught a couple hours on the couch." In truth, after the complete ass he'd made of himself the night before, there was no way he could go home and sleep. Self-recriminations plagued him for hours, eventually devolving into a base litany of caustic name-calling. After a fitful two hours on the station couch, he came to the conclusion he had to see her again and try to make things right. "I just wanted to offer my condolences."

"Thank you." She looked at him with red-rimmed eyes. For a moment, their gazes locked and held, causing his heart rate to jump, but the connection broke before he could find the words to erase the damage he'd done the night before. She glanced over his shoulder and said, "Didn't Grant come with you?"

"No. He's back at the office following up a couple leads." He swallowed. Why did she make him so nervous?

"A lead? I thought I was the only suspect on your list." Her eyes flashed just as they had last night right before she'd slammed the door in his face.

"No. Your alibi checked out."

"My alibi?" Her lips thinned, and her eyebrows knitted. "You checked up on me?"

"Yes." Ethan ground his teeth. How the hell did he always end up on the defensive? "I had to check your alibi, and because it checked out, you're cleared of being a suspect. I'm sorry if that offends you, but it's my job. I have to check every lead and every alibi in order to narrow down the list of suspects."

"I see." She chewed her bottom lip and glared at him.

"If you want to feel less like I'm singling you out, then you should know that I also checked both fiancées' alibis as well. We're checking co-workers, neighbors, the members of your therapy group—anyone who might have known both victims. Anyone other than you."

"Because my alibi checked out. Well, thank you, Detective. That makes me feel so much better." Sarcasm laced her words. She moved to the side, intent on storming past him.

He reached out, laid his hand on her arm to stop her, but she jerked away. The hurt in her eyes was almost more than he could bear, and he found himself fighting the urge to pull her into his arms again. To do so would be utter disaster at this point.

"What, Detective Parker? Now that you've cleared me of murder, you think you have the right to touch me?"

Ethan jolted. "No."

Icy satisfaction glazed her eyes, and she turned to storm off.

Ethan couldn't help himself. He couldn't just let her go off like that, so he snagged her hand and spun her toward him.

"Let go of—"

"Just hush a moment, will you?" He towered over her, stared at her until she shut her mouth so tightly her lips paled. "I know I messed up last night. I admit that. I should've questioned you and left."

"So, you're saying you never should've tried to comfort me?"

"Yes." He huffed in frustration. "No."

She arched her brow.

"It was the order of things." He sighed and wished he'd been smarter about this, had gotten more sleep up front.

"Oh, now I understand. You should've interrogated me first and then tried to seduce me." She tugged her hand free from his.

"Funny, but I don't remember Grant mentioning anything about that when he went through his academy training."

"I'm trying my damndest to apologize."

"Well, keep trying, Detective. Because this one didn't come close to clearing you off my list." She pivoted on her heel and strode away from him, her long, angry strides accentuating the sway of her hips.

Ethan stared after her, his mouth agape, his palm cold where he'd once held her hand. Just the night before he'd held her in his arms, and the memory of how her supple body had pressed against him tumbled through his mind, multiplying his frustration and catapulting it to a whole other level. He shook his head and swallowed an exasperated growl.

No woman had gotten to him like this before—irritated and excited him, gave him icy glares that left him hot with need—all in a single breath. Damn. He hadn't even known a woman like that existed.

Not until Abby Montgomery, anyway.

Chapter Ten

*W*ell over halfway through her shift at Red River Hospital, Abby locked the wheels of the gurney and scrutinized the teen who lay on the table to ensure he remained sedated. Myriad cuts and bruises marred his handsome face, and a contusion the size of a tethered volleyball covered his right shoulder and extended across his chest. Such a senseless accident for a boy so young, but for some reason, ice-covered parking lots tended to bring the hell-raisers out of the woodwork.

"What do we have?" Head Nurse Mary Jenkins asked as she strode through the doorway. She swept her sharp gaze over the teen. "Jacob Morris, your mom's going to tan your hide when you wake up." Nurse Jenkins flicked her gaze up to Abby. "What's his status?"

"Stable," She said and reached over to smooth the kid's dark hair from his eyes. "Dr. Marsh said it looked like a broken clavicle and fractured left femur. Should be another minute or two before Don confirms that from X-ray."

She nodded and took the boy's pulse. When she finished, she patted his hand. "You best come through this in one piece, boy. After your daddy lost his job, your mom doesn't need anymore bad news." She looked up at Abby, her unspoken request clear in her eyes.

"Mr. and Mrs. Morris have been notified," She said. "I'll let you know when they arrive."

Nurse Jenkins nodded again. "My Betsy goes to school with him." She looked at the boy, grimaced, and a slight shudder shook her frame.

Red River High School wasn't that big. From her reaction, it was obvious she realized her daughter could've been in the car with Jacob and possibly lying broken on a table in the next room.

"We'll prep him for surgery," Nurse Jenkins said. "By then, Don will have pictures, so we'll know what we're up against."

A moment later, two other nurses entered the room, and knowing Jacob was in good hands, Abby stepped out to give them space to maneuver. She trod silently over the highly polished tiles to the waiting room door and peeked through. After the mad rush with Jacob Morris' arrival, she sighed with relief to find less than a dozen people remained, and of those, only four had injuries. She approached the check-in station where Kelly took personal and insurance information for patients.

"Who's next?"

Kelly held up a manila folder. "Miles Freemont jumped off the top bunk of his bed. Mom thinks his arm may be broken. If you have don't have any films to take at the moment, I sure could use the help. We have room three open."

"No problem." She took the folder, called the name listed, and led the six-year-old boy and his distraught mother down the hallway.

"I was a superhero and tried to fly," Miles said as she helped him onto the examination table. The boy screwed his face up and looked down at his swollen wrist. "I think my cape didn't fly me like it should have, though."

"I guess it didn't." She gave him a sympathetic smile and took his pulse. After verifying pertinent information, she moved toward the door. "The doctor will be in to see you in just a few minutes. And you, young man...." She pointed at Miles, who stared back with big eyes. "Stay on that table. There's no flying allowed in the hospital."

He gave her a solemn nod, and she fought not to grin as she closed the door. With a shake of her head, she dropped the folder into the bin on the wall to alert the doctor of his next patient and headed back to the check-in station. What was it about death-defying acts that intrigued boys, bringing out the daredevil in them?

"You look tired. Why don't you take your dinner break while it's slow?" Kelly rose from her steno chair, another manila folder in her hand. "I can handle it for a bit while you eat."

Abby peered into the waiting room. The remaining people sat quietly, perusing magazines while they waited for their name to be called.

"Okay. If it gets busy again, just page me." She headed toward the cafeteria and passed Don on the way.

"You headed for dinner?" he asked.

She grinned at the brawny X-ray technician. "Yep. You want to join me?"

"I could eat." He held up a large white envelope. "Gotta get these shots to Doc Marsh first, though. Shouldn't take too long."

"See you there." She turned and headed down the main hallway to the far side of the hospital, the smell of freshly brewed coffee and garlic guiding her.

Halfway to the cafeteria, the memory of Jud's funeral jolted through her mind, and her heart ached as though she'd been stabbed with a knife. She leaned against the wall to catch her breath, the memory of him ensconced within the coffin in a dark blue suit, crisp white shirt, and striped tie vivid. The small smile on her best friend's lips tore at her, and tears welled in her eyes. Had they buried him only yesterday morning?

Abby pulled out the tissue pack she'd tucked into her pocket and yanked two free. She dabbed the corner of her eyes and took several deep, cleansing breaths. Now was not the time to fall apart. Better to hold it off until later when she could cry in the privacy of her bedroom.

She sniffled, blew her nose. Why would anyone want to kill Jud?

Of course, that question prompted an image of Detective Parker to spring into her mind. She closed her eyes, envisioned him from yesterday at the cemetery. He'd stood near that huge cedar tree, waited while she'd finished her goodbyes to Jud. She'd seen him from the corner of her eye, and her heart had skipped a beat. He'd looked so official, so serious—and yes, so handsome—bundled in his police-issue winter jacket. So much so, she'd been ready to dismiss the hurt and anger his actions had caused her the night before. But then he'd swaggered over, offered his half-hearted apology, and expected her to be grateful.

Fury flew through her, and she pushed away from the wall. Turning, she stormed down the hallway.

Yes. Anger was much easier to deal with than sorrow.

On entering the brightly lit cafeteria, she marched to the beginning of the food line, grabbed a colorful teal tray, and slammed it onto the metal counter. Snatching a fork, knife, and spoon, she dropped the utensils onto the tray, the tinny clang of metal reverberating through the room. When she arrived at the immense pan holding the night's specialty, she passed it by. The thought of heavy Italian food made her stomach churn. She moved toward the breads and pastries, clutching the sides of her tray until her knuckles showed white.

"How's it going, Abby?" A sweet-faced, grandfatherly man stood behind the counter and grinned at her. He wiped his hands on the towel he held. "What can I get you tonight?"

"I was thinking toast or something light." She forced a smile to her lips, but found it became genuine when he held up a large bagel.

"Aw, toast isn't good enough for a beautiful girl like you. My wife brought a dozen of these to me just an hour ago. Multigrain with oatmeal on top."

He deftly sliced the bagel in half and popped it into the toaster oven. He wiped the counter down while Abby grabbed a mug and filled it with fresh-brewed coffee. A minute later, a bell sounded, announcing the bagel had toasted.

"Why she thinks I need twelve bagels," he said as he opened the oven, "I'll never know."

"That was very sweet of her."

"Forty-eight years of marriage and the woman still brings me gifts." He slid the bagel halves onto a plate. "She's the light of my life, I tell you."

Her own parents had died when she was young, and Uncle Marty had come to live with her and Grant. He'd been unmarried. The idea of a lasting relationship full of love sent her mind and heart whirling. "You're very lucky."

"Luck doesn't have anything to do with it. We had our ups and downs. But trust, commitment, and a lot of hard work saw us through forty-eight years. Here you go." He handed her the plate along with two containers of cream cheese. He smiled, the corners of his eyes crinkling. "And don't worry. You'll find that man that makes your heart sing the way Jen makes mine."

She carried her tray to a nearby table. After adding a packet of sweetener and a dab of milk to her cup, she sat stirring her coffee, mesmerized by the creamy swirls in the dark liquid. How would anyone make her heart sing? The closest she'd come was when Detective Parker held her in his arms, and her heart had lightened ever so much. She was a broken person. Hopefully, therapy would mend her. But would she even recognize love if it happened?

Setting her spoon aside, she sipped the hot coffee. She'd cared for Jud, he'd made her feel special once upon a time. But that had been so long ago.

With a sigh, she let her eyelids drift closed. Her heart ached with missing him. But instead of the expected mental picture of Jud in her mind, an image of Ethan burst forth. He stared down at her as he had last night, his dark gaze intense and filled with longing. He reached for her, pulled her into his arms. The warmth of his body pressing against hers sent tingles of desire zinging through her body.

Her eyes flew open, her breath stuck in her throat. Ethan

Parker. How could that be possible? Yes, he drove her crazy, but more in an arrogant and insulting type fashion. Not romantic. He was a detective and didn't have a passionate bone in his body. Except for when he'd held her close, his heart pounding beneath her ear.

No. He'd realized that had been a mistake. He'd made it clear he wasn't interested. And she wanted nothing to do with him.

She shifted, crossed her legs. Although it seemed the heat coursing through her body indicated otherwise. And what a shock that was. To have felt nothing for so many years, the long forgotten sensations excited and unnerved her.

Her cell phone rang, and she jumped. She snatched it from her pocket, thankful for the distraction.

"Hello?"

"Hey, Abby. This is Elliot, Elliot Swanson. I took you out to dinner."

"Umm." God, what could she say?

"You freaked out over the peppermints. Remember?"

"Yes." She swallowed. "I remember."

"Yeah, sorry about that." He paused, cleared his throat. "I was just calling to reschedule our date. I'll see if I can find a restaurant that's peppermint-free this time around." A raucous laugh ended with what sounded like a pig's snort.

She sighed. "You don't know what happened to Cal?"

"No, darlin'. Why don't you tell Elliot all about the man responsible for bringing us together."

"He was...um...." She toyed with the spoon she'd used to stir her coffee, rubbed her thumb over the smooth metal handle. "He's dead. Murdered."

"Good God." His words came long and drawn out across the line. "Cal Gibson is dead?"

"Yes."

"Well, I better go see his fiancée, umm...."

"Kelly Lowell," she supplied.

"Yes. I need to offer my condolences to Ms. Lowell. See if she might be in need of my services."

Abby cringed. Hopefully, Elliot meant his lawyer services. But after his blatant flirtation with the waitress, she wouldn't put anything past him.

"So, how's about Friday night?"

"What?"

"You and me. Meet at a different restaurant for our date." His bawdy laughter came over the line. "Can't let ole Cal's hook-up go to waste, now can we?"

Her stomach clenched. He wanted to go out on a date? She gritted her teeth, her mind whirling for a plausible excuse. "Elliot, Cal is dead. I need some time to grieve. It might, uh, be awhile before I go out on another date."

"Oh." The line hung silent for a long moment, then with a jaunty tone, he said, "Well, you take a couple days and grieve, darlin'. Then Elliot Swanson will show you a good time. We'll dance and drink in honor of our dear deceased buddy. I'll call you."

Before Abby could respond, the call ended. She stared at her cell phone. What an arrogant, self-absorbed idiot. Why had Cal ever believed she and Elliot would hit it off? Maybe Elliot had saved Cal's boyhood dog from an oncoming car or something, but then she couldn't imagine the self-absorbed lawyer caring about anything other than himself. Truth be told, he probably had just felt sorry for the guy.

"I can't believe you're going to make me eat this delicious spaghetti all by myself."

She looked up into a pair of warm brown eyes. "About time you got here."

Don set his tray on the table and sat in the chair next to hers. "Girl, I can't believe all you're having is a mangy old bagel. You need sustenance."

She grinned. "I'll have you know this is a fresh, multi-grain bagel chock full of goodness."

"I hear you." Don twirled his fork in his pile of spaghetti and inserted the wad of noodles, dripping with garlic-infused marinara sauce, into his mouth. His eyelids fluttered closed. "Mmm. God, that man can cook. If he wasn't straight and married, I'd be all over that."

Abby laughed and dropped her cell back into her pocket. Grabbing one of the cream cheese containers, she pulled the top flap back and spread the contents onto one bagel half.

"Of course, Bobby would have a fit, the jealous little snit. He'd kill me if I even looked at—" Don's eyes grew wide, and he reached out, grabbed her arm and squeezed. "Oh, God. I am so sorry. I wasn't thinking. It just came out...."

She patted his hand and forced a smile. "It's okay, Don. I know you didn't mean it."

"I should just stuff my face with spaghetti and stop talking."

"Tell you what." She picked up half her bagel. "Let's call a truce. Spaghetti for bagel."

His gaze flitted down to his brimming plate then back to her. "Deal." He held up a second fork. "Figured you'd want some anyway, you moocher."

She laughed, grabbed the fork, and twirled it in the noodles. Pushing the mound into her mouth, she savored the sweet, tangy flavor.

"So, how was the funeral?" Don stared at her, his gaze filled with sympathy.

She swallowed, blinking away the rush of tears. "It was nice. I mean, lots of people attended, the flowers were beautiful, the service was thoughtful."

He nodded and took a bite of bagel, crunching through the toasted crust. They ate in silence for a few minutes, then Don sat up straight, his face lighting, and said, "I just had a fabulous idea."

Abby eyed him. "What's that?"

"You need to get out, take your mind off everything for a few hours. Why not go dancing with Bobby and me this Friday?"

The glee brimming in his face brought laughter burbling up her throat. "Dancing?"

"Absolutely!" He set his fork onto his plate. "And with a

gorgeous man on each arm, you'll be the envy of every woman in the club. What's not to love?"

"I don't know." She clutched her coffee cup, held it with both hands. "My last date didn't turn out so well. I'm not sure I'm the dating type anymore."

"Who? That schmuck, Elliot Swanson? He's an ambulance whore." Don's mouth twisted into a distasteful grimace. "You need to class it up, darling. And Bobby and I are just the guys to get you out and about Red River again."

Dancing with no strings attached, no sexual pressure? That sounded wonderful.

Don leaned toward her, his voice low and conspiring. "You can join in the festivities of marital bliss." When she met his gaze with raised eyebrows, he said, "I'm asking him to marry me Friday at lunch, and we'll celebrate that night."

"Wouldn't you two rather be alone?"

"Honey, I want to shout it to the world. I want to sing, dance. And my man can shake the rafters. So, don't make me grovel, because you know I'm not above that. Say yes."

"Goodness," Abby said then giggled. "How can I say no?"

ଔ

Closing the door against the howling wind outside, Abby locked the deadbolt and shrugged out of her coat. The warmth of the house embraced her, twining around her limbs like a long lost lover. She sighed, thankful to be home after an arduous day at the hospital.

"Abby, that you?" Grant's voice wafted down the hallway.

She ambled toward his room, leaned against the doorjamb, and offered him a tired smile. "It's me."

"Tough day?" He laid the novel in his hands against his chest, his full attention on her.

"Yes." She crossed the room to sit on the edge of his bed. The mattress eased beneath her, beckoning her to lie down and sleep. "A stupid kid cutting donuts on an icy parking lot ended up in surgery. Sprained ankles, bruised knees, a broken arm. Just an endless stream of injuries that kept us hopping all night."

"Did you get dinner?"

"I shared some spaghetti with Don."

"Don?" He set his book aside and sat up higher in the bed.

"Yes. He's an X-ray technician." She grinned, giddiness bubbling through the exhaustion, and flopped back on the bed. "We're going out dancing Friday night."

"Dancing?" A mischievous gleam sparkled in his eyes. "Sounds serious. Maybe I should run a background check on this guy, make sure he doesn't have any outstanding parking or speeding tickets."

Panic at the thought of Don discovering her brother had investigated him rushed through her, and she bolted upright. He'd never let her live it down. "Don't you dare!"

He held up his hands. "Okay, okay. I was just joking."

"Better be. He's a good friend, and I'd like to keep it that way."

"Whatever. I'm just happy to see you smiling again."

She sobered, her thoughts turning to a more serious subject. Grant's brow furrowed. "Did I say something wrong?"

"No." She took a breath then let the air whoosh between her lips. "Just thinking about Jud's funeral."

"Oh." He ran a hand through his hair. "Sorry I couldn't be there."

"That's okay." She offered him a tremulous smile. Unable to hold his gaze, she looked toward the door. "Detective Parker was there and offered his condolences."

Grant grunted, picked up his book. "That was nice of him. Though really, he had to be there for the service. You know a lot of killers go to the funeral to see the grief they've caused."

The idea that Jud's murderer had attended the funeral, might have stood right next to her, set her stomach to churning. "That's just sick."

"True. Unfortunately, Ethan said no one appeared

conspicuous." He opened his book, flipped a page. "Didn't mention he saw you."

A bevy of butterflies fluttered in her chest at the memory of how he'd looked, standing next to the snow-covered cedar tree. She rose from the bed and moved toward the door, hoping to hide the flush burning her cheeks. Attempting to appear nonchalant, she turned back to him, shrugged, and said, "Nothing to mention."

He turned another page of his novel. "I figured."

Anxious to escape, Abby forced a yawn behind her hand. "I think I'll head to bed. I'm exhausted." She turned and stepped through the doorway.

"Hey, can you switch my light off on your way out? Now that I know you're home safe and sound, I can get some shut-eye, too." He closed his book and set it aside.

"No problem." She reached back and hit the switch. "By the way, I'm a big girl. You don't have to wait up for me."

"Heck, some days it's the only time I get to see you." He chuckled. "Sweet dreams," he called, his words chasing her down the hallway.

She pushed her door closed behind her, the latch clicking home. Her heart pounded as thoughts of Ethan tumbled through her mind. His eyes. His touch. His arms around her, holding her close.

Her cheeks heated further.

She moved to the side of her bed, removed her watch, and placed it on the nightstand. A swarm of butterflies fluttered inside her stomach. Her legs trembled, threatened to give way. She eased onto the edge of the mattress and bit her lower lip, thoughts of the handsome detective sending enticing warmth to settle between her thighs.

She shook her head. It made no sense. The man was arrogant, infuriating. He'd questioned her as a suspect, believing that she might have killed Jud and Cal.

After clicking off the bedside lamp, Abby flopped back on the bed. Impossible. There was no way she could be even remotely

attracted to Detective Ethan Parker. Could she?
Sweet dreams indeed.

Chapter Eleven

*D*on Bledsoe shrugged out of his coat and tossed it and his keys on the table by the door. "Love you, too, and I think I'll get to the hospital half an hour early, so we can have breakfast together," he said into the cell phone he cradled to his ear.

"Sounds great, babe. I'll see you in the morning, then."

With a sigh, he disconnected the call and ambled into the bathroom to wash up for the night. Lord but he was blessed to have a man like Bobby Higgins in his life. Now that same-sex marriage had been legalized in Vermont, he counted the days 'til he could propose. Friday night would be perfect. And who better to help them celebrate than Abby? She was the one who'd introduced them after all.

After brushing his teeth, he spat the minty toothpaste into the sink and splashed his face with warm water. With droplets clinging to his chin, he reached blindly for the face towel that hung next to the sink.

Except it wasn't there.

What the hell? Don forced his eyes open in time to see the dark shadow of a man and a white towel rushing toward his face. A sweet odor assaulted his sense of smell.

Instinct took over, and he fought off his unknown attacker. He threw his weight backward and rammed his elbow hard into the ribcage of the man behind him. The hand holding the cloth against his nose and mouth released its pressure, and Don knocked the foul material away, inhaling a much-needed breath of fresh air.

Still pinned against the marble sink, he brought his heel up and kicked out, hitting his assailant's knee. The man cried out and took a step back.

Don was free.

He used the split second of freedom, spun around, and kicked the stranger in the groin. Pain traveled up his leg from the impact, but he didn't stop. He shoved the man aside and bolted out of the bathroom.

Don sprinted for the front door, grabbed the knob, and pulled. He was going to make it. Holy shit, he was going to make it out of this alive.

The door opened an inch and jolted to a stop. Crap. The security chain. He fumbled with it, pushed it off the slide plate, and....

Freedom.

He yanked the door open wide. The dark night yawned before him, and frigid air rushed to him, curled around his bare legs, and embraced his naked torso. Smoky white puffs spewed from his mouth as he struggled to catch his breath. He looked left then right. What could he use as a weapon? Where could he hide?

Headlights. Coming up the road.

His breath jammed in his throat, and hope swam in his chest. He ran down the first two steps, oblivious to his state of undress. Almost there. Almost safe.

Pain exploded in the back of his head. His feet faltered, and he tumbled down the stairs, crashing face-first onto the cement sidewalk with brutal intensity. A horrible crunching sound filled his ears followed by a sharp ache from his broken nose.

He squeezed his eyes closed, and a starburst of colors erupted behind his eyelids. Moaning, he pushed from the ground on shaky arms and fought to stay in the moment, to fight the black hole that threatened to swallow him.

A hand dug into his hair, yanked his head back, and a cry of misery gurgled from his throat.

So close. Tears overflowed and fell down his cheeks. He'd been so damn close.

"Why?" he said, amid the blood that gushed over his lips and into his mouth.

"She's mine," the man said, his deep voice filled with rage. He shoved Don's head forward, releasing his hair.

Don's arms buckled, and he slammed into the concrete a second time. He slumped against the icy sidewalk, the rough texture scraping across his cheek. Blackness swirled into his vision, dragging him down until nothing remained.

೦೪

Don strained against the fog muddling his mind. The familiar scent of jasmine and the plush, overstuffed down comforter told him he lay on his bed. Bobby loved jasmine, said it was like making love on a tropical beach or in the rainforest.

Don attempted to sit up, but his arms and legs didn't work right, like they'd gone numb or something. And, God, he hurt. All over, his muscles ached, his joints cried with pain. At last, he forced his eyes open.

Oh, dear sweet God.

He turned his head, found his hands lashed to the headboard with duct tape twisted into a silver rope, except where it had been wrapped several times around his wrists, the wide, sticky adhesive holding taut. He jerked his knees, only to find they wouldn't move. His feet had been tied to the footboard, rendering him immobile.

And he was naked, spread-eagled on the bed.

Fear bubbled up his throat, threatened to choke him. The sound of his harsh breathing filled the bedroom as the air wheezed through the nostrils of his shattered nose, his mouth covered with the same duct tape that trapped him on the bed.

This wasn't a game. No. Bobby knew how much he hated bondage games.

Images of the man in the bathroom mirror rushed back to him. The softness of the hand towel as it slammed against his face. The sweet smell of...chloroform?

But he'd been free, damn it.

His face and head throbbed. The memory of his assailant attacking him outside rushed back to him. Not so free as he'd thought.

Don yanked at his restraints. He had to get out of this. A cold sweat broke out on his forehead, and his heart beat in triple time. How could this be happening? The rasping sound of his breath grew quicker and louder until the room began to tilt in on him. Slow down, buddy. Think.

There was still time to get out of this. He scanned the room, searching for something to help him. Something to cut through those damned restraints and set him free.

And that's when Don spotted him.

Dressed in black, the man who had attacked him leaned against the doorframe. Just stood there, so still. He stared at Don through what appeared to be a stocking that he'd pulled over his head.

A glint of light caught Don's eye and drew his gaze lower. In the man's hands, which had been cloaked in black gloves, a sharp carving knife gleamed. Fear squeezed Don's throat, and he struggled to breathe.

Oh, sweet Jesus.

"You're awake. Good. I was about to get started without you, but I didn't want you to miss all the fun." The man sauntered over to the bed.

Through the stocking, Don glimpsed the guy's smile. Dread pooled low in his gut.

"You should've left well enough alone. This really is your fault, you know." He tightened his grip around the knife's handle, the leather gloves creaking as he flexed his fingers.

A tremor set up in Don's chest, causing his breath to hitch.

His entire body shook uncontrollably. His mind reeled with the possibility that he'd pissed some crazy guy off, and now he was going to die. Except he had no idea who this man was or what he was talking about.

"If you'd just stayed away from her, we'd have never had to meet. Unfortunately, you tried to take what's mine, and that's unforgivable."

Powerless, Don watched the man lift the knife and plunge it downward. Sharp, burning pain radiated through his chest as the blade sliced through his skin. His body tried to curl in on itself, drawing his constraints tight, and beneath the tape that covered his mouth, he screamed, the noise going nowhere.

With mounting horror, Don watched the man carve into his chest. The stranger concentrated on the knife in his hand, his movements swift and surgical as he whittled away at his flesh. Don screamed and shook at each incision until all that remained were whimpers and tears. Drops of blood from his broken nose ran over the duct tape on his mouth, dripped off his chin, and spattered onto his ravaged chest, mixing with the crimson puddle already there.

Through the torture, his mind sought refuge, and his thoughts turned to the only true haven he'd ever known. Bobby, their love, their life together.

Don sobbed. All gone. He would never hold Bobby in his arms again, never feel his slow, rhythmic breath as he drifted off to sleep, never hear the laughter that sent swirls of warmth through him.

Dear Lord, don't let him find me like this.

The crazy man stepped away and stared at Don's chest. Don tried to look into his eyes, to create some kind of connection, to plead for his life the only way available to him. But the bastard only nodded and, even through the stocking that covered his face, satisfaction with his handiwork glimmered in his eyes.

"This next part might hurt a little, but it's unavoidable. Men like you think only with their dicks." He stepped to the end of the bed, tested the hold of the makeshift ropes. "They see a hot woman and think only of what that woman can do for them. They don't think of the pain they can cause her, only of their own pleasure. It's disgusting."

A woman?

Don shook his head, tried to convey to the madman he was wrong. But it did no good. All that came out were unintelligible sounds muted by the gag.

He had the wrong man. Christ, couldn't he see that? But the bastard wouldn't even look at him, turning to scan the room instead. When his dark gaze paused on the framed photo of him and Bobby in an embrace, Don's heart stuttered.

Oh, please, please don't let him hurt Bobby.

The bastard strode over to the photo and picked it up. He traced his index finger gently over Bobby's face. Don's stomach seemed to rise into his throat. He wanted to shout to the man to do what he wanted to him, but leave Bobby the hell alone.

The man slammed the frame down on the dresser and spun around to face Don. Eyes wide through the stocking, he marched toward Don.

"You're gay? You're fucking gay? How is that possible?" He ripped the tape off Don's mouth—a minor displeasure compared to what the bastard had already done to him. With a sharp twitch of his wrist, the man flung the tape away, Don's blood and spit spattering against the wall. He turned back to his captive and growled, "Answer me. How is that possible?"

He stared at the man. What the hell was he talking about? "I...I—"

"How do you know Abby?"

"Abby Montgomery?" He cringed. Was this guy a confused, jealous boyfriend?

"Yes." He brandished the knife, held the point beneath Don's chin. "How the hell do you know her?"

"I work with her." Nervous and anxious to explain, he glanced toward the picture of Bobby and himself. "She introduced me to the guy you saw in that picture. I was going to propose to him this weekend. She was going to be there. It all seemed so—"

With a growl, the man lifted the knife to Don's mouth and pressed the blade against his lips, silencing him. "Perfect," the man snarled, his angry sarcasm sending sweaty chills down Don's back.

The guy straightened, and there was a slight clack as he set the knife on the bedside table. Don flinched when a sharp ripping sound filled the air.

"Please," he whimpered. "I won't tell. I sw—"

The new strip of tape slapped over his mouth, cutting his pleas short. He squeezed his eyes closed and heard the tinny clatter of metal sliding over wood as the murderer retrieved his knife. Don's heart thudded heavily, the outcome to this night obvious.

His life was over. There would be no breakfast with Bobby at the hospital. No romantic proposal at the dance club.

He opened his eyes.

This was the man who'd killed Abby's friends. That knowledge brought a strange calm to him. This wasn't about him or Bobby. This man wouldn't go after Bobby next, and for that, Don was unbelievably grateful.

The man rubbed his hand over his stocking-swathed face. "Fuck!"

When the killer leaned over and brought his hand up, Don cringed. But instead of smashing his fist into Don's face, he covered his eyes, his leather-ensconced fingers cool against his warm face.

"I'm sorry. This was my mistake," the killer said. His words sounded more like a parishioner's confession than an apology. "But you know I can't let you live."

The sound of the knife slicing through the air reached Don's ears just before the blade pierced his chest. He jolted in response to the intense pain and as he struggled, his arms and legs became heavy, his fingers and toes numbing.

Oh damn. I wish....

He closed his eyes, picturing sweet Bobby's smile.

Chapter Twelve

"Damn it," Ethan grumbled as his eight-hour-old nuked department coffee burned its way down his throat. He knew better than to drink the crap, but at five a.m., and operating on a scant four hours of sleep in the last forty-eight, the bitter, caffeinated sludge was a necessity.

Leaning back in his chair, he rubbed his jaw where it ached from grinding his teeth so much. The case had no new developments, and it frustrated the hell out him. Who had killed these men? Ethan's chair squeaked as he leaned forward to read Gary's forensic report again. He flipped open the autopsy results on Jud and Cal and paused to massage the bridge of his nose before focusing on the details.

Both men had died of exsanguination after their femoral and carotid arteries had been cut. Both men's eyes had been removed as well as their penises filleted. Jud had been dead for approximately three hours before he'd been found, Cal five hours. No foreign fibers or hairs had been found on either body. That alone proved premeditation. Crimes of passion happened on the spur of the moment and always left trace evidence. This killer was intelligent and had prepared for each murder.

He placed the victims' autopsy photos side by side. The blood had been cleaned away, revealing what lay beneath. The word carved in the first victim's chest was YOU, the second victim had ARE. A sentence? Some kind of sick message? If so, how many more men had to die before they knew what it said?

He glanced at his watch—quarter of six. It was still early, but he took a chance and placed a call to Will Donovan in the FBI's Behavioral Analysis Unit. He needed some kind of insight into the man they were looking for. Expecting voicemail, he was surprised when Will answered on the second ring.

"Donovan."

"Hey, Will. It's Ethan Parker. Sorry if I woke you."

"Eh, you didn't wake me. I was just headed to the gym, trying to get an early start before the bad guys bog me down. What's up?"

"Listen, I've bagged this case that looks like it's gonna turn serial on me." He stared down at the reports on his desk and wished he were wrong, but everything pointed to the worst. "I'm wondering if you might be able to work up a profile for me?"

"Sure. Fax me the crime scene info and victimology, and I'll take a look when I get to the office. You still have my fax number?"

"I do, thanks. I appreciate the extra set of eyes." Maybe this would crack the case before the killer struck again. "I owe ya one."

A chuckle came through the phone. "You owe me more than one, Ethan, but I've lost count. I'll get back to you when I have something."

After hanging up, he gathered the reports and faxed the information off to Will. Each of these victims still had his own murder book where all photos and information were kept. But his gut told him they would soon be combined into one once he was ready to call a spade a spade and link the two murders to a serial killer.

Ethan sat at his desk, opened Jud's file again, and scoured the reports they had so far. The neighbor interviews revealed no one saw or heard a thing out of the ordinary. No unidentified fingerprints had been found at the scene. The DNA reports still remained outstanding, but it could be weeks before they came in.

He expelled a short burst of air and rubbed his hands over his face. Damn it. They had nothing. No evidence. Nothing to go on.

"Anything new?" Grant set a cup of coffee on the desk, draped his jacket over the back of his chair, and sat across from him.

"Morning. Glad you're here early." He tapped his finger on the open folder in front of him. "Nothing new really, just going over the interviews. Trying to find something that jumps out at me, but it's just not there. Did you find anything with the wedding lead?"

His partner leaned back in his chair and crossed his arms over his chest. "Still waiting on a couple call backs, but nothing so far. They both had different wedding planners, caterers, venues, and tailors. Still waiting to hear back from the wedding planners about the bands and ministers."

"Damn." He thrust a hand through his hair and stood. Shoving his chair out of the way, he paced behind the desk. "You know, basically we're having to wait for this bastard to make a mistake. And in order for him to do that, he has to kill again. We have to stand by while some innocent guy gets mutilated in order to get some kind of lead. Damn it, I hate this shit."

Ethan turned back just as his partner took a gulp of coffee.

"Oh, God!" Grant choked, swallowed, and then gagged.

"Pretty bad, huh?"

"Damn. That was foul." He swiped his mouth with the back of his hand. "You could've warned me."

"Yeah." Ethan chuckled, grabbed his chair, and dragged it to the desk. "But then I wouldn't have gotten to see you almost upchuck a lung." He dropped into the chair, which protested with a shrill squeak. He grimaced and scooted up to the desk. "By the way, I called in a favor with a profiler friend over at the FBI. I sent him the crime scene information and stuff, and he's gonna get back to me with a profile of the guy we're looking for."

Grant straightened in the chair. "A profile? Is that really

necessary? I mean, how often are they accurate?"

"Only fifty, sixty percent of the time. But it's another tool in our arsenal. Something else to give us a little insight. We need all the help we can get."

"Yeah." He reached up, pulled his earlobe, his brow furrowing. "But the FBI? Do we really want them all up in our investigation?"

Did the kid really know this little? "They won't come in unless asked or unless this thing crosses state lines. All Will is doing is giving me a profile, which he does from the comfort of his own desk. What is your real problem with this?"

Grant looked down at his desk calendar and reached over to turn his coffee cup in circles. "I don't have a problem."

"Really? Cause it seems like you do." He stared at his partner, tried to see inside his head and understand whatever might be going on in there. But before his partner could answer, Ethan's cell went off. He held the buzzing phone in his hand, still waiting for Grant to reply, but when no explanation came, he jabbed the answer button. "Parker."

The words that came over the line were both anticipated and dreaded. He just hadn't expected them quite this soon.

"Fuck!" He slammed his phone shut and motioned to Grant. "Grab your coat. We've got another body."

Twenty minutes later, they each signed the scene log, handed it back to the officer at the door, and entered the latest victim's house. Officer Moore met them in the foyer and led them directly to the bedroom. Inside, Don Bledsoe lay naked on his bed, his hands and feet bound to each bedpost with duct tape like the previous victims. Ethan yanked on a pair of rubber gloves, snapping them in place. Edging along the side of the bed, he leaned over and peered at the deceased. Something had been carved in his chest, but he couldn't make out the letters.

A distinctive clicking sound came from the far side of the room where Steve Gordon took the crime scene photos. Ethan scanned the body and immediate area, noting the similarities and differences between this victim and the other two. But when the clicking ceased, he glanced up.

Steve stood next to the window and stared at a framed photo sitting on the dresser. With a sharp inhale, he picked it up and studied the picture. The corners of his mouth turned down, and he ran a hand over his right eyebrow. After a moment, he returned the frame carefully to the dresser top and lifted his camera.

Did Steve know the victim? When the photographer looked over, Ethan nodded and altered his focus to the body. Now wasn't the time to ask that question. It was something that needed to be discussed in private.

He turned to Gary. "This scene looks different than the last two. Our vic's eyes are intact, as is his penis, and there's nowhere near the same quantity of blood. What have you got for me?"

"Yeah, there's a lot different." Gary pointed toward the bloodied face. "For the first time, it appears the victim retaliated, and there was a bit of a struggle. Looks like he was surprised in the bathroom. Put up one hell of a fight; the place is a wreck." He straightened and jerked a thumb over his shoulder. "From what I can tell, he made it outside where it looks like he either fell or was pushed. I'm sure you saw the blood spatter out there on the cement that we flagged."

"Yeah, I noticed the markers, and you're assuming that's the vic's blood and not the perp's. Won't know for sure till the samples are processed." Ethan scanned the bedroom. Nothing appeared out of place, so the fight must have been finished by the time Bledsoe had been brought in here. But one thing still nagged him. "His eyes are intact. So, what's all the blood on his face from?"

Gary moved up to the head of the bed. "His nose. It's broken. There's an abrasion on his forehead and cheek." He gestured toward the vic's torso and spoke with a calm, detached tone. "The killer carved the chest, and I can tell you now, the word is MINE. He's getting better at it, not so sloppy anymore. But after that, he strayed from his normal routine. He didn't touch Bledsoe's eyes or penis." He eyed Ethan. "And, I'm sure you've noticed the majority of the blood is contained to the bed."

He nodded. "Yeah, the other scenes had blood spatter everywhere." He leaned forward. "I see the guy's throat has been slit like the others. So, what's the deal?"

He pointed toward the deep slash. "Yes, but the lack of blood around the area indicates that the slicing of the throat and carotid artery was performed post mortem. He was already dead."

"Wait. How can that be?"

Gary gestured toward the vic's chest. "For some reason, your perp just ended the guy with a knife through the heart. Bledsoe was dead in minutes, less."

Ethan stared at the carnage. Why the change? What happened to make the killer stray from his plans? "How sure are you it's the same guy?"

Gary raised an eyebrow. "Looks like it might be the same duct tape used to tie him up and cover his mouth, but I won't know for sure till we test it against what was used in the other murders. The carving of the victim's chest, while slightly neater, shows similar characteristics of the first two murders. The cuts are smooth and shallow, suggesting a small, sharp knife such as a scalpel as opposed to say the deeper, more jagged edges a hunting or fillet knife would leave. It appears the killer's point was more intentional rather than to hack and slash. You're the detective here, but since nothing has been released in the papers about the crime scenes and with just the similarities in binding, the twisting of the duct tape, the deliberate mutilations performed on the body, I'd say there's more than an excellent chance all three murders were committed by the same guy."

Damn. There it was. Serial killer.

Gary shook his head and looked back at the corpse. "I'll send you my report as soon as it's done."

"All right, Gary. I'll let you finish up here." He sighed, shifted his focus to Grant, and said, "Let's go do our thing. I want to check out the rest of the house before we talk to the first responder."

As he turned to leave, Ethan noticed the photographer limp across the room. "What happened to you, Steve? Some woman get sick of you hitting on her?"

The wiry guy lowered his camera, and his face reddened. "Ha, ha, ha. No, I had a snowboarding accident Sunday. Took a bad digger and fucked up my knee and ribs."

"That'll teach ya for trying to slide down a mountain on a piece of flimsy wood. Next time, slap two of 'em on your feet. It'll work much better."

"I'll have you know, skis are for wimps. Snowboarding is where it's at, old-timer."

"Yeah, whatever." Ethan waved his hand, dismissing him, and laughed. On his way out of the room, he called back over his shoulder, "You don't see me limping around, do you?"

They stopped by the bathroom where the attack supposedly occurred and looked through the doorway. Various toiletries lay scattered on the floor. The throw rug was shoved against the wall. A hand towel lay on the floor by the toilet.

"Looks like quite a struggle," Grant said. He strode into the room and bent to pick up a bottle of hair gel.

"Wait a minute." He stepped back out in the hall. "Gary, has anyone worked this room yet?"

"No! We got here ten minutes before you," he said, his words harsh and clipped. "Give us a break here."

"Touchy, touchy," he mumbled under his breath and turned back to his partner. "Leave it."

After walking through the rest of the house and finding nothing notably amiss, Ethan and Grant went outside to speak with the responding officer.

"You were first on the scene?" Ethan asked.

Officer Reynolds pulled out his note pad and readied himself to give his report. "Yes. I got the call at six-forty this morning. The victim's boyfriend called for a welfare check. I was just down the road, so I took the call." He shifted his weight from one foot to the other. "The front door was locked. I rang the bell but got no answer, so I walked around the house, looking in what windows I could. When I got to the back bedroom window, I saw the victim on the bed and called it in."

"You didn't go in the house?"

"No, it was quite obvious the vic was dead. His throat had been slashed. Blood everywhere. So, I called it in and waited out front. No one but CSU and you and Detective Montgomery have entered the scene."

Well, that was a plus. Hard to get a more pristine crime scene than that. "That's good, Reynolds. Keeping the crime scene uncontaminated is a top priority. But, your first concern is to the victim. You always need to make sure there is no way you can help him. In this case, you were right. But just keep that in mind next time. If there's ever any doubt, you call it in, then enter the house and as soon as you have back up to check on the victim."

Reynolds nodded. "Yes, sir."

Ethan glanced over at Grant and found him scribbling on his notepad. God, the department needed to spring for a class in shorthand for him. At the rate he was writing, the guy would have a shoebox full every three months. He gritted his teeth, turned his attention on Officer Reynolds, and said, "So, why did the boyfriend call in a welfare check?"

"He told dispatch he'd been trying to get a hold of Mr. Bledsoe since midnight to tell him of a schedule change at the hospital. He'd been asked to do a double shift. Bledsoe was supposed to meet him for breakfast, and he wanted to let him know he couldn't make it."

"Midnight. Didn't he assume the guy was sleeping?"

"Apparently Bledsoe is used to getting called in to work and is a light sleeper. When the boyfriend couldn't reach him by the time they were to meet for breakfast, he called for the welfare check."

Ethan nodded. So, he should be in the clear, assuming his alibi checked out. "Has anyone notified him the victim was found dead?"

"No, not to my knowledge."

Damn. The guy must be out of his head with worry. He needed to wrap this up. "Anything else?"

"No." The officer shook his head and pointed down at his feet. "I've been here at the door the rest of the time."

"Okay, thanks." Ethan walked down the steps and out onto the snow-covered lawn with Grant trailing behind him. When he reached the rock garden with a freestanding, rough-hewn wood swing, he stopped and rounded toward his partner. "Why don't you go notify the boyfriend and get his statement? I'll work the house a couple more hours, try to get a feel for our guy while they finish up the scene. When you're done, meet me back here, and we can canvass the neighborhood, see if anyone heard or saw anything."

"Sounds good. See ya in two hours." Grant strode back across the yard to get the contact information for Don Bledsoe's lover from Officer Reynolds.

Ethan studied the footprints they'd left in the snow as they'd walked to and from the house. Deep, nondescript holes dotted the crisp, white ground cover. He walked around the house. No other footprints besides those of Officer Reynolds.

He pivoted around the way he'd just come and scanned the area. An unruffled blanket of snow. A line of trees to block winter winds, but none with sturdy branches that ranged close enough to the house to allow for a surreptitious entry.

He rubbed his jaw. So, how the hell is this guy getting in? None of the scenes showed any sign of forced entry. It was as though he'd been invited in.

Except, he hadn't been invited this time. Bledsoe had fought back.

And why had the killer changed up his M.O.? What the hell had happened to throw him off track? Besides the carving in the vic's chest, there'd been no torture like with the other two. Death had come quickly and relatively pain free. So something definitely had changed. But what?

He shuffled along the side of the house and came around to the front just as a white van with WCAX pulled up to the curb.

Just what I need now. The damn press.

The side door of the van slid open, and out jumped veteran reporter Mike Dalton, some big dude with a camera following on his heels. Dalton scurried up to Ethan, shoved a microphone in his face, and said, "Detective, is it true we have a serial killer in Red River?"

Chapter Thirteen

*F*riday morning found Ethan's teeth still on edge, the muddy sky outside the precinct window matching his mood to a tee. In two hours, Mikey would be released. Ethan planned to get out to the prison, pick him up, and drive him as far out of town as he could get him. He'd located the halfway house the probation officer had suggested and would set Mikey up financially one last time. Not because he gave two shits about his half-brother anymore, but because he didn't want him anywhere near Abby or this investigation.

Grant sat at his desk, weeding through reports, combining the three murder books on Jud, Cal, and Don into one. Now that they'd officially decided to call these murders serial, all information would be located in a huge single file instead of three individual ones.

He leaned against his desk and stared at the murder board, the various photographs, index cards, and strings that marked where the bodies had been discovered, and his gaze shot straight to Abby's eight-by-ten glossy. These murders were connected to her. How, he didn't know, but he worried for her safety. Sooner or later, this guy would stop killing the men in her life and go after her.

The day before yesterday, he'd expressed his concerns to Grant, tried to reinforce the point that this wasn't only a part of the investigation.

"You and Abby live in your parents' house."

"Yeah," he'd said. "We couldn't bear to sell it."

"The men she knows are dying." Ethan had drummed his fingers on his desk. "You're her brother."

Grant nodded and said, "I appreciate your concern, but don't worry. I can protect myself if this guy's stupid enough to come after me."

Ethan grimaced. Didn't he get it? "And Abby?"

"What about her?"

"This guy knows the men in her life. What will he do when he's killed all of them?"

"We'll have to catch him before that happens." Grant's face had sobered, and he'd leaned toward Ethan. "I've got the house locked down. And if he did manage to get in, he'd have to pass my room to get to her. I'd know."

Ethan had nodded, letting the conversation die. The man believed himself invincible. There was no convincing him otherwise.

But the problem was, thoughts of Abby plagued Ethan continually. During the day, he worried he wouldn't be able to discover her connection to the victims fast enough.

The nights were even worse.

Erotic fantasies filled his dreams, leaving him breathless, hard as a rock, and in need of a cold shower every morning. He couldn't get her out of his head. The exotic scent of her hair. The silkiness of her skin. The way her body had once curved into his and fit as if she'd been made for him.

He dreamed of cupping her full breasts in his palms, bending slightly to suckle the hard nipple that begged for his attention. His splayed hand traveled over her smooth, flat stomach and down to....

Shit! He had to stop this.

He abruptly sat behind his desk before anyone noticed the

sizable bulge behind the zipper of his trousers. Grant asked him a question, and Ethan looked up, his heart pounding as though he'd been caught with his hand in the cookie jar. Damn. Had he noticed?

He forced himself to focus. "I'm sorry, what did you say?"

"I said, I went to the hospital to inform Bobby Higgins of Don's death." Grant stared at him for a moment, his brow furrowing. "The guy was pretty broken up, could hardly speak. I had an officer drive him home. But, while I was there, I got access to Don's locker and found this." He held up a small velvet box. "According to the head nurse on duty, Don had been planning to propose. Several other co-workers corroborated." He set the box on the desk. "So, I've gone back over every conceivable aspect of the engaged couple theory. Still no commonalities. And, even though Don Bledsoe and Bobby Higgins were about to be engaged, they hadn't even begun to think about the ceremony or when it would occur. Bobby's alibi is firm. Co-workers and security cameras confirm he was at the hospital the entire night."

While he'd anticipated this outcome, he couldn't help the disappointment that curled in his gut. Did it make him an ass to want this case tied up into a nice neat bow so the woman he was interested in would be available for his pursuit?

Ethan's gaze cut to the murder board again. "This guy made a mistake with Don's murder. He didn't follow his ritual. Something happened to throw him off his usual path."

"Like what?"

"The obvious difference between this vic and the other two is Don Bledsoe was gay. But the murderer went there with the intent to kill. So, we can't assume that has anything to do with this."

"Right." Grant gestured toward the board. "He still carved the next word in the vic's chest."

"Exactly. And the message You Are Mine is pretty damned intimate, leading me to believe he knew the vics. My guess? Looks to me like he got interrupted. Had to leave in a hurry." He sighed. "Damn it. I wish we could find the common link between these vics other than the fact that they all knew your sister. The moment we figure that out is when we find out who the bastard is."

"Yeah well, it better happen soon. The press is breathing heavy down our necks. So are the chief and the mayor." Grant looked down at the mass of papers and photos he had yet to compile into the single murder book and threw up his hands. "Like we're fucking miracle workers here or something."

"The press lives and breathes blood and gore. They've got every neighborhood within fifty miles scared out of their minds." He pushed back from his desk, the bulge in his pants having disappeared. Nothing like the mayor demanding the killer's head on a platter to take the *umph* out. "Listen, I've got something personal to do. I doubt I'll get back for the one o'clock autopsy on Don. I need you to stand in for that, and you can brief me when I get back." Ethan rose, shrugged his coat on. "Oh yeah, that profile on our guy just came in. I'll read it while I'm out and fill you in later."

His partner nodded and continued to shuffle papers around his desk.

He snatched up the report Will Donovan had faxed from the FBI's Behavioral Analysis Unit and tucked it inside his jacket. On his way out, he paused at the door. "By the way, how is Abby handling Don's death?"

Grant scowled. "How the hell do you think she's handling it? This is the third guy connected to her who has met with a brutal death. She gets it now. She knows it's somehow about her. She's scared and feeling guilty her friends are dying. How the fuck would you be feeling, Ethan?"

"Whoa there, buddy." He held his hands up. "I was merely asking if she's okay. I know she's not responsible for this, some whack job is. I'm not questioning her innocence."

Grant shoved a hand through his hair. "Sorry. It's just I'm worried about her. She even skipped her meeting yesterday, never left the house. I think she took a leave of absence from work. I told her to get out of the house today, get some fresh air, but I doubt she will."

Ethan nodded. They needed to catch this bastard. Quick. "I'll be back this afternoon. Meantime, you know what to do."

Before turning away, his gaze flicked to Abby's photo on the murder board. Of all the feelings running through his head and body about her, the overwhelming need to protect her overpowered them all at the moment. Yes, she had Grant, but it wasn't enough. She was in danger—his gut screamed it. He hadn't talked to her since they'd found Don's body, and he still needed to, but first he needed to get Mikey the hell out of town.

෬

Half an hour from the prison, traffic came to a stand still. What the hell? Ethan grabbed his radio and called dispatch. "Any idea what the holdup is on County Route 22?"

"Sand truck turned over on its side. They're just cleaning up now. They just reported it. Shouldn't be more than ten more minutes, and they can clear the road."

"Thanks." He pulled out the papers Will had sent him and used the time to read them over. The report itself was short and sweet.

From the small amount you have from the crime scene, you are looking at either a white female, age twenty-five to thirty-five or gay male in the same age bracket. I say this because of the damage being done to the penis. It is unlikely a straight male would do this—he would identify too much with his own appendage to do that to another male.

Also, I would label the killer in the low to mid-level education bracket and not overly intelligent. They possibly wouldn't work in a white-collar job and probably aren't mobile. More than likely a loner and not married. Probably has too many social issues to have long-term relationships, although when in a relationship, is overbearing and controlling. In other words, a non-social killer. I don't think you'll find him or her contacting the press or police looking for attention. With the carvings in the chest, this feels much more personal to me.

All this being said, you need to take into account what you're seeing. Profiling isn't an exact science, and the person responsible for your murders might be nothing of what I've noted here.

Let me know if I can be of any more help to you, and I'll catch up with you next time I'm your way. Good luck with this one, Ethan. It sounds pretty nasty.

William Donovan.

Female? No way. A woman couldn't overpower these men and tie them to a bed. Even if she managed to incapacitate them in some way, he just didn't see it happening.

Gay male? That was entirely possible, as was the rest of the profile. Unfortunately, it could fit many of the guys, gay or straight, in all the neighboring counties. This was a poor, low-income part of the state. There weren't many white-collar jobs available, and many guys quit high school before graduating to go work in the slate and marble quarries.

Well, crap. So basically, he was right back where he started.

A horn honked behind him, and he looked up from the papers to see the line of cars moving again. Tossing the information to the passenger seat, he shifted into drive and continued on his way to the prison. Damn, he'd be glad when this day was over.

Twenty minutes later, he veered into the Pine Valley State Prison parking lot. After signing in, he looked around for Mikey. Ethan was a half an hour late due to the sand truck, so his half-brother should have been all processed and waiting for him.

He walked up to the desk sergeant. "Michael Greene? He's supposed to be released today. Can you check how long he'll be?"

The guard spun his chair around and grabbed a thick binder from the shelf behind him. "Greene, ya said?

He mentally rolled his eyes. "Yes, Michael Greene, with an E."

The guard ran a thick index finger down the page, stopping

at the last name. "Oh, yep, here we are. Michael Greene, with an E. He was released an hour ago."

His heart stuttered. "An hour ago? Then where the hell is he?"

The guard flipped the binder shut and gave Ethan a hard stare. "'Bout as far away from here as he could get, I'd imagine. Once they're on the other side of those bars, they usually don't stop to tell us thanks and have a nice day."

"This is ridiculous." he stuffed his hands in his pockets so he wouldn't slam his fist on the counter. "You don't even know who he left here with?"

"Look, pal, the guy did his time and was released. The only person he has to answer to now is his probation officer. I'm not his babysitter anymore. There's still three hundred guys in there I'm reliable for, so go look for your friend somewhere else."

He gritted his teeth, knowing the guy meant liable.

The guard tapped his pen twice on the desk blotter then jabbed his finger toward the exit. "He ain't here no more."

Ethan shoved the door open so hard it rebounded back into his face. He caught it, strode through the doorway, and gave the damned door one last heave. The ear-splitting bang that followed gave him a bit of satisfaction. Sons of bitches should keep a closer eye on the people they release—especially known rapists who've already made threats to repeat their crimes.

Frigid air enveloped him, a few stray snowflakes swirled in his path, and none of it did anything to improve his mood. With slush and icy muck splashing beneath his feet, he stomped across the parking lot to his truck, jumped in, and slammed the door.

"Dammit all shit to hell!" He smacked the steering wheel with his open palm then grasped it in his hands and shook it. "Where the fuck is that little sonofabitch?"

Ethan sat in the truck, blood pounding in his ears, his gut roiling with anger, and scanned the surrounding area. Maybe stupid-ass Mikey had decided to play a joke on him. But after a few minutes, he growled and hit the steering wheel again. The bastard was gone.

He started the Tahoe, shoved it into reverse, and twisted around to peer out the back window. But as he turned, his peripheral alerted him something wasn't right. He glanced down at the passenger seat, and nausea bubbled up into his throat. The profile he'd tossed there was gone.

"Aw, shit."

Ω

Ethan arrived back at the precinct to find everyone gone except Steve, who was dropping a manila folder onto his desk.

"Whatcha got there?" he asked while he shrugged off his coat.

Steve started and glanced up at him. "Just Bledsoe's crime scene photos. Gary asked me to drop them off to you since you didn't show at the autopsy."

Ethan locked his gaze on the folder and said, "Why didn't he just give them to Montgomery?"

"Montgomery? He never showed." The photographer's gaze flitted to the photos and back to him. Reaching up, he tugged his earlobe and edged toward the door, bumping into a chair. "Called and said something about truck trouble."

Ethan threw his jacket on his desk, covering the envelope. Just one more thing to pile onto an already crappy day. Anger seethed in his gut. He yanked his chair out to sit in but managed to fling it across the room. "Fuck. I ask him to do one damn thing. Am I the only one around here who wants to see this bastard caught?"

Steve backed away. His hand moved from pulling his earlobe to massaging the back of his neck. A minuscule smile twitched the corners of his mouth. "Don't shoot the messenger, buddy. I'm just here doing my job."

Ignoring him, he pulled out his phone and dialed Grant. After five rings, it went to voice mail. *Shit.* He slammed his cell shut and chucked it on his desk. When he looked up, he spotted the receptionist draining the rest of the coffee into her cup and stomped over to her. "Did you happen to see when Montgomery left?"

"Right after you," she said and set the empty pot back onto the burner. "I'm surprised you didn't meet in the parking lot."

He whirled around, amazed his head hadn't exploded yet, and shouted to Steve, "Come on. We're going on a coffee run." He snatched his jacket off his desk and shoved his arms in. "I can't drink this crap one more day."

As they headed out, they met Grant coming through the station door. Ethan stopped so fast, the wiry photographer crashed into his back. "Where the fuck have you been?"

His partner's mouth thinned, and his upper body stiffened. "You're not the only one with 'personal' problems. Abby called. I had to go take care of a few things. I called the coroner and explained. He taped the whole thing." He rolled his shoulders. "Chill out."

"Really?" He took a step toward him, jabbing his finger in the asshole's face. "This whole cluster-fuck of a mess is because of her. It's your sister in danger, and you want me to chill out? Maybe you ought to be a little less chilled."

Grant grabbed Ethan's coat lapel. "Are you blaming this shit on my sister? You think I don't know what's at stake here?"

He brought his arms up in a fast move, knocking the idiot's hands away. Taking hold of Grant's shoulders, he shoved him up against the wall. "No, I really don't think you have a fool's clue in hell of what's at stake here. I think—"

Steve tried to wedge between the two men. "Let's all take a step back here. Tensions are high 'cause we want this guy found. Taking it out on each other isn't going to solve a thing." He reached up and placed a hand on Ethan's shoulder. "Hey man, let's go get that coffee."

He jolted Grant's shoulders one last time to drive his point home then let go. "Right. The autopsy report and photos are on my desk. Why don't you go through those while I'm gone?"

Grant's glare never wavered. "Yes, sir."

Chapter Fourteen

Still fuming, Ethan trudged across the slush-covered parking lot and jumped up into his Tahoe. He was sick of the snow, sick of the cold weather, and sick of Grant's smug-ass attitude. The guy didn't get it at all. This bastard they were after was psychotic, and Abby was the center point of the whole damned case. For some reason, everything the killer did revolved around her. But the idiot acted as if they were after a freaking flasher or something.

Damn, this had been one screwed-up day. First Mikey, now Grant. Here it was, well after three o'clock, and he hadn't even had lunch. Maybe the coffee shop would have a snack to tide him over—not that he was hungry after all this bullshit.

Glancing into the rearview mirror, Ethan watched Steve limp through the icy muck that covered the parking lot. The photographer huddled into his jacket and seemed to twitch with each step, his gaze flicking around in every direction. He took great crime scene photos, but the guy reminded him of a caffeine junky or a jittery squirrel.

At the last three crime scenes, Steve had been there, scooting about and snapping pictures. The guy always seemed to be in motion. Except....

Ethan recalled the way the guy had been distracted by the

photo of Don Bledsoe and Bobby Higgins. He'd been motionless, his gaze fixed on the male couple. Why? And then there'd been the fight that had occurred between Don and his killer, a brawl that had ended in murder. The evidence indicated there was a more than reasonable chance Don got a good punch or two in, maybe cracked the killer's ribs or something. Hadn't Steve arrived at the scene, banged up and bruised, claiming some type of accident?

The wiry photographer opened the Tahoe door, and icy air swirled into the vehicle. He gingerly slid into the passenger seat and twisted to fasten his seatbelt, a grimace marring his face.

He started the Tahoe to warm the engine. Damn it. He had to ask, had to get it out of the way. After the photographer finished strapping in, he said, "How the hell did you say you got hurt again?"

Wide-eyed, Steve glanced at him. "Uh, a snowboarding accident."

"So what were your injuries?"

Brows furrowed, he kept his gaze directly on Ethan. "I messed up my knee and cracked a couple ribs." The fingers of one hand lightly drummed on his thigh. "Why the sudden interest?"

He studied Steve. The guy was always in motion. "Excellent question. Why the sudden interest in the framed photo at the Bledsoe crime scene?"

Steve jerked his head back, breaking eye contact. "What the hell are you talking about?"

"The picture on Bledsoe's dresser, the one of him and Higgins in an embrace. It caught your attention, had you off-guard. You picked it up, rubbed your thumb over one of their faces, and set it back down." Unable to let up, Ethan leaned toward him, his tone darkening. "I repeat, what was your interest in the photo?"

His face reddened. He jerked his hand up to tug on his ear and huffed out a laugh. "What is this, an interrogation?"

"Yes." He gave the photographer a pointed stare. "Answer

the question. What was your interest in the photo?"

Steve's jaw clenched, the muscles visibly working. He turned his head, looked out the passenger-side window. For a long moment, only the thrumming of the engine filled the SUV's interior, leading him to think the guy might just not answer. But then Steve faced him again, eyes cast downward, voice small.

"Bobby Higgins and I dated for over two years." He lifted his gaze and swallowed hard. "That's right, I'm gay."

Ethan blinked. Well, damn. That explained a lot.

"Bobby and I broke up a year and a half ago, and I hadn't seen him since. I knew he was dating Don, but when I saw the picture...." His gaze drifted to the windshield, where snowflakes danced across the glass. "I guess I was just startled to see so much love between them. I still miss him, ya know? It was hard enough to see the man he loved dead on that bed, but then to see Bobby in that picture...." He shook his head and looked down at the hands he wrung in his lap. "I have my receipt and the ski-pass if you need to see it. I can also give you the name of the guy I was with the day Don was murdered...if that's necessary."

Christ, I am such an ass. "I apologize for making you uncomfortable, but you've got to understand where I'm coming from. Don obviously fought back, and you were visibly shaken by that picture, and you'd been injured. I had to ask. I have no idea who I'm dealing with."

"Yeah, I know." Steve turned back to him. "Is knowing the truth about, I mean, the fact that I'm gay, is that going to change how you handle things?"

He put the Tahoe into reverse and gave him a hard stare. "Is the fact that you're gay going to change how you take pictures?"

"No."

"Well, I don't see as there's a problem then." He eased the SUV out of the parking space, the tires splashing through the slush.

A genuine smile lit Steve's face. "Man, you're making friends all over today. I hope this caffeine run puts you in a better mood."

Ethan laughed, shifting the Tahoe into drive. "You and me both, man."

ભ

Bundled in her jacket, a scarf around her neck and a hat pulled down over her ears, Abby exited the local pharmacy. She stuffed the bag containing a bottle of ibuprofen into her coat pocket and scurried down the sidewalk, another round of snow swirling about her. Sleep hadn't been a regular visitor as of late, and the few hours she'd managed to get hadn't been enough to stave off a headache. Add to that her lack of desire for food, and the whole thing left her drained.

My God, the people around her were dying. Murdered, one by one. Three in six days. Guilt crashed onto her shoulders. She wasn't stupid. She knew she was the one thing the three dead men had in common. What had she done to trigger this madman's killing spree?

As she approached Main Street, a car horn blared, and she twisted around to see why. She plowed into something solid, and before she realized what had happened, she lay flat on her back on the sidewalk. She stared up at a man holding a briefcase.

"I'm so sorry," he said, concern etching his brow. Leaning over, he helped her to her feet.

"No," she said as she brushed herself off. "I wasn't looking where I was going."

"Abby?" He stared wide-eyed at her. "Abby Montgomery?"

She squinted, her mind trying to place his face, when wham, she recognized him. "Nick? Oh, my God. Nick Colbert?"

"Yeah." He laughed. "Haven't seen you in forever. How have you been?"

"Great." She hugged herself, suddenly self-conscious. "I remember you were captain of the football team, graduated *summa cum laude*, prom king with, let me see...."

"Dorie Marx," he supplied.

"Yeah. Dorie Marx was prom queen. Wow." She shook her

head, and the old high school anxiety that had plagued her whenever she stood in the presence of the popular crowd reared its ugly head. Nick Colbert had been near god-like over the student body. Compared to him, her life had been insignificant. Her nerves coiled in anticipation of questions. "So, what have you been up to?"

"Well for starters, Dorie dumped me." He laughed, his dark eyes sparkling amid the twirling snowflakes. He glanced at his watch. "You want to get a cup of coffee?"

Stunned, she stared at him and stammered, "What?"

"Coffee. There's a shop just down the block." He gestured behind him. "We could sit and talk, catch up."

She glanced around, her brain scrambling for an excuse. "I don't know."

"Oh, come on," he said and hooked her arm through his. "I'd love to hear what Bunny Montgomery has been up to since high school."

Ten minutes later, Abby found herself sitting across the table from Nick Colbert, sipping a cup of steamy, Brazilian nut-flavored coffee, and grinning from ear to ear. Oh, how she would've loved this attention in high school, but now it all seemed so grown up, so...uncomplicated.

"I can't believe you even remember that stupid nickname I had."

Nick grinned. "I remember a lot of things. Like drama class for one. I always figured you'd move off to Hollywood and make yourself famous. You were great in all those high school plays."

Yeah, I'm still good at acting. "Thanks. They were fun, but it was nothing I ever took seriously. I work at the hospital now as an ultrasound technician." She concentrated on her cup of coffee, trying to think of a way to get the conversation off herself. "What about you? What have you been doing since you moved away?"

"Well, after Dorie dumped me, I went to business school, moved to New York City, and made a small fortune on Wall Street." He blushed, which Abby found endearing. "Sounds like it was a breeze and that I take it all for Granted, but it was a lot of hard work and a little bit of luck. Actually, I've been very fortunate to have the life I do. Only thing missing is a woman at my side who loves me."

It was her turn to blush, but she pushed past it. Picking up her coffee, she said, "So, what brings you back to town?"

"Mom and Dad's fiftieth wedding anniversary this weekend. My Aunt Stacy and I are throwing them a huge party over at the Lake House Inn." His eyes grew wide, and his face lit up. "Hey, why don't you come? That way, I'll have someone beautiful to talk to and dance with."

Abby choked on her coffee. Grabbing her hand, Nick slid his chair over and patted her back.

"Easy there. Did it go down the wrong pipe?"

Too busy trying to breathe, all she could do was nod. Somewhere through the coughing fit and trying to catch her breath, she realized Nick's arm was around her and was surprised she had no real reaction to it one way or the other. She wasn't frozen in fear, nor did she find herself attracted to him.

The only crazy thought she had was wishing Ethan was there. She squeezed her eyes closed. Good Lord, here she sat, choking to death, a handsome man's arm around her, and all she could think of was Ethan? She must be losing her mind.

"Well, isn't this a cozy little picture?" came an angry male voice behind her.

Abby twisted around, and her breath caught. Oh shit. Elliot.

The lawyer strode to their table but remained standing, towering over them. His face red and mouth grim, his gaze bore a hole in her.

"Elliot." She conjured up a smile and forced a pleasant voice. "How are you? Um, this is an old friend, Nick Colbert. Nick, this is Elliot Swanson."

Nick stood and offered his hand, but the lawyer ignored him. With his full attention on Abby, he said, "Well, well, well. Nick Colbert. Your reputation precedes you. Local boy makes it big on Wall Street." He gave Nick a cursory once-over then returned his focus to her. "Really, Abby? You tell me you can't go out because you're grieving, and I find you here, sipping lattés and yukking it up with this schmuck?"

Her face burned. "Elliot. That was uncalled for."

"Not really. These Wall Street boys are a dime a dozen. One day they have a fortune, the next day they've blown it all on bad investments." He jerked his thumb toward his chest. "Elliot Swanson is a lawyer, Abby. Everyone always needs a lawyer at some point. You're not seeing the bigger picture here."

She clutched her coffee cup, her knuckles whitening. God, this guy was just so over-the-top that she wanted to crawl underneath the table and hide until he was gone. Her gaze flitted toward Nick, who hadn't said a word yet, and her stomach knotted.

Oh, crap.

Nick had widened his stance, squared his shoulders. Take off fifteen years, and he would look like that Friday night quarterback he used to be. Anger flared in those dark eyes, and his mouth twisted into an *I'm-gonna-kick-your-ass* sneer.

Her heart pounded. This wasn't good. Needing to defuse the situation, she took a deep breath and in her firmest voice said, "Elliot, I think you need to leave. Who I have coffee with isn't your business, and to come in here and insult my friend like this is just beyond rude."

He snorted and smirked down at her. "Really, Abby? Do you think this blockhead would give you the time of day if he knew about your past or your wacky obsessions? It takes a real man like Elliot Swanson to overlook your...shall we say...abject history and peculiar fixations."

She gasped, and in a blink of the eye, Nick had him by the shirt, fist drawn back before she could utter a word.

"Whoa, there. What the hell's going on here?"

Abby whirled around to find Ethan and another guy striding toward the enraged men. He pushed between Nick and Elliot, all but shoving the lawyer into her lap. Good Lord, could this day get any worse?

"It was all a misunderstanding," she said, rising to her feet. "Elliot was just leaving."

He pivoted toward her, his face livid. "*I* was just leaving? I think you better rephrase that, darlin'. Elliot Swanson is the best chance at a normal life a woman with your past is gonna have."

She recoiled.

He stared down at her, a smug sneer on his face. "Yeah, after our little date, I did some digging into your background. Get real, Abby. Do you think any other man is going to want a used-up woman with all the issues you have? You're lucky Elliot's willing to give you the time of day."

In a blur of motion, Ethan grabbed the man and slammed him face-first into the wall. The sound of the impact exploded throughout the coffee house, and patrons jumped from their chairs and scrambled out of the way.

"Damn," Nick muttered, bumping a chair as he backed off.

Ethan wrenched the lawyer's arm behind his back and, with a growl, crammed his forearm against the base of Elliot's neck.

"Easy, man!" The guy who'd accompanied Detective Parker bounced from one foot to the other. "Don't mess him up too bad."

Ethan pressed his weight against his captive, crushing the side of Elliot's face into the wall. He leaned down to the lawyer's ear and, in a menacing voice, said, "You owe the lady an apology, mister."

The lawyer squirmed beneath the detective's grasp.

"Ethan," Abby said, afraid he might really hurt Elliot. "It's okay. He's not worth it. Just let him leave."

He increased the pressure. "Apologize first."

"All right, all right! I apologize to the...lady."

"Good. Now, you need to get your ass out of here before I haul you in for disturbing the public and any other charges I can come up with." He jerked Elliot back a fraction of an inch and smashed him into the wall again before releasing him.

Elliot stumbled, nearly fell to the tiled floor. Catching his balance, he swung around toward Ethan, his face indignant.

Pointing a finger, he said, "You're a cop. I'll have your badge for police brutality."

"Go right ahead, pal. I'm sure I can help Ms. Montgomery and her friend in filling out their complaints against you."

"Fine. Have it your way." The lawyer's shoulders slumped. But a moment later, the gleam returned to his eyes. His gaze, cold and hard, fell on Abby. "I'll see ya around, darlin'." Pivoting on his heel, Elliot Swanson stormed out of the café.

Shocked rolled through her and her gaze moved from Ethan to Nick, to the strange wiry guy, and back to Ethan. Tears burned the backs of her eyes, and she fought to keep them at bay. Sinking into her chair, she shook her head, unable to speak.

Nick held his hand out to the detective. "Nick Colbert, and I just want to say thanks for stepping in. That guy is seriously deranged."

"Detective Parker." He shook the high school quarterback's hand. "No problem. And if you want to press charges, you'd be well within your rights."

"I'll consider it." Nick turned to Abby, his face much paler than it had been when they'd entered the café. "I'm sorry for what happened here, Bunny. Listen, I've got an appointment, but I'll give you a call sometime, and we can catch up again."

Abby nodded, watched him turn and practically run out of the shop. She squeezed her eyes closed. Oh, what he must think of her. Elbows on the table, she put her face in her hands and tried to disappear.

Ethan's arm came around her shoulders. Internally, she sighed, knowing his touch without having to see him. He drew her close against his strong chest, and his warm, musky scent enveloped her. It only took a moment before she relaxed into him, absorbing the comfort he offered.

"Are you okay?"

Still unable to speak, she shook her head.

"Come on, let's get out of here."

He helped her into her coat and, ready to leave the horror, she rose with him. Letting him guide her through the café, she kept her head bowed, unable to meet any of the other patrons' curious gazes. She just wanted to forget any of this had ever happened.

Outside, cold air wrapped around them while snowflakes peppered from above. Abby drew in a deep breath, welcoming the invigorating, icy atmosphere. Turning to Ethan and his friend, she said, "I'm so sorry you had to get involved in that, but thank you for coming to my rescue."

He squeezed her shoulder. "That guy was a jackass. Believe me, it was my pleasure."

"Believe him," the skinny guy said with a chuckle. "He's been spoiling for a fight all day. That was probably a better stress reliever for him than sex."

Ethan knocked him upside the head. "Ignore my friend here. He's good at taking crime scene photos, but not much else."

Abby's face heated, and she giggled. "Well, thank you anyway."

"So, how 'bout it? Want to get something to eat?" He glanced at his watch. "It's almost suppertime, and I haven't eaten all day."

She didn't think twice. "I'd like that."

Turning to his friend, Ethan said, "Listen, why don't you grab the coffee and take my Tahoe back to the station? I'll pick it up later." He glanced back to Abby. "You don't mind driving me around, do you?"

"Not at all."

They left the wiry guy at the café and walked the block to the nearby parking lot. As they drew closer, she hesitated, fear tickling the back of her neck. Something had been spilled all over the hood of the car. Squinting, she gasped when she figured out what had been done.

No.

She trembled. Her heart thrashed. She drew in breath after breath until her head spun. Knees weakening, she clutched Ethan's sleeve.

He guided her around the car, opened the passenger side

door, and helped her to the seat. Gently, he urged her to bend over and let her head hang between her knees. "Just breathe, honey. Nice and slow, in and out. That's a girl."

When her head settled and her breathing evened, she sat up and looked at him, who knelt on the ground in front of her. The stark concern that filled his face unlocked the tears she'd struggled to hold at bay. One huge drop after another poured from the corners of her eyes and trailed over her cheeks.

"I know sweetheart. It's going to be okay," he said. His voice soothed, reassured. "Give me your keys. I'm taking you home."

She handed over the car keys and managed to slide fully into the seat and buckle in. Ethan strode around the front of the car, his mouth grim, his brow furrowed. With a single swipe, he sent more than two dozen peppermints flying off her car hood and skittering across the parking lot.

Chapter Fifteen

After Abby's reaction to the peppermints on the hood of her car, Ethan decided to skip dinner at a restaurant in favor of a quieter, secure setting. He didn't need to ask her about the candies. Unfortunately, he already knew why she'd hyperventilated. Glancing over at her, he realized she'd stopped shivering. That was a good sign. He kept his mouth closed and his focus on the road. He would allow her to work through the incident on the ride to his house. He'd use the time to process what had happened at the café.

He remembered entering the coffee shop, Steve on his heels. The door had just clicked shut behind them when he'd heard what Elliot said to her. He couldn't get to the lawyer fast enough. Being closer, that Nick guy had gotten to the lawyer first, but not by much. And when Ethan had gotten his hands on the loudmouthed idiot, he'd wanted to smash his face through the wall, not just into it.

Gritting his teeth, he had to admit only the panic in Abby's voice had stopped him from putting a serious beating on the guy. Steve was right. He'd been spoiling for a fight since losing track of Mikey at the prison.

But his reaction hadn't been solely because of the insults Elliot had hurled. His gaze flitted to the attractive blonde. She evoked emotions in him he'd never experienced before. Protective, yes, but it was more than that.

He wanted her, and for that, he felt like an ass. But he couldn't get past the overpowering need to hold her in his arms, to taste her mouth. Heat rushed to his abdomen. Damn. He was like a randy teenager who couldn't control his urges.

Turning into his driveway, he shut off her car and unbuckled. He hadn't brought a woman here in years. He'd built his life around his career, he hadn't allowed much time for women. Abby was different. He wanted her here, wanted to take care of her. He rotated in his seat and risked a glance. He'd said he was taking her home. He just hadn't said *his* home.

"No pressure here." He took a breath, tried to put the words he wanted to say together in his head. "I just wanted to get you somewhere where you could decompress, maybe get some food in you. You're looking a little pale there."

Her fingers twisted together in her lap. She stared out the windshield, her face solemn. "This is your house?"

"Yes." He placed his hand on her shoulder. "Is that okay? The last thing I want is for you to feel uncomfortable."

"I'm fine now." She offered him a weak smile. "I promise I'm really not the basket case I appear to be. Well, on second thought, maybe I am, and you should run as far away from me as you can. Unless you've forgotten, it's kind of life-shortening to be around me."

Ethan focused on her deep blue eyes. She may have sounded sarcastic, as if she was trying to make a joke, but her eyes revealed the truth—she was afraid she might be right.

"I'm not running, Abby. It's way too late for that." He leaned across and unbuckled her. "Come on, let's get inside. It's getting colder and darker out."

Coming to her side of the car, he offered his hand to help her out. He held her close, draping his arm around her shoulders, and ushered her along the shoveled path. Inside, he took her coat, hung it up, and led her to the living room.

"Have a seat while I start the fire and go throw on some

soup. Clam chowder okay?"

She kicked off her shoes, sat on the couch with her legs tucked under her, and shivered. "Clam chowder is great. I'm chilled to the bone."

He lit the kindling beneath the logs he'd set the day before, grabbed an afghan from the recliner, and brought it over to her. Wrapping it around her, he pulled her hair free, his fingers winding through her silky, golden tresses. He fanned out her long hair over the tightly woven fabric, the multi-hued strands glinting jewel-like in the firelight. His hands lingered on her shoulders. "Is that better?" he asked, his voice a tad huskier than normal.

Placing her hand over his, she met his gaze. "Thank you."

His skin tingled beneath her touch. The intensity of the sparks flying between them overwhelmed him. He stared at her and swallowed. God. She was so amazing.

He leaned in, hovered his mouth over hers, and when she didn't back away, pressed his lips to hers. Damn, she tasted good. Like hot, sweet honey with a hint of coffee.

Trailing his hand up her arm, he twisted his fingers through her hair. Lust arrowed through him, hot and intense. More than anything, he wanted to lay her down on the rug in front of the fire and make love to her.

Reluctantly, he lifted his head from hers, breaking the kiss.

It was too soon. They needed to talk first.

"You're so damn beautiful, Abby. I could go on kissing you for hours." He traced her lips with his finger, his desire for her urging him to take her mouth again. "But I guess that won't get the soup warmed up, will it?" His chest tightening with regret, he grinned, pushed to his feet, and headed for the kitchen.

From the freezer, Ethan grabbed the container of chowder and stuck it in the microwave to defrost. Using the time, he tried to gain control of his raging hormones. Just being near her did things to him. A simple touch sent his self-restraint spiraling out of control. And her kiss....

A high-pitched beep announced the clam chowder needed to

be stirred. Retrieving a spoon, he swirled the contents in the bowl and set it to heat for another minute. Hell, forget the microwave—his rising body temperature alone would probably boil the soup in no time.

When the chowder had warmed, he poured it into two bowls, grabbed the crackers from the cupboard, and put everything on a tray to carry out to the living room, including two large cups of hot cocoa. He found her in the same position on the couch, transfixed by the roaring fire.

Sitting next to her, he set the tray on the coffee table and offered her a bowl of steaming soup. As they ate, his gaze continued to drift to her face. He couldn't keep his eyes off her. Watching her savor the warm soup was as erotic as kissing her soft lips. Lord, he was half hard just sitting near her.

Her words broke into his thoughts. "What brand is this? It's great."

Unable to hold back a huge grin, he said, "It's Parker brand."

Her eyes widened. "You made this?"

This time he laughed out loud. "Is that so hard to believe? I made a batch last week and froze it. I do a lot of cooking on my downtime and throw it in the freezer. Then all I have to do is heat it up in the microwave on the nights I'm too tired to cook."

"I'm very impressed, Detective Parker." A smile curled the corners of her luscious mouth. "You keep amazing me. I think I sorely misjudged you after our first couple meetings." She set the empty bowl down and picked up the mug.

He nested his bowl with hers and got up to stoke the fire. "Yeah, you did, but that was my fault. I didn't give you much to go on." He sat by her again and took the mug from her hands, placing it back on the table. Angling toward her, he grasped her hands in his. "I handled things badly, and I want to apologize for that."

"There's no need, Ethan. I know you were just doing your job. In order to catch whoever is committing these horrible crimes, you need to be as thorough as possible." She lowered her gaze to their hands. "It's quite apparent this whole business is somehow related to me. I don't want anyone else hurt because of something I may have done."

Placing his fingertips beneath her chin, Ethan lifted her head to meet his gaze. "One thing I want you to understand right now is that the murders this sick bastard has committed are not your fault. Who knows what demented reasons he has running around inside his head? But those are *his* sins, not yours." Wiping a tear from her cheek, he leaned in and kissed the edge of her mouth, and a mix of protectiveness and desire spiraled through him. "Please don't feel guilty for something that's not in your control."

Abby sniffed and nodded, staring into his eyes. "I need to explain what happened at my car. My reaction to the peppermints. There are some things you need to know about me."

Ethan gritted his teeth, his jaw popping as he ground his molars. He didn't want to hear it. He'd read the reports. Hell, once behind bars, Mikey had all but bragged about his conquests, filling in the details. Listening to her recount that horrific incident was something he didn't want any part of. "I know everything I need to about you, Abby. You are a beautiful, kind, caring woman."

"I have to tell you, or whatever this is between us can't go any further. Frankly, I'm not sure it can anyway." She looked at him, her eyes round with worry. "But I want to try if you do."

He framed her head in his hands and trailed gentle kisses over her forehead and down to the tip of her nose. "You have to know I do."

She pulled back from him. Rising, she paced in front of the fire. Dear Lord, he didn't want her to have to go through this, to relive it. But maybe she needed to say it, get it out, and get rid of it. And maybe he needed to hear it, so he might fully understand what a monster his brother was.

She stopped in front of the window and kept her gaze on the falling snow. "Seven years ago I was raped. It was a vicious, brutal attack." Her voice held no emotion, sounded hollow, robotic. He remained silent, giving her what time she needed. After a moment, she wrapped her arms around herself and said, "He did things I don't think I will ever be able to talk about...."

Ethan's breath jammed in his throat. He had to stop her, had to tell her he already knew, and how he knew. "Abby, you don't need to put yourself through this."

She faced him. The tears streaming over her cheeks tore at his heart. He rose from the couch, intent on gathering her in his arms, but she held up her hand.

"Yes I do. If I want any chance at a normal life, I do."

He stopped, remaining near the couch. His hands clenched and unclenched at his sides. She'd prevented him from comforting her and left him helpless to change the course she'd chosen. Frustration roiled in his stomach. Guilt squeezed his lungs.

"I remember trying to go somewhere else in my mind while he was...while he was hurting me." Her gaze left his and moved to the dancing flames in the hearth. She swallowed. "Tried to imagine myself someplace safe and warm, but every time I got there, he'd move his face back to mine, and the rancid smell of bad whiskey and peppermint would break through the walls and bring me back to where he was hurting me. The whole time he attacked me, he had one of those peppermint candies in his mouth." She looked up, met his gaze directly. "He even had the audacity to offer me one, like what he was doing wasn't wrong. Like he hadn't beaten me, ripped my clothes off, and used me like...like an animal."

Rage consumed Ethan. This time, nothing she did or said would stop him from reaching her. In two long strides, he was at her side, his arms wrapped around her. It wasn't until she pulled back, peered up at him, and brushed the tears from his cheeks that he realized he'd been crying.

"I'm so sorry for all you went through," he said, his voice coarse with emotion. He kissed the wetness from her cheeks. "I wish I'd been there to stop him."

"I didn't tell you this for you to feel sorry for me. I just wanted you to understand the peppermint reaction." She inhaled and released a soulful sigh. "And, well...me."

He guided her back to the couch, and they sat together, his arm a shawl of protection around her shoulders. "I don't feel sorry for you, honey. I'm just sorry something like that happened to you."

She swiped her cheeks with the backs of her hands and said, "Elliot knew about the peppermint thing. I kind of freaked out on him when we went on a blind date last week. The waitress brought the mints with the bill, and I wigged out." A derisive laugh spilled from her mouth. "You'd think that would've scared him away, but he's got this idea I still want to go out with him or something. He probably put them on my car after the incident in the café." She became quiet, thoughtful for a moment. "You don't think he's the murderer do you?" Her brow knitted, and she shook her head, her shoulders sagging. "No. Jud was killed before I met Elliot. He was just being mean."

Ethan placed a finger over her mouth. "Shh. It's not up to you to figure out who the killer is. Although I do want you to stay away from Elliot. I'll check him out."

"Oh, that won't be a problem. The guy is seriously freaky." She reached out and covered his hand with hers. Heat raced up his arm and straight down to his groin. "I'm sorry if I ruined whatever moment we were having."

"Moment?" He raised his eyebrows, tried for a surprised expression. "We were having a moment? Where was I?"

A husky laugh escaped Abby's lips. She gave him a playful shove, but he caught her hand, his fingers encircling her delicate wrist. With great care, he bowed his head and pressed his lips to the center of her palm. Her sharp intake of air told him she liked it.

"Is this the moment you were referring to?" He kissed her wrist. "Or this?" His mouth grazed along her skin, up the side of her neck to the tender point below her ear.

"Mmm." She shivered.

He inhaled, reveled in her unique scent. A mixture of spicy

vanilla and exotic flowers invaded his senses and sent the room slowly spinning. Primal lust roared through him, demanded he possess her in a rush of carnal passion.

But Ethan resisted.

Intent on enticing Abby into a wild, heated frenzy, he trailed the tip of his tongue along her throat. Her pulse hammered beneath his ardent attention, and he reveled in her response. His fingers slid over her supple skin. One hand sought the silky tresses adorning her head while the other coaxed her legs across his lap and then slipped around her waist.

He pulled back, stared into her lovely face. Eyelids fluttering, she sighed in his arms. When she looked at him, desire burned bright in her eyes. His heart stuttered at the sight, and hot need rushed to his groin.

"Abby." Her name rolled from his tongue in a mix of desperation and lust. A voracious hunger to taste every inch of her body washed over him. The urge to kiss the small of her back, to run his tongue along her skin, delving and dipping into her secret, sensitive places, all but overwhelmed him. "Tell me to stop. If you're not ready, honey, tell me to stop right now and by all that's holy, I will. But you need to know how much I want you right now."

Bringing her hands to the front of his shirt, she spoke clearly as she unfastened each button. "Stopping is the last thing I want you to do. For the first time in such a long time, I feel like a woman, and it feels wonderful."

Spreading his shirt apart, she pushed it over his shoulders and off his arms, freeing him of the offensive material. She laid her open palms against his chest, her fingernails lightly scraping his skin. His flesh burned in the wake of her touch.

Slowly, he opened her blouse, planting gentle kisses where buttons had once been. The pulse point in her neck. The hollow between her breasts. He even paused to swirl his tongue in her bellybutton. And when she arched beneath his lips, he kept going, running his mouth just above the waistline of her jeans and producing a breathy moan from her.

Ethan helped her out of the blouse, tossed it to the floor, and revealed a scanty pink satin bra. He made quick work of the clasp at her back, freeing her breasts. Mercy. His gaze took in the gorgeous woman before him. "You are so beautiful."

Taking one breast in his mouth, he nipped and sucked at the sweet offering, while his hand fondled her other pebbled nipple. The taste of her, the suppleness of her skin, had fire racing through his veins. His body demanded he plunge deep into her body and make her his own. But with great effort, he restrained himself.

Performing a little flip, he swapped places with her, so that she straddled his hips while he lay on his back on the couch. He eased her on to him, and damn, did she feel good.

A sly smile curved her lips, and she immediately took control, capturing his mouth with hers. Heat pooled in his groin, and he ground his hips up into hers. She answered by trailing her fingernails over his abdomen, unsnapping his jeans, and moving her hand down the outside of his pants to caress the bulge she found there. He wrapped his arms tightly around her.

"Abby," he said on a groan. God, he wanted her. Without warning, she started, and if not for his hold on her, she would have fallen right off the couch. It took a moment for the lust-filled haze to clear from his brain and realize the pounding wasn't in his head but at his door. Ethan twisted around, stared toward the entryway. Not only was his front door being practically battered off its hinges, but Grant's angry voice demanded entry from the other side.

Well, shit.

Grabbing her blouse off the floor, he tossed it to her and waited until she had covered herself. The lust that had pulsed through his body had morphed into the icy adrenaline of fight or flight—and fight had surged to the forefront. Three long strides took him to the entryway where he disengaged the deadbolt with a sharp clack. He jerked the door open, prepared to give Grant hell for interrupting them and causing such a scene.

"What the—?"

A fist crashed into Ethan's jaw. Caught off-guard, he stumbled backward, his hand rising to his now throbbing face. He steadied himself just as Grant reached him, only this time he was ready. Jerking his arm up, he deflected the bastard's fist, and in a swift move, shoved him face-first against the wall and pinned his arm behind him.

"What the fuck is your problem, man?" he growled.

Fumbling with a button on her blouse, Abby rushed to the two men, her eyes round with shock.

"Let me go," Grant bellowed.

"If I let you go, are you going to calm your ass down?"

"Yes." He struggled to break free again. "Just let the fuck go."

Ethan released him but took two quick steps back, his fists clenched in preparation for another round. The guy spun, his gaze shifting from Ethan's naked torso and unsnapped jeans to Abby's half-buttoned shirt. It didn't take a rocket scientist to realize what had been going on. Fire erupted in his eyes.

"Where the hell do you get off coming over to my house, ranting like a lunatic at the door, and then assaulting me when I open it?"

Grant swung his head back in his direction, his face the color of a fire engine. "Where do I get off? Oh, let's see. Steve comes back to the station hours ago, telling us all what happened, how my sister was almost assaulted. Hours later, I still haven't heard a word from her." He jerked his hand toward them, slicing the air. "But look at the two of you. It's easy to see just where the hell *you* get off."

With a growl, Ethan lunged at the maniac.

"No!" She scurried forward, moving between them.

Grant raised his hands in an act of surrender. "I'm sorry, Abby. That was uncalled for." He turned, pulled her into his arms. "Steve had me so damn worried about you, then after hours of waiting for you to call, wondering where you were and driving the streets looking for you, when I saw your car here...I guess I just lost it."

She moved from his embrace. "You owe Ethan an apology.

You practically break down his door and then punch him? You had to know if I was here, I was safe."

The muscles in Grant's jaw worked. Obviously, not only did he think she wasn't safe here in his home, but he also didn't want his sister anywhere near him. Her brother stood rigid, his brows drawn down. His stance had nothing to do with the murders, that much Ethan knew.

The asshole pondered something interesting on the floor then, then he shifted his gaze to the wall over Ethan's shoulder. The guy wouldn't look him in the eye.

"I apologize for acting like an overprotective brother," he grumbled. "But with this maniac running around out there, I was imagining all sorts of things." Then he did meet Ethan's stare. "Turns out she was safe in your arms. Huh, partner?"

He opened his mouth to respond, but before he could utter a word, his cell went off. He strode to the table and grabbed it up. "Parker."

Chapter Sixteen

*E*than slammed his SUV's door shut with a little more oomph than needed and trudged through the freshly fallen snow toward the latest victim's house. This was so not what he wanted to be doing right now.

The way he'd been forced to leave things with Abby had remained in the forefront of his mind since leaving his house. He wanted to get back to her and pick up where they'd left off—as it was, he stood at half-mast just thinking of having her back in his arms. Of course, she wasn't at his house any longer. While he grabbed his coat and keys, they'd decided he might be too long, and she'd just gone home.

What the fuck had Grant been thinking?

As soon as they'd left his house, Ethan told him to swing by the station so he could pick up his truck. No way would he be stuck inside a small, confined area with that sonofabitch for a moment longer than necessary. As it was, the short drive had been tense as hell. He hadn't said a word to his partner because he'd been too pissed to speak without knocking the guy out. It was probably the same for him.

The second this case was over there would be no more partnership. It was bad enough he would have to finish this out with him—as though Abby's brother had any real say in her life.

She was a grown woman, for God's sake. He'd known full well she'd been safe with him. The guy had a personal ax to grind, and he was damned sure going to find out what it was.

When Chief Hague first assigned Montgomery to him, Ethan had told the chief straight out that he was no mentor, trainer, rookie babysitter, or whatever anybody wanted to call it. He'd been solving cases just fine on his own and didn't need a partner. But the old man had insisted.

Damn, this case couldn't be over soon enough for so many reasons.

The rumble of Grant's truck pulling up brought Ethan back to the present. With a groan, he shoved his emotions aside and took in his surroundings. He had a job to do, and the sooner it was done, the better.

The victim's house was at the end of a long, private drive in one of the more influential neighborhoods. Ethan glanced back toward the road and gritted his teeth. Numerous tracks rutted the icy slush on the driveway. Even with the fresh snow, it was impossible to tell how many vehicles had been in and out with all of the emergency vehicles there.

He tromped up the walkway, letting the frosty air cool his heated temper. This was a crime scene, and he couldn't afford to let his disposition interfere with his job. He waited for Grant to join him at the front door then asked the attending officer for his report.

"The victim's name is Nicholas Colbert. He apparently grew up around here but moved away after college and was now some big shot on Wall Street. He was home to celebrate his parents' fiftieth anniversary. The parents had gone out with another couple to dinner and a comedy show then had coffee afterward. They arrived home around two a.m. The mother decided to look in on her son before she retired, and that's when she found his body."

Ethan stiffened. "What did you say the victim's name was?"

"Nicholas—or Nick, as his father called him—Colbert."

Pivoting toward Grant, who stood behind him, he searched

for any reaction, but the guy remained stone-faced. "I met him earlier today in the coffee shop. He was an old friend of your sister's."

A flicker of recognition shown in his eyes, and he nodded. "Yeah, I remember him now. He was a big football star."

Ethan clenched his jaw. Damn, another person Abby knew had been murdered. He glanced back at the officer. "Where are the parents now?"

"The hospital. The mother suffered a cardiac arrest after finding the victim. Paramedics had a heartbeat going when they left with her, but they said it wasn't looking too good. The husband rode along in the ambulance."

Ethan shook his head. For a mother to walk in and find her child like that? Unconscionable. Hopefully she'd pull through, but even then, she'd have a tough road ahead of her.

He glanced around. "Where are Officers Moore and Hanson? Out canvassing the neighbors?"

The officer shook his head. "Moore had a family emergency, and Hanson had a doctor's appointment. No one's available to canvass until after CSU is done."

Ethan eyed Grant. As usual, his partner stood staid next to him, but Ethan sensed the anger rolling off him in waves. The guy needed to take a walk, cool off. "Montgomery, go talk to the neighbors."

His partner blanched, his eyes flashing wide with fury. "What?"

"See if any of them heard or saw anything," he said, careful to keep his voice even and authoritative. "I'll go in and get the lay of the land."

Grant balled his hand into a fist and tightened his jaw. Ethan tensed, prepared for the idiot to throw a punch at any moment—and at a crime scene, no less. Yeah, his partner needed a long walk through the snow, needed to clear his head.

"Yes, sir," he said through clenched teeth. Pivoting on his heel, he marched out across the snow-covered yard.

The officer watched Grant walk off. He raised a brow in

comment but wisely kept his mouth shut as Ethan strode through the door.

Inside the house, he unzipped his coat then, slipped on the booties, and headed down the hall to the only bedroom with the door open.

"Hey," Steve said as he limped by, camera in hand. "Quite a mess in there."

Ethan nodded, his gut tightening in preparation of what lay ahead. He stepped through the bedroom doorway and stopped.

Blood.

Everywhere.

The walls were streaked with it. Crimson spattered the curtains in the window. The floorboards. The carpet. The bed.

Ethan swallowed.

He dragged his gaze to the body. There lay Nick, tied spread-eagled to the bed frame, his body mutilated. Damn. The guy had just thanked him for breaking up the fight that had been about to ensue at the coffee shop. And now his mouth hung slightly agape, his jaw cocked off to the side. His eyes stared sightlessly up and to the left toward his hand. Had he been trying to free himself when the killer slashed his throat?

"Same M.O.," he said to Gary, who stood hunched over Nick's body, examining the message the killer had carved in his chest.

"Yes," the forensics investigator said without looking up. "And I can tell you the next word in the killer's message."

Steve pushed by Ethan. "You got the chest cleaned up? Let me get a shot." He jerked his camera up, and a sharp flash filled the room. Leaning over and squinting, he said, "What does it say?"

"FOR." Gary turned and rummaged in his work case.

"Yeah," Steve said. "Maybe. But it looks like the guy was going to add something else but changed his mind. That or maybe he slipped."

He moved closer to the bed and stared at the victim's marred chest. A slip? Had the killer made a mistake or been interrupted?

"Oh, he didn't slip," the forensics investigator said, standing. "That mark is too straight to be a mistake. It was intentional."

Steve looked up. "Intentional, huh? F, O, R, and a line. That makes no sense."

Ethan nodded. "Maybe not to us. But this guy is precise. He knows exactly what he's doing and how he wants to do it, even with the variations of the last vic who fought him. The killer tied him up with duct tape, slit his throat, and left the next word in his twisted message." He glanced over at Gary. "How long you figure you and your guys got here?"

"Jesus, Ethan, you just got here, and you're giving me shit already?"

He sighed. "I don't mean to push you—scratch that, I'm not pushing you. Not giving you shit. It's just with no available patrol or help other than Montgomery, I'm already behind the eight ball with this one. You know I can't leave until you close the scene. Just looking for a timeline is all. Stop getting your panties in a wad."

The older investigator met his gaze. "Just so you remember this is my crime scene."

"Damn it, Gary, I'm too tired to get into a pissing match with you. You know me better than that. Just give me a fucking estimated time, would you?"

His lips cracked into a smile. "A little testy this early in the morning? Two more hours tops. If this scene is as consistent as the others, anything we find will be in this room. The other rooms always come up with nothing, and my guys are just about done with the rest of the house. I have a few more things to do in here, then we can move the body to the morgue, and CSU can finish up in here. Okay with you?"

"Fine, thank you. I'll be checking out the rest of the house if you need me." Ethan shook his head and left the room. He walked through the dining room, kitchen, living room. It was a grand house. Of course, now with it covered in black soot from the CSU and their fingerprinting crap, there was a hell of a mess to clean up.

His heart ached at what this poor guy's parents had ahead of them. Damn it, he had to get a lead on the bastard doing this. Something to go on. This needed to be the last victim. He didn't give a shit about the heat coming at him from the mayor and the chief. There shouldn't be another family who had to go through this.

Two and a half hours later, Grant walked through the door while the CSU packed up their equipment. His narrowed eyes and hardened features remained. The long walk and cold air had done little to rectify his demeanor. He was just as pissy as when he'd left.

Irritation flared in Ethan's gut. He couldn't deal with his partner's cocky-ass attitude now any more than he could three hours ago. Attempting to remain professional, he leveled his gaze and said, "Got anything?"

"No, nothing. No one saw a thing. No one heard a thing. No one believed such a bad thing could happen to such a wonderful family." The last was said with a sneer in his voice.

"You got reason to believe they aren't a wonderful family?" Ethan asked.

"Nope. Don't know them. Wouldn't know if they were wonderful or not."

He stepped toward his partner and lowered his voice so no one else would hear. "Then your attitude must still have something to do with me," he gritted out. "Is that the case? You still have something you need to say to me?"

"Nope."

He stared at him long and hard, and Grant glared back, never breaking eye contact. Apparently, his partner remained angry about what had transpired earlier, but Ethan decided not to call him on it. A crime scene was not the place to hold that conversation.

"Fine. We're just about done here. I want you to head over to the hospital and check on Mr. and Mrs. Colbert." To ensure the rookie understood his next words, he deepened his voice to a commanding rumble. "Just stay with them. I don't want you questioning Mr. Colbert at this point. You call me as soon as there's news about Mrs. Colbert. You got that?"

"You want me to go over there and babysit the husband and do nothing else?" Grant narrowed his eyes, the childish temper returning. He stepped back, swiping his hand through the air toward the door. "You're kidding me, right? And just what the fuck are you going to be doing?"

Ethan's whole body tensed, and he widened his stance. "You know what, Montgomery? This isn't up for debate. I'm the lead on this case. If you don't like it, take it up with the chief. Otherwise, go over to the hospital and do your damn job."

Grant stood there, eyebrows drawn down as he glowered. He opened his mouth as if to speak, but then a spark glimmered in the rookie's eyes, and his lips twisted into a petulant sneer. Had he realized pursuing this discussion at a crime scene was unprofessional after all? Or was he planning some other type of altercation or revenge?

"Off to the hospital, sir." He took a crisp, academy-style step backward, his dark gaze never wavering. "I assume I can get you on your cell when the parents are ready to talk?"

"That would be correct."

Grant spun on his heel and stormed off to his truck. Gunning the engine, he fishtailed all over the driveway as he pulled away.

Damn. Why was everything so difficult with him?

Thirty minutes later, Ethan locked the door behind the last of the CSU team and headed to Abby's house. As much as he hated it, he had to question her about Nick. She was one of the last people to see him alive. He needed to know what their conversation had entailed and go back over the details of the argument with Elliot.

Elliot.

That guy needed some looking into. He kept popping up in this investigation, and to say he looked good for the perp was an understatement.

And, just where the fuck was Mikey? He'd been released

from prison, and it was as if he'd walked out the gates and disappeared. No phone calls with parting jabs of guilt about how his dear, toe-the-line detective brother hadn't taken good enough care of him.

Ethan rubbed his hand over his beard-stubbled jaw. What was Mikey up to? He had no money, no place to live. So, where the hell had he gone? Was he responsible for those mints on Abby's car? Damn it, he needed to find him.

He pulled into Abby's driveway, shut his truck off, and sat there for a minute. He didn't want to tell her about Nick. She'd already shouldered the blame for these crimes, and he'd only just reassured her, helped her to feel a little better about herself. Would this cause a backslide?

The porch light came on. Ethan sighed and slid out of the truck.

The door opened, and she met him, wearing a pair of light blue sleep pants and matching tank top. He stared at her, his hunger for her increasing. God, she was gorgeous. She reached for him, and he pulled her into his arms, holding her tight against his chest, breathing in the fresh floral scent that was her.

She felt like home.

Chapter Seventeen

*E*than nuzzled his face into the crook of Abby's neck and inhaled deeply. He'd yet to let her go, and the warmth of her body wrapped around his enabled him to briefly forget the horror of the crime scene earlier.

She giggled, pulled back, and looked up at him. "You're going to give me a stubble burn with all that scruff on your face. Frankly, Ethan, you look like hell. I know how tired you've got to be. You should've just gone home and gotten some sleep. But I'm glad you didn't."

He ran a hand over his chin, and sure enough there was a full day's growth. "I'm sorry. I didn't realize I was in this bad of shape. It's been a rough night."

She frowned. "Another victim?"

He silently nodded.

"Come in. You can use my brother's bathroom to clean up while I put on a pot of coffee." She closed the door behind him, took his hand, and guided him to the bathroom.

With a sweet smile that caused his heart to beat double-time, she left him alone. Ethan turned the water on, braced his hands on both sides of the sink, and took a long, hard look in the mirror. Dark shadows under his eyes, deep creases on his brow. When the hell had his life gone to shit? He wanted more than the endless hours he put in on the job, more than the lonely, hollow walls of his house. Walking into Abby's arms at the end of such a messed up night had been a balm to his tortured soul. Her touch had rendered him whole again.

That was what he wanted.

But could he have her? Or, the better question, would she have him? He was a cop. What the hell could he give a woman like her? She deserved everything life had to offer, but instead, she'd received the worst. Could she forgive his part in her painful past, his relationship to her attacker?

Ethan let out a deep sigh and scrubbed his face with handfuls of cool water. It helped to wake him up a bit and wash the melancholy away.

She was right about his scruffiness. Almost a full day's growth covered his face. He grabbed Grant's razor and cream and shaved away the remains of an awful night. Placing the razor back where he'd found it, he chuckled. Bastard would be madder than hell when he realized he'd used his stuff. Too bad.

Feeling much better, he left the bathroom to find Abby. He'd get her through this latest news about Nick and then figure out how to tell her about Mikey. He wanted this woman in his life, and he prayed to God she wanted to be part of his.

Allowing the rich aroma to lead him, Ethan ambled into the kitchen and saw her at the counter, pouring two mugs of freshly brewed coffee. He walked up behind her and wrapped his arms around her, once again breathing in the wonderful scent that was her.

She turned in his arms to face him and smiled. Bringing her hands up, she cupped his face and smoothed her fingers over his jaw. When her thumb grazed his bottom lip, she swallowed, and said in a sultry voice, "You clean up mighty fine, Detective."

He couldn't help it. With her so close, the sexy glint in her eyes. It was more than he could take. Threading his fingers through her silky tresses, he cradled her head and captured her mouth with a kiss that stole his breath away.

Ethan skimmed his hand down to the small of her back and

tugged her up tight against him. He slid the other behind her neck to tangle in the silky hair of her nape. His tongue warred with hers as she matched his fervor and then some. Blood rushed from his head straight to his groin where he grew impossibly hard. God, he wanted this woman.

She moaned, molding against him. When her hips ground against his, she made it more than apparent she knew how she affected him.

Dear Lord, if he didn't stop this now, he'd take her right there on the kitchen floor. Pulling back with a groan, he cupped her face. "God I've missed you."

She beamed up at him and laughed. "It's only been a few hours, silly man. But I've missed you, too. I was unhappy we had to end things where we did."

No sooner had the words left her mouth than he slammed back into the present. Dread filled his chest, and his heated veins cooled with the thought of their impending conversation. "Yeah, about that and the victim. We need to talk."

Abby took his hand and led him out of the kitchen, leaving the coffee behind. They reached the couch and she gestured for him to sit.

Tension coiled inside him. He didn't want to tell her another person she knew had been murdered. And as soon as she sat next to him, her eyes became soft and something else he couldn't describe.

She reached up, slipped a button on his shirt through its hole and then another.

He grabbed her hand to stop her. "Baby, as much as I want this, you know we have to talk about what happened tonight."

Abby sighed, dropped her hands to her lap, and studied them for a moment before raising her head to search his face. She saw the pain in his eyes and her throat tightened.

Another victim.

He'd told her that when he'd gotten here. She would know the victim, too. That much was a given. But what she wanted now was the man sitting next to her. She needed to be happy, to feel the pleasure he could give her before she had to face more heartache. Was that selfish of her? Probably. But she'd just started to feel whole again because of him. She needed to get lost in his arms, be swept away by the touch of his hands on her body before she could endure more devastation.

Twisting her fingers together, she tried to explain. "I know, but I need you. I know you're not here with good news. But I want this small slice of happiness before I have to deal with more pain." Abby stared into his warm brown eyes and swallowed. "Does that make sense to you? You've made me feel like a woman again, and I just really...don't want to lose that."

"Aw, honey, I'd never take that away from you."

"Make love to me, Ethan." She slipped another button free on his shirt, but he ceased her actions once again.

"You have to be sure about this. I want you more than I've ever wanted anything before. But are you sure you want me or just an escape from the grief?" he asked, releasing her hands.

She splayed them across his chest. Heat radiated through his shirt, the thumping of his heartbeat strong beneath her hands, and his solid muscle incited butterflies in her stomach to take flight. Her fingers slid over the cotton fabric, itching to explore every inch of his body.

Was she using him to delay the bad news that was sure to come? *No.* She didn't have to think twice about it.

"For seven years I've been barely alive, going through the motions of life because I couldn't see the point of getting excited about the next day let alone the next hour. That was until I met you. From our first meeting, you woke something in me." She laughed. "Yeah, maybe it was anger, but I began to feel a spark of passion for life again. Since then, that spark has grown into a full-blown, five-alarm fire." She resumed her work on his shirt, sliding each button through its hole. When he didn't stop her, a ripple of pleasure coursed through her. Once she had it open, she slid his shirt off those broad shoulders of his and dropped it on the floor, leaving only a T-shirt tucked into his jeans.

"What happened in the past has had a huge hold of my life for years, and I've lived with unbearable pain. Am I afraid of what you have to tell me? Yes. Am I using sex to prolong the inevitable?" She met his gaze, all but falling into the depths of his deep brown eyes. The desire that swirled there matched her own and sent heat radiating through her body. The truth of their connection shone bright and real, so tangible she had but to reach out and touch it. "This is the inevitable. This, you and me, the passion and fire between us. It's not an escape. It's a homecoming. Whatever you have to tell me will be there later. Make love to me, Ethan."

Tugging at his T-shirt, Abby lifted her mouth to his, and he met her more than halfway, eagerly taking charge of the kiss. He traced her lips with his tongue, leaving open-mouthed kisses along her jaw to whisper in her ear.

"Absolutely."

The tremble of his voice caused a shiver to cascade down her spine. A rush of molten lava sped from the hollow in her throat to pool at the very soul of her being. *Yes, this is where I belong.*

She pushed the shirt up his abdomen, touching every rippled muscle along her way. Helping her, he leaned back and, in a single, swift motion, pulled it over his head, revealing sculpted abs and a firm, powerful chest.

Unable to resist, she trailed her fingers through the fine dusting of hair to his hardened nipples. A rushed intake of air from Ethan left her in awe of the power her touch had over him. Tracing circles around the tight buds, she created a path of hot kisses across his chest. Emboldened, she brought her mouth to linger over one of his nipples and blew a whisper of warm breath.

He groaned and tangled a hand in her hair, pulling her closer. With a quick flick of her tongue, she tasted the sweet saltiness of his skin. Another groan from him, and she swirled her tongue around and around while her nimble fingers tortured his other nipple at the same time.

"Good God, Abby, you're killing me."

She smiled up at him, momentarily startled by the dark hunger in his eyes.

Tucking a finger under her chin, he lifted her face up to meet his gaze again. "Know one thing, baby. I will never hurt you. You're in control here. You say go, we go. You say stop, we stop, no matter what."

"I say go."

He leaned down and kissed her neck, then shoulder, trailing tender, wet kisses over her skin. With one finger, he slid the strap of her tank top off her shoulder, tracing the length of her arm until he reached the bottom of her shirt. He glanced at her and lifted the tank top over her head, revealing her bare breasts.

Her heart pounded in anticipation, her nipples so hard they ached.

"So, so beautiful."

He lowered his head to her breast and twirled his tongue around the tightened bud in a soft caress. Her breath caught. Then he took her nipple fully in his mouth, laving and sucking while gently stroking her other breast with his hand.

She arched and, threading her hands through his hair, she pulled him in closer. He lowered his head, blazing a trail from her chest to her belly button down to the top of her sleep pants.

Fire burned from within, and her body yearned for his touch. The heat of his skin beneath her hands. The sight of him, all muscles and hardness. And God, the hot, musky maleness. Unable to wait any longer, she reached for his pants and made quick work of the belt and zipper.

"Now, Ethan. Please."

He stood, shimmied out of his jeans and dark briefs, and reached for her. As he helped her to her feet, she waited while he bent and slowly drew her sleep pants down her legs. He skimmed his hands over her calves and up her thighs, slipping his fingers into the sides of her panties. His touch sent tingles low in her abdomen, and when he removed the lacy undergarment, leaving her fully nude in front of him, her body quivered with realization.

He was the one.

Ethan knelt and slowly glided his palms up her legs. He stared up at her, the intensity of his gaze alone causing her body to quake with anticipation. Oh, how she wanted him, because for them to join, to become one, would create the intimacy her soul craved.

His hands trembled, and he shifted his thumbs to the insides of her thighs. Oh, how she wanted this. On shaky legs, she widened her stance and placed her hands on his shoulders for leverage. He moved in quickly, like a starving man ready to devour her, and she squirmed under his attention.

"Oh, oh, Ethan." She threw her head back, her eyes shut tight. She stood on the edge of an abyss. Clawing his shoulders, she fought the oncoming tsunami, afraid to let go.

He pulled slightly away, his fingers still teasing her most sensitive spot. He'd built a fire inside her, and she trembled with the intense need he'd brought her to.

"I want all of you, Abby," he said, his gaze locked on her, his dark eyes reassuring. "Let it go, honey."

His husky voice was her undoing.

A kaleidoscope of light flashed behind her eyes, and her knees buckled. If not for his other hand on her thigh holding her up, she'd have collapsed to the floor.

When the undulating waves of pleasure coursing through her body subsided, she sank to her knees, and Ethan wrapped his arms around her. He held her against him while her breathing returned to normal, his own heart thudding in an even rhythm beneath her cheek.

"You were gorgeous." His hands slid down her back, over her hips, and cupped her bottom, pulling her against him. Inclining his head, he nuzzled her neck, his tongue branding a trail up to her ear. "I could never get enough," he said with a lust-filled growl.

His words sent a hot rush of hunger spinning through her. She moaned, a mix of desire and destiny twining around her heart.

She could never get enough of Ethan Parker. Never.

He moved to the couch, and the loss of his warmth caused her to reach for him. His fingers still intertwined with hers, he lay on his back and coaxed her to him.

"I want you to be in control of this, Abby. I don't want to be some looming figure hovering over you. I want you to look me in the eyes when we join."

Her gaze roved over his taut body as he lay there, magnificent in his nakedness, totally open and vulnerable. Her heart swelled at his gesture. He truly was an amazing man.

She trailed a finger over his chest and down his muscled abdomen. He was hot and hard, and his entire being beckoned to her. She licked her lips, desire racing through her. But it'd been so long since she'd been with anyone. Would her body accept what she wanted so badly?

He urged her to him, and she straddled his thighs, her knees pressing into the couch cushions. "We'll do this slowly," he said.

His hands descended to her thighs, helping her into position, but made no move to lower her. His arms and chest trembled, and with his gaze glued to hers, he silently begged her to take him.

"Don't worry," he reassured her. "You're ready for me, sweetheart."

Gradually, she lowered herself. He groaned and clearly fought to hold himself still, gripping her hips to the point of pain. But being joined with him wasn't painful. It was wonderful.

"Abby," he managed through gritted teeth. "Please, honey."

A thrill of power rushed through her. He'd relinquished control, gave it all to her. She reveled in the gift and his ability to let go. Lifting her hips, she moved, all the while keeping eye contact with him. She was okay, this was okay. Joy swirled with lust, and she leaned forward to capture his mouth as he moved with her in a torturously languid rhythm.

Except in her heart, she didn't want all the control—although for a long time, that was all she'd believed she wanted. But tonight, with this man, it wasn't about power. It was about giving and trust, healing and wholeness. It was about two people destined to become one.

Realizing the only way to reach true fulfillment, she tilted her head to the side, nipped at his ear, and whispered, "Take me, Ethan."

She rose up, smiled at him, and lust flared in his eyes. His movements grew harder and faster, and tingles rippled deep inside her. As his rhythm increased, his pelvis pounded her thighs with each fervent stroke, bringing her to the brink once again.

"Ah, God, Abby," he growled. "So good."

Lost in the passion, she met him thrust for thrust and threw her head back. Her body burned for him, and the quivering pulse inside her grew into a scorching wave of rapture that threatened to consume her. When he pushed her over the edge, she clutched him, her entire body bucking at the intense sensations searing through her.

"Oh!"

He bolted upright and wrapped her legs fully around him. Sheeted in sweat, his breath coming in ragged gasps, he pumped his hips. With a feral growl, he buried his face in her neck and ground into her a few more times before finding his own release.

Breathless, they collapsed onto the cushions, still twined together. Ethan reached back and grabbed the afghan off the back of the couch to cover them.

Snuggling close, she sighed. "Thank you."

His chest rumbled with a chuckle. "The pleasure was all mine, ma'am. You okay?"

"Perfect." She trailed a finger over his shoulder and down his arm.

He held her close, his fingers twining through her hair until she drifted off to sleep.

◌⃝

When she opened her eyes again, the first vestiges of the

sun's morning glow streamed through the windows. With her head on his chest, peace stole over her while she listened to the slow, even thump of his heart. Shifting, she lifted her head and peered at his handsome, tranquil face. If only it could be like this forever.

He opened his eyes and saw her, and his lips curved into a soft, satisfied smile. "Hey."

"Good morning." She traced a finger over his eyebrow. She swallowed, knowing the spell had been broken and reality had tracked them down.

Ethan's arms tensed around her as if sensing the same. He stared at her, concern creasing his previously smooth brow. "Abby...."

"It's okay." She sighed. "I'm ready. Who was it?"

He reached up, pushed a loose strand of hair behind her ear. "Nick Colbert."

"Nick?" Shock rolled through her with surprising force. God, she'd seen him just yesterday, smiling, laughing. "No. No, it can't...."

He pulled her against him and held her while silent sobs wracked her body. Tears coursed over her cheeks, landing on his bare chest. He rubbed her back, murmuring words of comfort until she stilled.

Grief morphed into anger, and Abby clutched his arm, her nails digging into his skin. So many wonderful people in her life had been taken from her. It was wrong. So despicably wrong.

Pushing from his embrace, she sat up, snatched her clothes off the floor, and yanked them on. "This has to stop."

Ethan bolted upright, the afghan sliding down his thigh. "What?"

"The murders. It has to end." She turned, leveled her gaze on him. "Use me."

His brow furrowed. Shoving the afghan aside, he snagged his briefs. "What are you talking about?"

"It's simple. Use me as bait to stop this guy."

"What?" His eyes widened, and his mouth opened then

closed. "No. Absolutely not."

"Why not?"

"Because it's damned dangerous, that's why." He grabbed his T-shirt and shoved his arms through the holes, then yanked it over his head.

"But he's killing everyone I know. It's me he really wants."

"Which is exactly why you're not doing this." He glared at her. "Just cause he's only killed men so far doesn't mean he wouldn't hurt you."

"There must be some way to use that to our advantage." She moved toward him, got in his face. "The people I love are dying. Why won't you even consider letting me help you stop this bastard?"

"Oh, hell, fucking no." He stood and thrust his legs into his pants. "I repeat. No. Fucking. Way."

"You're not being reasonable. I—"

His voice rose. "Reasonable? Are you kidding me? There is no way in hell I will ever put you in harm's way. Especially not in the path of a psychotic killer. So just wipe it out of your mind."

"Ethan, just hear me out." Before she could say anything more the phone rang. She pointed a finger at him. "You stay right there. We're not finished discussing this."

"Uh, yeah. We are."

She glared at him, stomped over to the coffee table, and snatched up the phone. "Hello?" she snapped into the receiver. Who the hell could be calling at six in the morning?

"Could I please speak with Abigail Montgomery?"

"Speaking," she said, allowing her irritation to flow across the line. "Who is this?"

In the background, Ethan's cell rang. Grabbing it, he stalked off toward the kitchen and barked his name at whoever was on the other end.

"Abby, this is Trevor Lewis. I prosecuted your case."

Without warning, her knees weakened, and she sank into the chair next to the phone. "I remember."

"I've been meaning to call you," he said and cleared his

throat. "Actually, I thought my secretary had already done so a week ago, but I just found my memo to her buried on my desk. I'm sorry to call so early, but I'll be in court all day and didn't want to miss you."

"That's fine." She gripped the chair arm until her knuckles whitened, and her hand shook. A ball of icy dread formed in the pit of her stomach. "What is it you need to tell me?"

"Michael Greene, the man prosecuted in your case for, um...."

"Yes," she whispered. "I remember what he did."

"I'm sorry, Abby." Her attorney cleared his throat again. "But he was released from jail a few days ago. Last Friday, I think." He paused, and the sound of a pen tapping on a desk rang like a string of firecrackers over the line. "I just wanted you to know. He'd served his sentence. It was time. I really do apologize for not telling you sooner."

The phone dropped from her grip, clattering to the floor, and a small whimper escaped before she covered her mouth with her hand. Strong arms wrapped around her and pulled her into a warm embrace.

"Honey?" Ethan's voice rang with concern. "What is it? Who was on the phone?"

She blew out a shaky breath. "Michael Greene, my...my rapist has been released." She turned in his arms to face him. "My God, he's been out since Friday. I didn't even know."

He hugged her tighter, and she felt a shudder run through him. "I've got you now, Abby. I promise, he'll never hurt you again."

She buried her head against his chest and tried to absorb all his strength. But she couldn't shake the feeling that if Michael Greene wanted to get to her, all the promises in the world wouldn't stop him.

Chapter Eighteen

*E*than jerked the SUV's steering wheel, turning into St. Vincent's parking lot. He drove toward the Emergency Department while his stomach continued to churn over Abby's proposal. She'd looked him square in the eye and said she wanted to lure out the crazed killer who'd murdered four people.

And to top things off, her damn lawyer called to inform her Mikey was out. Ethan gritted his teeth. And hell if he knew where to find his half-brother. He gripped the wheel, his knuckles whitening, and glanced toward the employee lot. Abby had parked her compact and emerged with her purse over her shoulder. A breeze blew her hair from her face, revealing a pinched expression and wary gaze.

She wanted to be bait? Had she lost her mind?

He exited the Tahoe, his shoes immediately immersed in the gray slush that still covered the ground. Adjusting his sunglasses against the bright winter sun, he rounded the SUV and waited for her to cross the lot.

She traipsed toward him, one hand holding her hair to the side while she picked her path across the ice-mired asphalt. Lithe. Graceful. Even amongst the sludge and snow-covered cars, the harsh light glaring from above, she was beautiful. How could she offer to place herself into such a perilous position?

Didn't she realize how much he cared for her?

Well, one way or the other, he would talk her out of that harebrained scheme. He'd employ whatever methods necessary to catch the deadly sonofabitch, but using Abby as bait was out of the question.

"How late do you work tonight?" he asked when she reached him.

"Till five." Her brow furrowed. "Why?"

"Just wondered if a pretty girl might want to have dinner after she gets off work." He shoved his hands into his jacket pockets to keep from touching her. And, oh God, how he wanted to touch her. It was maddening.

"That sounds nice," she said in a thin voice. She glanced across the parking lot toward her car and her jaw tightened. Tension vibrated off her like a fire bell clanging. Swallowing, she looked up at him. "I'd like that."

"You didn't have to come to work," he said. Unable to stand her being so wound up, he reached over and caressed her shoulder.

Her lips curved, but the smile wasn't genuine. He'd seen her smile, and this wasn't it.

"I'm fine." She looked toward the hospital entrance.

"All I'm saying is you could've stayed at my house for the day." Ethan slid his hand to her back. Realizing she probably felt exposed out here in the parking lot, he ushered her toward the door. "I could've told your boss it was police business."

"I appreciate that." She stepped through the doorway, and her shoulders relaxed. "But if I'd stayed home, all I would've done was worry about where...." She crossed her arms over her chest and swallowed. "Where the guy who ruined my life is. From what my attorney told me, he's been out several days, which makes me sure it was him and not Elliot who left all those peppermints on my car." They pushed through a set of double doors and ambled down a long hallway. Abby's damp, rubber-soled shoes squeaked lightly against the tiled floor. "At least here I'll be distracted. And with all the people around, I'll be safe."

They stopped at an open doorway with a sign that read, *Ultrasound.*

"This is me." She rounded toward Ethan, and before he realized it, she popped up on her tiptoes and pressed her lips against his. When she pulled back, she stared at him with soulful eyes and said, "Thank you. I look forward to dinner."

"Sure," he managed to respond, unused to such a public display of affection.

After she'd disappeared into her office, guilt speared through his chest. Mikey. Damn it. That was a whole other problem. He had to tell her Mikey was his half-brother, but damned if he knew how. Their relationship was so new. How in hell was he supposed to drop a bomb like that?

Uh, I just wanted to tell you the guy who raped you seven years ago and ruined your life is a member of my family.

Shit. Talk about destroying any chance of a future together. And now, he was out, God knew where, doing God knew what. Was he the one who'd littered Abby's car hood with peppermints? After all the comments he'd made when Ethan had spoken to him in jail, there was an excellent chance he'd done just that. The mints had been a message to her that he was out and could get to her whenever he wanted. And a message to Ethan that he'd do whatever the hell he pleased.

He shoved his hands into his jacket pockets. With a sharp exhalation, he tromped down the hall to the main desk and requested the room number for Nick Colbert's mother. Taking the elevator to the Intensive Care Unit on the third floor, he continued to brood about the way life was determined to screw over any chances he had at love.

Stepping off the elevator, he all but ran Grant down.

"Whoa!" His partner sidestepped and lifted his arms into the air, a steaming cup of coffee in each hand.

"What the hell, Grant?" he barked.

He lowered his arms and glared at Ethan. "I was getting a cup of coffee for Mr. Colbert while he waited for news about his wife's surgery. Thought he could use it after sitting up all night."

He tightened his hand around one of the cups, the hot liquid rising dangerously close to the lip. "Or are you gonna punch me for being civil to a grieving father?"

"No." He sliced the air with his hand. Crap. Now, he looked like the asshole. "No," he said again, forcing the agitation from his voice. "He said he's ready to talk?"

"Now that Mrs. Colbert's out of danger, he wants to catch the guy who killed his son."

Grant led him to a private waiting room where the vic's father sat hunched over in a chair. The man raised his head as they entered, revealing purplish slashes beneath his eyes. Grief marred the man's face, and he held his hand out to Ethan while he struggled to his feet.

Ethan shook his hand and said, "Mr. Colbert. I'm Detective Parker, and I'm so sorry for your loss. Have you heard anything regarding your wife?"

"She's stable, but the next few hours are critical." He sank back down into the chair.

"We don't have to do this now. If you'd rather wait—"

The man raised a wrinkled hand to cut him off. "Detective Parker, the next few hours will pass whether I'm sitting here alone in this tiny room or answering your questions. Honestly, I believe Margie would prefer I spend the time helping catch the bastard who murdered our son."

Ethan nodded, took a seat in a chair across from the grieving, older gentleman, and pulled his pad and pen from his inner jacket pocket. Taking it slowly, he asked his questions, followed leads as far as he could, and made sure to allow plenty of time for the man to think between answers. Shock had a way of blocking details out, and this man had endured a double dose in less than twenty-four hours.

Two hours later, Ethan wound up his questions, having learned little more than what he'd known before entering the miniscule waiting room. Saying his goodbyes, he altered his focus to Grant. "Come on, let's go grab some coffee and food in the cafeteria and go over what we know so far. I'm thinking we should have a patrol pick up this Elliot character and bring him in for questioning. There's something about him that just doesn't feel right."

"Sounds good. I'm starved and definitely need the caffeine. It's been a damn long night."

His remark sounded genuine, not full of the anger like it had been last night. Apparently sending him over here to cool his heels had done the trick. "By the way, the coroner messaged me. He should have the body ready for autopsy in about ninety minutes, so we can head downstairs to the morgue as soon as he calls."

Grant hit the elevator button for down. "I'll meet you in the cafeteria. I just want to stop off and tell Abby good morning."

Ethan wanted to go with him—she never strayed far from his thoughts. But the rookie appeared to be in a good mood. Seeing him and her together would no doubt send her brother spiraling into Pissed-off Land again.

Besides, Ethan smiled to himself, *Abby and I have a date for dinner.*

ଔ

Abby sat in the dark ultrasound room, her patient's protruding, bare belly covered with warm goo. All day she'd struggled to focus on her job. The one thing that kept her going was the memory of her and Ethan and the magnificent love they'd made.

While sitting in the low-lit room, she realized for the first time that day, faceless evils hadn't rushed to the forefront of her mind. Right now, all she could do was smile at the woman on her table.

"So when are you due?"

Her patient all but glowed in the dark from excitement. "Four weeks. We can't wait."

"Is this your first ultrasound?"

"No. I had one when I was three months along just to make

171

sure the dates were correct. My friends tell me I should have had more than just the one, but my doctor didn't see the need for it."

Four weeks. Four weeks and this woman would be holding her beautiful baby in her arms. Ultrasounds on pregnant women were one of Abby's favorite things about this job, seeing the newly forming life tucked away in the safety of its mother's womb. What job could be better?

Then she jolted, realization shooting through her mind. She and Ethan hadn't used protection. She hadn't realized that fact until just this moment. The night had been so intense, and she'd been so swept away by her feelings that she'd never even thought about using a condom. Not once. How stupid was that? She shook her head, remembering she'd sat there at home, hoping he would show up after his crime scene just so they could finish where they'd left off—and, boy, had they ever! Yet protection had never even entered her mind.

Ethan had come to tell her bad news—he'd probably never imagined they'd end up making love. Yet looking at the joy on this woman's face and the baby moving around in her womb, she couldn't find it in herself to be all that worried. She wanted children and a family. Wanted them so much. If it happened, it happened.

The truth was, she was falling in love Ethan Parker.

Abby continued to measure the woman's baby. "So what brings you in at this point?"

"My mom had a very small cervix. She was in labor with me for thirty-six hours and still ended up with a cesarean section because my head wouldn't fit. So, the doctor just wants to make sure the baby's head won't be too big to fit." A nerve-laden giggle erupted from the woman.

Moving the wand over her belly, she pointed out the beating heart and how the baby was sucking its thumb. "Do you want to know the sex?"

The woman lifted her head and stared at the screen. "Can you really tell? It was too early the first time, and the doctor thought the baby may be too big to tell this time."

She grinned. "Oh, I can definitely tell if you want to know."

"Ohhh, I wish my husband could have made it today. Yes. Yes, I want to know."

Abby pointed out the essential parts on the monitor. "You're going to have a beautiful baby boy, Mrs. Collins. We're all done. Here's a towel to wipe off the gel, and I'll be right back with some cool pictures for you to take to your husband. He can show off to all his friends."

She drew the curtain closed and left the room with the first genuine smile of the day. After processing the film and leaving the prints for the patient, she left to check out for lunch. Although the quick hello from her brother had been nice, it had still been a long morning, and she was overdue for her break as it was. But taking the last patient for Missy had been a godsend.

Entering the deserted employee room, she punched out on the time clock then opened her locker to retrieve her purse. On the edge of the top shelf sat a folded piece of paper. Had Ethan left her a note? Excitement rocketed through her as she reached for it. She grinned, her heart tapped out a wild rhythm, and her cheeks heated with anticipation. *God! I feel like a schoolgirl.*

Unfolding the paper, her hands shook. She trembled, but not enough to miss the big, bold letters on the paper.

YOU. ARE. MINE. BITCH!

The room seemed to tilt. She reached out to steady herself. Sliding down the wall, she blindly reached for the cell phone in her purse and dialed Ethan.

"Hey, you." The warm timbre of his voice washed over her, reassuring her she wasn't alone. "This is a nice surprise. I didn't expect to hear from you until later."

"Ethan." She swallowed, and her head lolled back against the cool wall. "He left me a note. In my locker. He left me a note in my locker." She was losing it, she knew she was losing it but couldn't stop. "How did he know? How did he get in here? God. He left a note *in my locker.*"

"Where are you, honey?" His voice broke through the thundering in her head.

"The break room. At my locker. He was here." She heard him mumble something to someone else, then horror struck again. She bolted upright, her gaze scanning the area. "Ethan? What if he's still here? Oh, God, what do I do?"

"You sit tight, honey." His voice resonated over the line. "I'm almost there. Just keep talking to me. Are you okay?"

Abby stared at the note in her hand. No, she wasn't okay. Far, far from it. Before she had a chance to answer him, the break room door burst open. Ethan stormed in, gun drawn, and swept the immediate area. As soon as their gazes met, he slid to the floor and grabbed her up in his arms.

Safe.

It was then she spotted her brother, gun still in his hands as he searched each bathroom stall and changing area.

"All clear," Grant said.

"How did you get here so fast?" she managed to grind out past the lump in her throat.

His arms tightened around her. "We were still in the building, wrapping up some business. Are you okay?"

She huffed out a half-laugh. "I am now. Pretty sad reaction for someone who wants to be bait, huh?"

"Bait?" her brother barked. "What the hell are you talking about?"

"Hold on," Ethan said, his stern voice vibrating the walls. "Before we all get into it again, let me make something perfectly clear. There will be no bait. End of story. Now, let's see the note." He pulled a clean hanky from his pocket and took the paper by the upper right corner, read it, and handed it to Grant. "Okay, we'll take it from here. Right now, I want you to call it a day, and I'll follow you over to my house. You can stay there."

"What the hell?" He stepped toward Ethan and glared at him. "You think I can't take care of my own sister? She can go home."

"You don't have the security system I have." Turning toward his partner, he spoke in a calm and reasonable voice. "Are you really willing to risk her life over your pride? This guy is threatening her now. We have to process this letter and have the locker dusted for prints, not to mention the interview we have to do. She'll be safer at my house."

Grant clenched his jaw and flicked his gaze toward her. With his brow knitted in question, he stared at her, his eyes displaying the trust they'd shared over a lifetime. "Abby, what do you want to do?"

Her heart ached over being forced into a decision. But a crazed psychopath roamed the halls of the hospital, leaving her threatening notes in her locker. Safety was the determining issue. She looked from the man she'd fallen in love with to the brother who'd watched over her all her life and back. "I'll go to your house."

Chapter Nineteen

*A*bby followed Ethan to his house. Now that the initial shock had worn off, she felt like an idiot for the panicked call she'd made to him. Then to have Grant and him argue over where she should go? Lord, the whole thing was pathetic. Their partnership seemed tense enough already. They didn't need her getting between them as well.

The fact remained, He had won.

She pulled into his driveway, parked her car alongside his, and for a brief moment she let her earlier fantasy of being a family invade her thoughts. What would it be like to be here every night, to greet Ethan at the door with their baby on her hip?

Baby.

Damn. She needed to stop thinking that way. It was one time. It was foolish and irresponsible to have unprotected sex and wouldn't happen again. But that didn't stop the dream from popping into her thoughts when she dropped her guard.

Truth be told, she'd wanted to go to his house—though his security system had nothing to do with why. She wanted to be with him. He made her feel safe, wanted, adored. She peered through the car window, watching him emerge from his SUV. His gaze shifted toward her, and that sexy smile curled his lips.

Yeah. She could get used to that real quick.

She grinned at him and shut the car off. All foolishness aside, and now that the scare of the letter had faded, she would have an active role in finding this guy. Her life couldn't move forward until he was apprehended. Therefore, catching him just became a priority to her—no matter what Ethan or Grant had to say on the matter.

Abby removed her keys from the ignition, scooped up her purse and gloves, and stepped from the car. Icy air enveloped her, swirled around her legs, and caressed her cheeks with frosty fingers.

He was at her side the moment she shut the car door. He wrapped an arm around her waist and guided her toward the house. "I'm glad you choose to come here. You scared me half to death with that phone call. I don't know that I could concentrate on the job if I didn't know you were safe."

He leaned down and brushed his mouth over hers then went about unlocking the door and shutting off the alarm. He led her through the foyer to the living room and took her coat. "I'll show you around then I've got to get back to the station. Your brother is sending the letter off for analysis, and we've got a suspect we need to interview this afternoon, but I should be no later than six."

"Slow down, cowboy. You have a suspect? Who?" This was a new development, and she prayed it would pan out.

"It's Elliot Swanson." His jaw tightened as he hung her coat on the rack near the door. "I've had patrol bring him in for questioning. He did threaten Nick and you in that coffee shop. He's cooling his jets in the interview room as we speak, probably foaming at the mouth already."

She cringed at the thought of Elliot sitting at the police station, waiting. She had no doubt he'd raised a fracas. The man was too self-important for the likes of the police. "Do you really think he could do something like this?"

Ethan shrugged. "There's something off about the guy. I guess I'll find out soon enough." He grasped her by her hand.

"Come on, let me show you around here."

He showed her through the house, apologizing for not having much food and promising to rectify that when he got home tonight. Upstairs, he showed her two bedrooms. "But only the master bedroom has a bathroom. If you're more comfortable, I can take the guest room, so you don't have to go all the way downstairs for the bath."

She peered into his room, taking in the masculine beige and blue color scheme, the utilitarian chest of drawers, the lack of adornments on the walls. A single framed photo sat on the dresser—a young boy and girl with their parents, smiling at the camera. But somehow, the room was warm, inviting. Like him. She inhaled and smiled. The air even smelled like him.

He moved behind her, trailed a hand up her arm, his fingers feather light against her skin. "Aw, hell, Abby," he said, his voice deep with desire. "Who am I kidding? A gentleman is the last thing I want to be. What I want is for you to share my room, but I'll understand if you don't feel comfortable doing that."

Butterflies batted about in her tummy once again. She didn't want to appear too eager, so she walked into the room, casually looking around. "Hmm." She sat on the bed and bounced once then laughed and patted the bed beside her for him to sit. "This room will do, as long as you're in it with me."

He sat, placed his hands on her shoulders, eased her back onto the mattress, and moved to cover her body with his. Placing kisses along her jaw line to her ear, he whispered, "That's exactly what I'd hoped you'd say."

Dear Lord, she loved the feel of his body on hers. She wrapped herself around him and angled her head to meet his mouth. He opened immediately for a deep, toe-curling kiss that ended way too early.

He gazed down at her, lust swirling in his eyes. "I hate to do this, but I really need to get back to the station. I promise I won't be long." He rolled off her and helped her sit up. "By the way, I wanted to talk to you about last night and my disrespect for you."

"Disrespect? What do you mean?"

He looked away, appearing to find his carpet very interesting. "We didn't use protection, and for that I apologize. I, uh, wasn't prepared for the situation, and I can't say that even if I had been, I'd've had the wherewithal at the time to use it. I can tell you I am disease-free, and it's been a good year since I've been with anyone. But I promise to protect you from now on."

Heat rushed to her face. What would his reaction be if she told him she didn't care? "Well, it takes two. I was right there with you and never thought one thing about it. I do have to tell you though, I'm not on the pill." She glanced at him, waiting for him to process the obvious.

"No worries." He brushed a kiss across her cheek and stood. "We take it one day at a time. You are in my life to stay, honey, no backing out now. I'll see you in a few hours." He moved to the doorway and said, "Why don't you take a nap as long as you're up here?" Leering over his shoulder, his gaze raked over her body, and a lascivious smile curved his lips. "We certainly didn't get much sleep last night."

A few moments later, the sound of his feet pounding down the stairs and the alarm being set before he departed wafted to her ears. Abby rolled to the middle of the bed and curled up in the spread. Now *this* she could get used to.

෫

Ethan trailed Grant into the interrogation room, and the door closed behind them with a resounding click. Crossing to the table in three strides, Ethan pulled out the chair, the metal legs scraping over the linoleum floor. He sat, and scrutinized the man on the opposite side of the table.

His partner placed a recorder on the table and pressed the record button. He stepped back, folded his arms across his chest, and leaned against the wall.

Elliot Swanson's dubious gaze traveled from one of them, to the other, and back again. A wry smile curled the corners of his mouth. "Really, boys? This is how you're going to play this?"

"What d'ya mean, Swanson?" Grant said. "No one's playing here."

A sharp bark of laughter erupted from Elliot's throat. "You must've forgotten who you've got sitting in here. I'm Elliot Swanson, Red River's number one defense attorney."

"So?" He straightened, moved away from the wall.

Ethan kept his partner in his peripheral, trying to gauge whether he was under control or about to detonate. The case revolved around his sister, so the man's desire to go ballistic on their number one suspect was understandable. Hell, Ethan barely held his own emotions in check. But roughing up Elliot wouldn't aid in a conviction. They needed evidence. Or a confession.

"Well, Elliot wrote the book on emotional manipulation," Elliot drawled. He focused on Grant, but not a hint of worry or bother stirred his unwavering gaze.

"I'll just bet you did." The rookie detective crossed the room, slamming his fists onto the table. "You sonofabitch."

Elliot didn't flinch. "Whoa, there. Best be careful not to take this good cop, bad cop routine too far. Might find yourself on the nasty end of a lawsuit." He grinned, the right side of his mouth pulling slightly higher than the left, depicting a pompous, self-righteous attitude. "'Cause Elliot Swanson knows the law."

Grant lunged.

Ethan dove between them, his quick movements toppling his chair behind him. He shoved his partner back, giving him a stare laden with the definition of police decorum. His partner looked at him, sending his own message.

I get it.

Ethan hoped so.

"You know, though," Elliot continued, his tone as smooth as ever, "I wouldn't have cast you as the bad cop, Detective Montgomery. Not after Detective Parker manhandled me in the café." He reached up and rubbed the back of his neck, his gaze settling on Ethan. "Why, the way you slammed me into that wall? All those witnesses? Sounds like Elliot just might have a case for police brutality."

"Let me take you out behind the station," Grant growled, "and I'll show you police brutality, you bastard."

Elliot sucked air between his front teeth. "Well, well. That sounds like a threat, Detective Montgomery."

"Damned straight it is." He took a step toward the lawyer and pointed a finger at him. "And you better leave my sister the hell alone, or Elliot will get more than he bargained for."

The lawyer grinned, completely unperturbed. "While your sister is quite pretty, she's a bit off-kilter."

"Sonofabitch!" Grant roared. But instead of going for the man's throat, he punched the wall. The resounding thud vibrated through the room. Turning, he folded his arms across his chest, took a wide stance, and glared at the suspect.

"So, you're not interested in her?" Ethan asked as he righted his chair and took a seat.

"Not in the least."

"So, you're saying you didn't dump a bunch of peppermints on her car hood in retribution?" He studied the man's face for any hint of untruth.

"Peppermints?" The egotistical lawyer raised his eyebrows. "I can only imagine how she might've reacted to something like that."

"So did you put them there or not?" Grant barked.

"An act like that is beneath me," he replied.

Ethan leaned forward. "But attacking Nick Colbert isn't?"

"Ah, well." Elliot rubbed his jaw, and Ethan could almost see the gears grinding in the man's head. "That was unfortunate. Nick Colbert verbally accosted me."

"And then you physically accosted Nick," Ethan concluded. He narrowed his gaze on the man.

Elliot shifted in his chair, glanced toward the door. "Mr. Colbert manipulated my emotions."

"Thought you wrote the book on that, Elliot," he said and leaned further forward. "Thought you were the master of emotional manipulation."

"I am the master," he said, spitting out each word while his features warped with anger.

"What d'ya think, Grant?"

He shook his head. "Sounds like a confession to me."

"A confession?" Elliot hollered. "To what?"

"To the murder of Nick Colbert." Ethan folded his hands on the table, giving the lawyer a hard stare.

"Murder?" His gaze oscillated between the two of them. "I didn't murder anyone. You have no evidence to prove otherwise."

"We have witnesses to the argument and subsequent fight with the victim in the café," Grant gloated. "You dumped peppermints on Abby's car for some twisted revenge. But that wasn't enough for you, was it? Nick Colbert had made the mistake of talking to her, and it pissed you off. You couldn't have anyone outwitting the great Elliot Swanson, so you murdered him."

Elliot shook his head. "You're as insane as your sister, Detective." He waved a hand, dismissing him, and turned to Ethan, his controlled demeanor returning. "What you have is circumstantial. Nothing."

"Where were you between the hours of eight p.m. and two a.m. this morning?" Ethan asked.

The lawyer's chest puffed out. "That's easy. With a hotter woman than you'll ever be able to get."

"We'll need her name and phone number, so she can verify this."

"Absolutely. Elliot Swanson has nothing to hide."

He pushed a pad of paper and a pen across the table to him. "Then you won't mind writing a couple of words for me."

The lawyer eyed the paper. "What words? Because if either happen to be confess or murder or a derivative of, then Elliot Swanson would have to decline."

Ethan chuckled. "I like you, Elliot." *For murder.*

"Well, I like you, too, Detective." Elliot toyed with the pen and grinned.

He raised a brow. It was clear the man wanted to know the words and to write them on the paper. But why? Did he really think he was smart enough to get away with murder?

Elliot tapped the pen on the pad—an answer to Ethan's question.

"*Are* and *you*."

The lawyer's eyes widened, intrigue dancing in their depths. "*Are* and *you*. Like a question. Are you the killer? Or are you guilty?"

"Yeah," Grant chuffed from the other side of the room. "Just like that."

Elliot smirked, turned his attention to Ethan. "I would be happy to oblige." He scribbled the words at the top of the paper then pushed the pad across the table.

Ethan slapped his hand on the notepaper, stopping it halfway. "Not like that," he said. "I'd like to see it in all capital letters, not cursive."

Elliot drew the pad back to himself, his gaze locked with Ethan's. "All caps you say?"

"This big." He held up his hand, squeezed about two inches of air between his index finger and thumb to represent the letter height.

The lawyer smiled, but it didn't reach his eyes.

Ethan's hackles raised. The man across the table was intrigued. It was all a game to him, and he sat there, assessing his opponent and determining his next move.

"Why of course, Detective." He glanced at Ethan's hand then wrote the words on the pad in crisp capital letters.

Satisfied, Ethan took the paper and pen and shoved to his feet. "We'll be back in just a few moments."

Their suspect said nothing, but Ethan sensed the heat of his gaze burning against his back as he and Grant exited the room. When the door clicked behind them, the rookie rounded on him.

"Damn, but you got the sonofabitch." A triumphant grin stretched across his face.

Ethan handed him the pad Elliot had written the words on. "Take this down to the lab. Have them do a comparison with what was written on the note Abby got. If it matches, we've got our guy."

"What are you going to do?"

"I've got to see the captain, tell him what's up. Might not be enough to convict, but it's a damn good start." He met Grant's gaze, kept the smile plastered on his face. What he'd told him was the truth. However, he'd just neglected to add the part where after he spoke with Captain Hague, he would head home to Abby. Anticipation sent his heart racing.

Grant jerked his thumb toward the interrogation room door. "What about him?"

"Witnesses have him at the hospital this morning."

He nodded. "Chasing ambulances, drumming up business. One of the EMTs said he hit on her. Asked her out for a steak dinner."

"A nurse in admission said he hit on her, too. Same steak dinner." Ethan snorted. "Seems our lawyer fancies himself a player."

"He was definitely on site. He could've left that note in my sister's locker." He tapped his finger on the pad. "So?"

Ethan glanced toward the door. "We have enough to hold him for twenty-four hours while we do the handwriting comparison and check his alibi. Try to get something substantial."

"Overnight in lock-up." Grant chuckled. "I like the way you think."

"Yeah." He turned toward Captain Hague's office. Over his shoulder, he said, "But Elliot Swanson won't."

Chapter Twenty

*E*than juggled the grocery bags in one arm and silenced the house alarm. The interior was dark and too damn quiet. Where was Abby? Heart stuttering, he dropped the bags on the couch and bolted up the stairs. Storming into the bedroom, he stopped short at the sight of her curled up in the blankets and inhaled deeply.

It took a moment for the adrenaline rush to subside and his body to stop shaking. Lord, she'd just scared him, and she didn't even know it. He leaned against the doorjamb, the wood creaking beneath his weight.

She rolled over, peered up at him, and smiled. "Hi, there."

In three strides, he stood at the side of the bed. Leaning over, he kissed her forehead. "Hi there, yourself. Did you get a good nap?"

Abby stretched and sat up. "I did. I feel much better. You, on the other hand, look like crap, and I mean that in the best possible way. What time is it?"

Ethan glanced at his watch. "A little after six. Are you hungry? I grabbed some groceries on the way home. Got the makings for spaghetti if you like it."

"Love it, but why don't you let me take care of that? By the looks of you, a long hot shower is calling first." She crawled to the edge of the bed, sat up on her heels, and put her arms around his waist. "Get some strength back for later."

Capturing her in his grasp, Ethan lifted her off the mattress and into his arms. "When it comes to you, Abby, I've got plenty of reserves left."

She wrapped her arms around his neck, pulled him toward her, and closed her mouth over his. She'd been right. He was dead tired—at least he'd thought so until he'd discovered her lying on his bed. Now, with her tongue tangling with his and her warm body pressed tight against him, sleep was the last thing on his mind.

The tightening in his groin was proof positive of that. Blood raced throughout his body, and all he wanted was to lay her back down on the bed and get naked with her. But, she'd also been right about him needing to shower first—if for no other reason than to scrub off the slimy residue of Elliot Swanson.

Ending the kiss on a groan, he placed her down on the bed. "If you give me five minutes, I can be right back here to pick up where we just left off."

Damn she looked beautiful staring up at him.

"It's a deal," she said and ran her tongue over her lips.

If she kept that up, he'd forgo the shower. Chuckling, he dropped his pants where he stood and hurried to the bathroom, his remaining clothes trailing in his wake. Any other night, he would've been so tired it would have taken all his effort just to eat and fall into bed. But with Abby here to greet him, he found himself laughing and running to the shower.

Adjusting the water to a suitable temperature, Ethan stepped beneath the spray and grabbed the washcloth and soap.

"Why don't you give those to me?"

He snapped his head in the direction of her voice, the soap slipping from his hand to bounce on the porcelain floor. There she stood in front of him, not a stitch of clothing on, holding out her hand.

"Abby."

He reached for her and guided her under the warm cascade

to him. His heart beating double time, he bent for the soap but stayed on one knee, lathering the bar till it became frothy and slick in his hands. Slowly, he massaged her calf, caressing his way up her thigh to slide his fingers over the luscious curve of her buttocks. Eyes level with her silky thatch of curls, he swallowed, his mouth watering to taste her.

"Hey, I came in here to help you. No fair," she complained halfheartedly.

"Oh, honey, believe me, you are helping me. I am so damn hungry for you." Cupping water in his hands, he washed away the soap and, unable to wait any longer, he moved his hand between her thighs. She rewarded him with a groan as she braced her hands on his shoulders. Greedily, he went to work pleasuring her body.

"Oh, please, Ethan. I need you."

He rose and backed her against the shower wall. God, the sight of her. Her hair, dark and wet, skimmed her shoulders. Water sluiced over her firm breasts, down her stomach and thighs beyond. Need trembled through him, driving him to possess every inch of her. He dragged his gaze up to hers and found the same intense desire that barraged every nerve in his body swirling in her eyes. A spear of lust shot low in his gut.

He covered her mouth with his, dueling tongues, and deepened the kiss, pouring his very soul into her. He loved the taste of her, how she tangled her fingers in his hair, pulling him closer.

His hands roamed over her water-slicked body, memorizing every curve, every dip. He couldn't get enough, and he ached to plunge into her over and over. Grabbing her hips, he lifted her off the floor.

"Wrap your legs around me," he ground out.

She did as he asked, and he lifted her higher still, back tight against the wall for leverage. She placed one hand against the wet tiles and the other on his shoulder. And oh, so slowly he took her—the sensation nearly his undoing. Sweet torture!

"Ah, God, Abby. Don't move." He tightened his grip on her

hips to hold her still. "Right there."

He bent his head and took her nipple in his mouth, sucking hard until she moaned. When she squirmed against him, all control broke, and he thrust upward at an unrelenting pace.

The steady patter of the shower spray disappeared. Only her moans filled his head, her cries of pleasure.

On the edge, he fought to hold out for her, to hold on. But everything inside him screamed for satisfaction. He bucked beneath her, each thrust deeper than the last.

"Oh. So damn good."

When her body tensed, his release came hard and fast. He jerked, sparks flashing behind his closed eyes while she clutched him, whispering his name over and over. Leaning his face into the crook of her neck, he kissed her collarbone and waited for his breath to even out. Damn. He could stay just like this forever, holding her warm softness against him.

Unfortunately, his body betrayed him. His efforts had left his legs trembling. Slowly, he lowered Abby to her feet.

"Damn, woman, I could get used to coming home to you. You're amazing." He trailed a finger along her damp jaw line and stared into her limpid, satisfied eyes. "You know that, right?"

A contented smile curved her lips. "I know you make me feel amazing."

He kissed her soundly then grabbed the shampoo off the shelf and went about working her hair into a lather. They bathed each other, soapy hands skimming over wet skin. After thoroughly rinsing beneath the tepid spray, Ethan shut the water off and wrapped her up in a towel. "Hungry? Or would you like to continue this in an actual bed?"

She laughed. "How about some food first then the bed to work it off?"

"I like the way you think." Suddenly he remembered the box of condoms he'd left in the bags downstairs, and his heart stuttered with guilt. "Damn it."

"What?"

"I promised I would protect you. But once again, I let my

urges bypass my brain." Ethan tightened his jaw at his lack of responsibility. It wasn't like him to break his word, no matter the situation. "Abby, I swear I was prepared. I bought condoms. But when I came home to a dark house, I got scared and dropped the bags on the couch. I never thought of it again." He ran a hand through his damp hair. "God, I'm so sorry."

He followed her out of the bathroom, and she sat on his bed, dressed in nothing but a towel, looking innocent and beautiful. His heart skipped a beat at the sight of her.

"Like last time, Ethan. It takes two. You haven't been with anyone else, and you know I haven't, so there's no worry of disease. If you're concerned about pregnancy, I think it's the wrong time in my cycle. I'm not sure. But you should know, I'd never force a baby on you. I would never ask you for a commitment you didn't want." She looked down, toyed with the edge of the towel. "That's not to say I wouldn't have it. But I think we're getting way to ahead of ourselves anyway. From now on, we make sure we use condoms until I get on the pill. No biggie."

"Sounds like a plan." At one point in his life, the thought of children had scared the crap out of him. Now, however, not so much. Not with her.

"Ethan? Just so we're on the same page here—I don't want a whole relationship conversation—but what we have here...together...." She peered up at him. "It's real to you, right?"

He pulled on a pair of sweats and sat next to her on the bed. "Honey, we wouldn't be here right now if it wasn't real to me. I've never brought anyone here. This is my home. I've never wanted anyone here before." He took her hand, lifted it to his lips, and brushed a kiss over her soft skin. Gazing into her eyes, he realized she'd twined herself through his very soul. "What we have may be new, but have no doubt it's real. I want you here with me. Understood?"

A pounding at the front door triggered a jolt through both of them. The doorbell rang, the chimes keeping time with the constant thumping.

Ethan bolted to his feet. What the hell? Tossing Abby his robe, he said, "Here. Put this on. I'm going find out what the big problem is."

He jogged down the stairs to the front door. "Hold your horses." After shutting off the alarm, he yanked open the door and jolted, shock coursing through him, at what stood on the other side.

"Grant?" He grabbed his partner's arm and pulled him inside from the icy wind blowing outside. In the warm glow of the foyer, Ethan blinked, stunned by his partner's disheveled appearance. "What the fuck happened to you?"

"Oh, my God," Abby said from behind them. She rushed to her brother's side, and he slumped against her.

"Abby?" he croaked.

She guided him to the couch, kneeling before him. "What happened to you?"

"I...." He raised his head, his gaze searching her face. Looking toward Ethan, he grimaced. "Shit."

Ethan sat on the edge of the coffee table, took in the guy's ripped shirt, his mussed hair, the darkening bruise on his cheek. "Who did this to you?"

He stared at him over his sister's shoulder. "Some asshole jumped me outside the bakery."

"Crap."

"Yeah," he said, rising to his feet. "I was coming here to tell you about it. Certainly didn't expect to find the two of you half naked."

Ethan straightened. "Easy there, buddy."

"I'm not your buddy," he snapped. Fire filled his eyes. "I can't believe it." Glaring, he pointed a finger at him. "You've been here this whole time fucking my sister?"

His stomach knotted. Aw, shit. This wasn't what they needed to discuss at this moment. They needed to find clues to who was behind the attack.

Grant looked at his sister and swept his arm from her in an arc toward Ethan. "Tell me you didn't let this jerk seduce you,

Abby."

She stared at him, eyes wide with surprise. Her hand moved up the front of the robe, drawing it tighter across her bosom. "My relationship with Ethan is between him and me. I don't see—"

A bark of laughter erupted from Grant's mouth. "Relationship?"

She seemed to find herself and threw her shoulders back, her gaze meeting his. "Yes. Relationship."

"My God, Abby." His focus rolled to Ethan, a glare of daggers emanating from his eyes. "You've known him less than two weeks. How can you be in a relationship?"

She stepped toward him, placed her hand on his shoulder. "I love him."

Ethan's attention snapped to Abby, a mix of shock and fear rippling through him. Momentary worry abated when an overwhelming joy bowled him over.

By God, she loved him!

"Are you serious?" Grant shouted and jabbed a finger in his direction. "He doesn't care about you. He's just picking up where his brother left off." His head slewed toward Ethan. "Isn't that right, Parker?"

Barbs of ice assaulted his gut. *Shit!* He studied Grant, detected a hint of triumph in the bastard's eyes.

"Did you tell her?" he taunted.

Ethan balled his hands at his sides. He'd tried to tell her. More than once. He hadn't wanted any secrets between them. But this was not the way for her to hear such devastating news.

"Well, your silence and shocked face scream volumes," he sneered. "You haven't said a word. Why the hell would you?" Rounding on Abby, he grabbed her shoulders, commanding her full attention. "The man you claim you're in love with, the man you just fucked, is the brother of the man who raped you."

Her brow knitted. "W-what?"

Ethan took a step toward them and growled, "Shut up."

"She deserves to know the truth, Parker," he shot back then

returned his attention to his sister, whose face had paled. "Michael Greene, the man who raped you seven years ago, is Ethan's brother."

"Liar," she hissed and wrenched free from his grip. Rearing back, she slapped her brother across the face. The resounding crack echoed off the living room walls. "Get out. Just get the hell out."

Grant raised his hand to his cheek. He turned to Ethan, a smug grin on his face. "Tell her, partner. Tell her the truth."

Chapter Twenty-One

*E*than sighed. "You are one sonofabitch, Montgomery. You didn't have to do it this way. What ever the hell your problem is with me, you didn't have to do this to her."

"Me? The only thing I've done here is opened her eyes and told the truth. You've got her so snowed, she wouldn't have believed me any other way." Grant pointed a finger at him. "So don't try to turn this around on me. This one's on you. You don't get to fuck my sister and lie to her face."

She backed away from both of them. The betrayal in her eyes ripped at his heart. He reached for her, but she shirked his touch.

"Abby, I'm sorry." Inwardly he cringed, the words sounding hollow in his ears. He rushed on, his ill-rehearsed explanation tumbling from his lips as he struggled to make sense of his actions. "There were so many times I wanted to tell you—God, *so* many times—but I didn't want it to come between what was happening with us."

"How long have you known?" she asked.

He hesitated. "From the beginning." Ethan stepped in front of her before she could make an exit. He laid his hand on her arm, but she jerked away. *God, she thinks I'm like Mikey.* "What my brother did—my *half*-brother—makes me sick. How the hell was I supposed to tell you I was related to him?"

"You sat there the other night, let me pour my heart out about that bastard, and said nothing. You must've been laughing your ass off inside. The poor rape victim, crying her eyes out to the brother, falling for the brother, trusting the brother of her rapist. My God, how could you have made love to me knowing that?" She jerked the collar of the robe tighter, clutched it closed at her throat, and glared at him. "You make me sick."

"Abby, please. I know I was wrong not telling you, but it doesn't change how I feel about you." His heart ached, and his chest tightened to the point he worried it might crack in two.

"Oh, really, and how is that?"

Ethan hesitated. Was he ready to say those words to a woman? Was it even truly love or just his fear of losing her? His moment of uncertainty was all it took.

"That's what I thought," she snapped, her tone laden with ice. "Get the hell out of my way." She pushed him aside and ran to the stairs, but Grant stopped her.

"Let me drive you home," he said.

She raised a brow. "And how long have *you* known?"

"I, uh—"

"And you call yourself family." A derisive sound emanated from her throat. "You didn't cause this whole scene out of the goodness of your heart or out of any sense of loyalty to me. You did it because you wanted to put it to Ethan. Well done, brother. A happy ending for all." Shoving him aside, she stomped up the stairs, slamming the bedroom door.

Grant rounded on him, his eyes narrowed. "Don't fuck with my family again. It won't be nearly as pretty."

Ethan stared back, stunned. How could he have let this happen? Twenty minutes ago, he was happier than he'd ever been in his life. Now, the jackass standing in front of him had blown his whole world apart with just a few words.

Grant stepped closer, getting nose to nose. "What's the matter, Ethan, nothing to say this time? Guess you can't save everyone, huh."

He clenched his hands. He should have told her. He'd left himself wide open for this. "You can get the fuck out of my house, Montgomery. Now."

"Not without my sister, hotshot."

Disbelief shot through him. The bastard persisted in goading him. "You can either leave of your own accord or leave here looking a lot worse than when you arrived. Your choice. But make it now before I make it for you."

"Funny how you didn't win this one," he said with a sneer. "Not so big and mighty now, are you?"

Ethan's blood boiled. This guy had been after him from the beginning. From day one. Why? Because he'd dared to have feelings for Abby? Because he happened to be his superior officer at work? Yeah, maybe he'd given the guy some attitude about being partnered with him. But did it warrant a full-out attack from him?

"What is your problem with me? What have I done to you?" He gave him a hard stare. "You're sick in the head to just lay all that shit out there on your sister."

"I gave you plenty of chances to tell her yourself, you self-righteous bastard. Not my fault you never got around to it. Do you really think I want my sister with the brother of the man who raped her?" He raised a brow and sneered. "So, who's the one sick in the head here?"

"You sonofabitch." Ethan lunged, brought his fist up and around, and connected with Grant's jaw, sending him flying into the wall. About to go in for the kill and pound the ever-loving shit out of the bastard, he drew his fist back again.

"Stop!" Abby ran down the stairs.

Ethan froze.

Abby.

Grant pushed to his feet and grinned. "You're just like him, aren't you?" He swiped at the blood that trickled down his chin, his eyes filled with fire and hatred.

"I'm nothing like him. I would never hurt your sister." He gritted his teeth. What Mikey had done was completely separate from his feelings for her.

"Seems to me you already have. You're pretty arrogant in thinking something like that wouldn't make a difference to her—or me, for that matter. You have big fucking balls to sleep with her, knowing what you were keeping from her the whole time. I should rip your damn head off." Grant moved toward his sister.

Ethan's cell went off, and he jerked it from its holster, his gaze locked on his partner. "Back the fuck off, Montgomery. It won't be me that's left bleeding." One hand out to stop the asshole from going anywhere with Abby, he flicked open his cell and barked into it. "Parker."

"Ethan?" came a voice over a line that resonated with a low side tone and crackled with static.

"Mikey? Is that you?"

Jesus, could this day get any worse?

"Ethan, you...." His voice warbled in and out from clarity to nonsensical noise. "Careful...after you...that woman."

He strained to make out Mikey's words, but the connection kept breaking up, and he only caught a few. "You're not coming through. Try—"

Catching movement in his peripheral, he glanced up. Eyes blazing, Grant rushed across the living room. He plowed his shoulder into Ethan's chest, knocking the wind from his lungs, and lifted him off his feet with a full-force tackle. They crashed to the floor, the impact sending the phone flying from his hand.

A jarring ache raced up his side to his shoulder. Stunned, he struggled to catch his breath. He took a knee to his ribs and a punch to the jaw before he realized what the hell had happened. Pain shot though his face, and bright pinpoints filled his vision. He shoved with all his might and forced Grant back. A solid jab to the guy's gut sent him doubling over. Although out of breath, Ethan spun on his butt and leg-whipped the back of Grant's knees. His antagonist hit the floor.

Gasping for air, Ethan scrambled to his feet as Montgomery staggered back up. He jerked his head, and a punch sizzled past. Grant's knuckles grazed his cheek, and air whistled in his ear.

Shit! The guy was a maniac. Rearing back, he swung, his fist connecting to the side of the guy's head.

Heated blood soared through his veins, taking place of any pain he should have felt. Rocking to the balls of his feet, Ethan prepared for him to turn for another round. Idiot didn't know when to call it quits.

True to his nature, Grant spun, fists cocked, eyes blazing. Ethan didn't hesitate. He brought up the heel of his hand and smashed Montgomery's nose.

Blood splattered Ethan's shirt. He grabbed his partner with both hands and jerked him forward. At the same time, he thrust a hip into him, pivoted, and launched Montgomery over his back. When he slammed on the floor, the room shook.

Grabbing him by the collar, Ethan straddled him and rammed his fist into his face several more times. The stupid sonofabitch should have known better than to start with him. He should have known better than to come in here and tell Abby about Mikey. Fist cocked, ready to pummel the shit out of the son of a bitch, he jolted at the sound of a car engine revving outside.

He released Grant, letting his head drop to the hardwood with a resounding thud. Dragging his gaze from his partner, he searched for her. But the room was empty.

"Abby?"

A gust of cold air swept over him. He looked toward the front door, found it gaping wide, exposing the darkness outside.

"Shit."

Ethan staggered out onto the porch and down the steps. Huge flakes swirled around him, pelted his hair, and caressed his naked torso. Fresh snow crunched beneath his bare feet as he hurried down the walkway.

At the driveway, he skidded to a stop. Her car was gone. He looked toward the end of the driveway and caught the last twinkle of red taillights blinking in the darkness.

She'd left him.

He squeezed his eyes closed. Clenched his hands. "Not this

way!" he growled to the surrounding blackness. He lashed out, his fist slicing through the icy air and sending fat snowflakes twirling with his sudden movement. "Not this fucking way."

Chapter Twenty-Two

*E*than shifted in bed for what must have been the twentieth time since lying down two hours ago. Restless, he bounced his legs off the mattress, expending excess energy in the hopes to calm enough to lay still. He rolled from his aching side to his stomach then back over onto his back. Nothing worked. Every time he closed his eyes, he saw Abby staring back at him, pleading with him to tell her what Grant said about Mikey was a lie. And every time, a fresh round of pain ripped through his heart.

With a sigh, he gave up, laced his hands behind his head, and lay there staring up at the dark ceiling. Damn it, he should've gone after her yesterday. But after seeing the look in her eyes, he knew she needed space, time to process the bombshell her brother had dropped. If he pressured her, she might run the other way, and that was *not* the outcome he wanted.

Glancing over to the alarm clock, he grimaced—only five minutes had passed since the last time he'd checked. 4:15 a.m. The urge to call her was so bad his hands itched. He looked back at the ceiling. He wouldn't call yet. But all bets were off after the clock displayed six a.m.

An hour and forty-five minutes. His heart thumped double-time at the prospect.

He had no clue how, but he would make her listen to him. Lord, he prayed she would forgive him.

He glanced over at the clock again. 4:18. The luminous numbers flashed at him, mocking. Snarling, he yanked the thin sheet back and staggered off the bed, his battered ribs aching in protest. Padding into the bathroom, he stopped short at the sight of his robe crumpled on the floor. He knelt, picked it up, and buried his face in the thick material, inhaling deeply. Abby. Even the short time the robe had been wrapped around her, she'd left her indelible mark behind. Her scent had woven its way through the fabric—much like her smile had woven through his soul.

If only he hadn't screwed up.

Another incoherent growl pushed from his mouth. Frustrated, he tossed the robe aside and fumbled his way to the sink.

He turned on the faucet and splashed his face with water several times, the ice-cold liquid soothing his bruised jaw. Drying off with the towel, he made his way back to his room and sat on the edge of the bed. Something kept nagging at the back of his mind.

He never really had much of a chance to question Grant about the guy who'd attacked him before things had spun out of control. Ethan shoved his hand through his hair, his brain trying to force what little he knew into a coherent picture. Who the hell would have balls enough to attack a cop in the station parking lot? Grant's shirt had been ripped, his faced bruised. Other than that, he hadn't complained of anything else. Just started in on him about Abby.

Now, he pondered the possibility the guy might have injured himself as an excuse to barge in here. It wasn't that far of a stretch, considering how he'd leapt right into his verbal attack about Mikey. He'd conveniently forgotten all about being roughed up. And after Abby took off, Ethan had gone back in, grabbed a shirt, shoes, his keys, and had barely been back to his SUV when Grant sped by him in his truck, fishtailing over the icy driveway. Christ, the guy had almost clipped him on his way out.

No, something stank about the whole damn thing. Maybe it was time he learned a little more about his partner. He glanced over at the clock. 4:45. Resisting the urge to launch the damn thing through the window, Ethan dressed and headed downstairs.

"Aw shit!"

The groceries he'd bought still sat on the couch, the mint chocolate chip ice cream completely melted and staining the cushion. He fisted his hands, renewed irritation prickling his nerves. The desire to punch something raged though him, quick and hot. Maybe he should go to the gym before the station, work out some frustrations. But a moment after the flash of anger, his scuffed and swollen knuckles throbbed, forcing him to ease his hands open.

He leaned over the couch, his ribs wrenching in complaint, and snatched up the soggy bag. Straightening, he stomped to the kitchen and chucked the entire thing into the garbage. What a waste. He wiped off a bit of ice cream that had smeared his palm then paused. Ethan lifted his hand to study his minor injuries. Curling his fingers into a fist, he remembered the rage from earlier. He'd never been a violent man, but Grant had pushed him too far.

He froze in place. Dear God, was the guy right? Was he just like his brother?

The room swam, and he leaned against the arm of the chair. How far would he have gone if he hadn't heard Abby's car start? He'd already beaten him bloody. Would he have stopped before the man had become unconscious?

Ethan crooked his neck from side to side, snapping things into place, the movement causing the pain in his jaw to intensify. No, damn it, he was not Mikey. Grant had goaded him, had kept goading him until he'd thrown a punch. One punch. It wasn't until the idiot had tackled him and kept coming at him that he'd fought back.

He could understand Grant's position, but the way he'd gone

about it seemed way over the top. How long had he known? He'd sure as hell been antagonistic for days, walking around with his ass on his shoulder and jumping on the slightest remark that could be twisted into something it wasn't. Had he known about Mikey all along and just waited for the worst possible opportunity to let it all out?

Ethan expelled a sharp burst of breath. Yeah, skip the gym. He needed to get to the office and do a little background check on his so-called partner. Stalking back to the living room, he grabbed his gun and holster and put them on. He shrugged into his jacket, snatched up his gloves, set the alarm, and locked the door behind him.

Grant was out to ruin him. Ethan was damned if he'd just sit back without knowing why.

og

Ethan hung his jacket on the detectives' room coat rack, bypassed his desk, and headed straight for the coffee pot. At five in the morning, there was no one in his part of the office, so he dumped the grounds from yesterday and started a new pot.

With a fresh jolt of caffeine to get all his synapses firing, he sank into his chair and pulled himself up to his desk. He set his mug on the upper corner of the blotter and started up his computer. While waiting for the ancient machine to boot up, he shuffled through the reports on his desk. The official autopsy reports on all four victims were there along with phone records from the first victim and his fiancée.

Trudging over to the board, he grabbed the dry erase marker and wrote the cause of death under each victim's name. Following that, he added the word that had been carved in each victim's chest. *You. Are. Mine. For-.* He stepped back and studied the words.

You are mine for...what? For good? Now? Ever? Keeps? Christ, it could be anything.

And, was there just one more word to go, or was there more

to the sentence? He squinted at the board, attempting to take it all in at once, maybe find a pattern. But nothing stood out. The killer had left behind no DNA or fingerprints. They'd found no evidence at all to tell them who this guy was. Elliot looked good for it, but if his alibi came through, they'd have to let him go.

Ethan shoved his hand through his hair. Damn it! They had nothing! Nothing to go on at all.

The words were a message for Abby, and it was obvious, at least to him, she would be his final victim. But that was where the guy was wrong. Ethan would lay down his own life before he let anything happen to her.

Abby.

At the thought of her, he glanced at his watch. 5:20 a.m. He needed to hold off calling her till six, but the desire to talk to her, to hear her voice, had all but shredded him inside. Crap. Would she even listen to him if he called? He shook his head, determined to wait until the appointed time.

Work.

He needed to focus on the job. Papers in hand, he sat at his desk again and skimmed through the phone records. Nothing jumped out at him as abnormal. Tossing the papers aside, he turned his attention back to the computer and plugged Grant Montgomery's name into the search engine.

Academy scores and recommendations popped up on the screen. The record of his years on patrol, loads of citations and awards. Seemed the guy was a go-getter.

Ethan grabbed his mug and took a big gulp of coffee as he stared at the screen. Damn. He sure would like to get his hands on Grant's psych evaluation. Obviously, Montgomery had passed it, or he wouldn't be here. But, that didn't mean there wasn't something hiding in his past—possibly a note in the margin about anger management.

Maybe.

He took another swallow of coffee, the much-needed caffeine seeping into his veins. He set the mug down and rubbed his jaw. Yeah, the anger might make sense if Montgomery had known all along about Mikey. But how could he? And if he did, why didn't he say something the first damn night? Why now? It was as though he'd waited for the perfect moment to hurt both him and Abby.

And the alleged mugging outside Main Street Bakery just didn't feel right. Something was definitely off with that story, but it was one he could check out. He hit print on Grant's file and shoved away from the desk. He'd go through the information at home in privacy. Gathering the papers off the printer, he shoved them in his coat pocket and headed over to the bakery.

Ethan parked on the street and strolled inside, the aroma of coffee mixed with fresh-baked cakes and pastries washed over him. He approached the counter.

"What can I get you, Detective?" Mrs. Fitzgerald smiled, recognition lighting her bright blue eyes.

"Coffee and one of those cherry pastries sure would be good."

The spritely senior crossed to the coffee urn, snagging a to-go cup on her way. Jane Fitzgerald had owned Main Street Bakery for as long as he could remember. She'd always been nice to him—even after Mikey had stolen cash from the register when they were kids.

She set the cup on the counter in front of him, and Ethan dumped three packets of sugar into the dark, steamy liquid.

"I heard Grant Montgomery was in here last night." He stirred the coffee.

While wrapping the pastry in a wax paper sheet, she glanced up at him. "Yes, he was. Came in around ten thirty, I'd say. Mr. Fitzgerald and I were closing up." Her gaze shot to the large window at the front of the store. "Had a few teens come in for some coffee and those power drinks they love so much right before him."

"Energy drinks?"

"Yes, that's it. They got a big box of donuts and rushed back across the street to that game place over there." She pointed.

He looked where she'd indicated and spotted two boys going

into Games Galore. He turned back and pressed the lid on his coffee.

"When I was a child, we played outside, rode bikes, climbed trees." She pursed her lips. "You ask me, all that stuff just rots their brains. That and all the junk food. Though, I do appreciate the business."

"What about Detective Montgomery?"

Her gaze shot back to him. "Well, he certainly didn't go into that shop to play games. He's a good boy."

Ethan nodded though his instincts whispered something wasn't quite right. "Did he buy any donuts or anything?"

"No. Just the coffee." She set the bag with his pastry on the counter and sighed. "Those were my only two customers last night. Pretty slow for a Friday night. Guess the cold kept everyone indoors. Except for all those kids. Wonder if their parents knew they were over there."

"So, nothing odd happened while he was here? You saw him get back into his truck out front?"

"Detective Montgomery?" She shook her head. "He went off down the sidewalk. I guess I thought he'd parked in the alley. But nothing odd happened that I recall. Why?"

"Just asking," he said.

She eyed him and then set about straightening the pastry trays in the case. "I'm sure you have your reasons, Detective."

He dug out his wallet and removed several bills to cover his purchase, but the woman placed a wrinkled hand on his to stop him.

"No need, Ethan." A smile curved her mouth and her blue eyes sparkled. "I remember that summer you worked here for free after your brother did that bad deed of his. Gus and I never forgot how you stepped up to make things right. Besides, you're keeping Red River safe. With the town growing so fast, we could use more men like you."

"Thank you, ma'am." He exited the bakery, a mix of guilt and pride turning through his chest. As he crossed the street, he made a mental note to come back Sunday morning, and he would be sure she let him pay.

Stepping inside the game shop, Ethan was hit with the rampant buzz of video games, music, and conversation. He paused, scanning the establishment for the manager and found a lanky girl behind the counter to his right. Glancing up, she caught sight of him and traipsed toward him. In an instant, he understood why the shop was packed with teen boys. The tight white T-shirt, schoolgirl mini skirt, white thigh-high socks, and platform heels were the stuff of a teen boy's wet dream.

She stopped in front of him, crossed her arms over her chest, and cocked her hip. "What's your addiction, dude?"

Ethan shifted one side of his jacket. Beneath too-long brown bangs, her dark gaze flicked to the detective badge clipped to his belt.

Her bright red lips curved into a smirk, and she arched a pencil-thin eyebrow. "You want to frisk or handcuff me? I don't get off till eight."

He bit back a laugh. "No. Just some questions. What's your name?"

"Missy Perkins. I'm twenty-four, so I'm all legal."

He just bet she was. "Who worked last night?"

"That would be me." She sighed. "Donny had a hot date last night, and I got to cover his shift."

"Donny?"

"The owner, Donny Yarbrough."

"So you were here around ten thirty last night?"

"Yes. Me and about a dozen customers. We're open twenty-four hours on Fridays and Saturdays." She eyed him. "Usually just geeks and the occasional vamp wannabe. Sometimes a cop stops by to check the goings on, but none like you."

Missy shifted her hips, her skirt flouncing with the movement. Three boys playing a game console split their attention between the screen and the girl's long legs. Yeah, Donny had some good marketing skills all right. Word of mouth alone probably kept this place packed every minute it was open.

"Did you see anything odd last night?"

She snorted. "I got plenty of whack in here to distract me. Besides, ten thirty it's dark outside."

Ethan gestured toward the camera mounted on the wall behind the counter. "That real or just for show?"

Missy peered over her shoulder. "Oh, it's real. Donny's caught a couple of these creeps trying to make off with the merch. He's got one on every wall to get all the angles. Even two outside. Caught the losers hightailing it to their parents' car."

"You think I could see the video from last night?"

"Sure." She pivoted toward the counter and sashayed through a door marked "Manager".

She sat in front of a bank of monitors and cued up the cameras outside the store. "What's your time frame?"

Ethan thought back on when he left the station until the time Grant showed up on his doorstep. He wanted to know exactly when he left the bakery and if the cameras caught the mugging. "Let's say five p.m. to midnight."

Missy tapped the keys on the computer, and a moment later, images of the sidewalk out front as well as the Main Street Bakery across the road appeared. "This what you're looking for?"

He nodded. "That's fine. Let her roll."

Slowly, the time elapsed from five o'clock on. He watched several teens go in and out of the Games Galore entrance, and around nine thirty, two boys crossed the street to the bakery just as Mrs. Fitzgerald had told him. When the time stamp read 10:12 p.m., he spotted Grant's truck turn into the alley and park. He got out, glanced up and down the street, and strode up the sidewalk and into the bakery. A few minutes later, he came outside, coffee in hand, just as Mrs. Fitzgerald had reported. He climbed back into his truck and started the engine, a puff of smoke issuing from the tailpipe. But he didn't go anywhere. He just sat there in the alley with the F-150 idling.

Ethan squinted at the vague outline of his partner's head and shoulders. What was the guy doing?

A moment later, the image in the cab shifted, and the whole

truck shook.

"Geez," Missy mumbled. "Talk about a perv."

"What?"

She shot him a sideways glance. "Pretty obvious the guy just got lucky with Rosey Palm and her five sisters." She shifted her gaze back to the screen and watched Grant back out of the alley and drive away. "Just hope he wasn't wacking off to the old lady in the bakery. That's just like, eww."

He frowned and supposed the video might have appeared as Missy said. However, he was pretty sure his partner hadn't been masturbating but slamming his head against the steering wheel to fake a mugging. He gritted his teeth. Damn, that seemed a bit extreme just to keep Abby and him apart. Or was he possibly playing the overprotective older brother, trying to keep her safe from anyone associated with her rapist?

He kept his thoughts to himself, allowing the video to continue to run. The girl next to him didn't need to know why Ethan had taken an interest in who came and went on Main Street—it would lead to a lot of questions, not to mention gossip and speculation. Regardless of whether Grant had jacked off in his truck cab or rammed his head against the steering wheel, the fact remained a serial killer was running amok, and he didn't need the added drama. He let the video play another ten minutes. It showed several cars passing by on the street. Nothing occurred out of the ordinary.

"Okay," he said and stood. "That should do it."

"No problem, Detective." She tapped the keyboard, and the video disappeared. Turning toward him, she said, "Did you find what you were looking for?"

"Nothing really to find."

Missy grinned. "You're pretty hot for an older dude." She rose from her chair and placed her hands on her head. "We've still got a couple minutes before anyone comes looking. You want to frisk me now?"

He strode to the door. "Thanks for the assist and the, um,

invitation, but I've got to get back to work."

Her shoulders drooped and she lowered her arms.

Ethan opened the door and tilted his head toward the sales floor. "I'm sure there's more than one guy out there who'd do the honors. Just take your time and choose wisely."

She pursed her lips. "Who are you, freakin' Yoda?"

He laughed. "Never been accused of that before. But yeah, I guess the force runs deep in me."

He headed back to the station, taking the stairs to his office two at a time, anxious to learn more about his partner. When he reached his desk, the clock displayed six thirty a.m.

Finally!

He picked up the phone and dialed Abby's number.

"Hello?"

"Hey, it's me. Can we talk?"

"It's a little late for that. The time to talk would've been the night I laid my heart open for you. There's nothing to say now."

"Abby, please—"

"Goodbye, Ethan." A sharp click filled the line as she hung up on him.

"Damn it." Slamming the phone down, he shoved his hand through his hair and stared at the telephone. God, she'd sounded pissed, her tone more frigid than the Antarctic.

She just needs time. That's all.

At that moment, Chief Hague cruised around the corner. "Rough morning already, Parker?"

"Guess you could say that."

"You look like crap. Why don't you go home? Shower, shave. Get some grub. We've got a press conference at one. Be back then and try to look better than you do now."

Ethan massaged his temples. A press conference. He so did not want to have to deal with that. It was the single thing he hated most about being a detective—the politics. "Fine. I'll be back by one."

In the parking lot, he scanned the area one last time for any signs that a scuffle had taken place. Nothing. No surprise. He'd known there wouldn't be. Shit! He flipped open his cell and tried Abby again, this time getting her voice mail.

"Hey. It's me." Ethan trudged through the parking lot, another fresh round of snow silently cascading around him from the darkness above. Inhaling the crisp, cold air, he gathered his thoughts and said, "Listen, I know you don't want to hear anything I have to say right now, but please, please just hear me out. I promise I never meant to hurt you. You mean the world to me. And I'm worried about you, Abby. With this killer out there, I'm scared to death for you." He swallowed and willed the ache in his heart to subside. "Anyway, I'll be home 'til noon or a little after. Please just give me a call. Give me a chance to make this right. I don't want to lose you." He disconnected, shoved the phone in his pocket, and prayed she would listen and not just delete it.

Climbing into his SUV, he slammed the door and started the engine. He stared out the windshield, the first vestiges of sunlight chasing the night over the mountaintops. Another day in Red River would soon commence.

So just how the hell had his life suddenly gotten so fucked up?

Chapter Twenty-Three

*E*than pulled into his driveway and shut the engine off. Instead of getting out, he dragged the papers from his coat pocket and read through them. His gut told him there was something in his partner's past worth digging up, and his gut was rarely wrong.

The engine clicked as it cooled, and a stiff wind buffeted the Tahoe while he sat and scoured the file. So far, though, everything appeared on the up and up. Grant had sailed through the academy, done some really amazing stuff on patrol, and aced his detective's exam. The model cop. But for some reason, the guy on paper and the guy Ethan had come to know didn't jive.

He skipped ahead to Montgomery's personal profile. His parents had been killed in car wreck when he was thirteen, leaving Abby and him under the guardianship of an uncle from the father's side, Martin Montgomery. They'd been provided with enough money from their parents' estate to put them both through college, with which he had earned a degree in Criminal Justice and joined the force.

Ethan continued reading, but nothing leapt out as abnormal. Maybe his gut had finally failed him. He couldn't fault the guy for wanting to keep his sister safe—she was all he had left after their parents had died. He also couldn't fault the guy for not wanting the brother of her rapist in her life.

However, what bothered him was the way he'd gone about it. It was...almost sadistic.

He shivered, the heat having abandoned the SUV. Staring through the windshield at his house, he forced himself to face the reality that he'd been wrong. Grant was nothing more than an overprotective big brother. He sighed and folded the report to stuff back in his pocket but paused. Reopening the papers, he scanned for the word that had caught his eye.

Murdered.

The uncle had been found murdered when Grant was eighteen. He'd been formally questioned, as had Abby, and ruled out, never really considered a suspect. He'd gained guardianship of his sister, who'd been fifteen at the time.

He flipped a page then another, searching for the details of the murder. Ethan scanned the pages again but found nothing. Other than the brief mention of the uncle's murder, no other facts had been listed in the report anywhere.

Odd.

His instincts on full alert, Ethan's gut demanded more information. Not through the station, though. No, it was time to call in another favor with his buddy at Quantico. No longer feeling the chill in the air, he darted from the SUV to his front door, shut off the alarm upon entering, and kicked the door closed behind him.

This was it. This was what he'd been searching for. He dialed Will Donovan's number.

"Donovan."

"Hey there, long time no talk. Thanks for the profile, by the way."

"No problem," Will said with a chuckle. "What is it you want now?"

"Sheesh, you act like the only time I call you is when I want something."

"It is. You know I'm keeping track, don't you?"

Ethan knew. He also knew if Will minded, he would say so.

"Yeah, yeah, yeah. So, anyway, turns out you're right this time. I need another favor. It's an easy one. So you can probably handle it."

"If it's so easy, why don't you do it?"

"Because for one thing, I'm at home. And for another, I really don't want anyone knowing that I'm asking questions just yet. If this ends up being a false lead, then no noses will be out of joint." He really couldn't risk Grant discovering he'd dug around in his background if this turned out to be nothing. The guy already hated him enough. He didn't need to add fuel to the fire.

"Fine, spill it," came Will's amused voice.

"Can your get me whatever there is on the murder of one Martin Montgomery?" He relayed the birth date as well as the date of his murder. "Anything you can give me would be great. Oh, and I need it ASAP."

Will laughed loudly this time. "Of course you do. Give me your fax number, and I'll see what I can dig up."

"Thanks, man. I owe you. Next time you're up this way, we need to get together."

"Don't you worry, like I said, I'm keeping track."

Ethan rambled off the fax number in his office upstairs, thanked Will again, and hung up. He rubbed a hand over his stubbled jaw and remembered the chief had suggested he get a shower and some sleep. However, the rush of knowing he might be on to something stemmed the fatigue.

On his phone, he pressed the key for Abby's number. One more try then he'd hit the shower. He prayed she would answer this time, but the call went to voice mail.

"Okay. This is the last time today, I promise. I don't want you to think I'm a stalker." He rolled his eyes. Could he sound any more lame? Taking a breath, he said, "I just want to talk. I hate the way we left things. I was wrong in not telling you about my half-brother. Believe me when I say I wish I'd been the one to tell you, but frankly...I'm a coward. I was afraid. I care for you very much, Abby. Please come talk to me. I'll be here at home 'til noon."

Ethan sighed and hung up. If he didn't hear from her today, he would try again tomorrow. No way would he give up on her. He took his coat off, tossed it over the back of the couch and climbed the stairs to his room. A shower would feel damn good right now.

Shedding his clothes as he walked through the room, he let them lay where they fell. All he could think of was Abby and Grant. Who gave a shit if he left a mess in his wake? By the time he reached the bathroom door, he stood naked.

Switching on the lights, he paused. Memories of her assailed him. Skin against silky skin, their lovemaking of the night before.

His stomach tightened, images of how the water had cascaded over her supple body filling his brain. Her sexy moans echoed against the tiles, the taste of her hot and sweet in his mouth. Her welcoming sigh when he'd thrust inside her. She'd been so responsive to him.

Ethan groaned. There was no way he would be able to take another shower in this room and not crave her body. Her laugh. Her touch. Damn, he missed her. His throbbing shaft bumped his abdomen, his need for her intensifying.

Shit!

In two strides, he moved to the shower and set the controls to cold. Stepping under the spray, he jerked the shower curtain closed and braced his hands on the tiled wall in front of him. Shutting his eyes and lowering his head, he let the icy stream flow over him.

Christ! Why had he screwed this up so badly? He should've been up front with her, told her the truth at the start.

And it'd been so difficult for her to open up to him, to confide the worst part of her life. The pain in her eyes had torn at his soul. And still, she'd given herself to him, had faith he wouldn't let her down. Yet that's exactly what he'd done. She'd entrusted him with her heart, and he'd crushed it.

"Damn it to hell! I'm such a fucking idiot!" He pounded the wall with his fist, his bruised knuckles singing with pain. Stupid,

stupid, stupid. If his mama had been alive today, she would kick his ass. It's what he deserved.

The cold water having done its job, he lifted his head and moved back out of the spray. A frustrated growl rumbled in his throat as he rubbed his face vigorously then ran his hands through his sodden hair. He needed to focus on making amends with Abby and finding the sick sonofabitch who continued to leave cryptic messages carved in the chests of the men in her life. No more feeling sorry for himself.

From the corner of his eye, he caught a sudden shadowy movement on the opposite side of the shower curtain.

What the hell?

A flash of black darted into the shower and caught Ethan around the neck, jerking his head back. His feet slipped over the wet porcelain. Adrenaline shot through his veins, and his heart jackhammered. *Oh shit! The killer!* With the shower curtain between them, Ethan fought desperately to turn and face his opponent, but the arm against his throat was like a vice and the tub floor too slick. He gasped for air, clawed at the arm crushing his windpipe. Dark spots danced across the walls, and the room spun.

Abby!

He rammed his elbow backward, hitting home with the crunch of a rib. The chokehold loosened, and suddenly able to draw in air, he took a huge gulp. *Holy shit!*

His respite was brief, the killer grappling his neck again. Reaching around the curtain behind him, Ethan attempted to find something on the guy to grab. His hand contacted heavy cotton where hair should have been.

A ski mask.

Digging in his fingers, he yanked the mask from his assailant's head. The disguise jerked free, but the abrupt shift caught Ethan off balance. His feet skated over the porcelain.

Damn it!

He regained his stability and dropped the mask. Thrusting his hand backward again, he found the soft hollow of his opponent's eye and jammed his thumb straight in.

The guy howled in pain and released him. Finally free, he turned and reached to shove the curtain aside.

"Ethan?" came Abby's voice from downstairs.

His breath stalled in his bruised throat. *No!*

Without warning, a series of sharp pings echoed in the bathroom as the shower curtain was jerked from its rod. Before he could react, the heavy plastic shrouded his head. Strong hands grasped his shoulders and shoved him hard, sending his feet flying out from beneath him. He slammed onto the tub floor, his head grazing the substantial porcelain rim. His side taking the brunt of the fall, he slid into the basin, pain exploding in his hip.

He fought against the shower curtain covering him, his hot breath fogging the shiny plastic. Icy water rained down from the showerhead. Ethan reached for the edge of the tub, attempting to drag himself to safety.

He had to warn Abby, tell her the killer—

The outline of hands snaked toward him, seized him by the throat.

He thrashed about, striking out against his attacker, but to no avail. The bastard wore a thick sweatshirt.

With a growl, the assailant pulled him upward and hurled his head against the metal water faucet. A burst of stars flashed behind his eyes. Twice more the killer smashed Ethan's head into the faucet before releasing him.

The room spun. Buzzing filled his ears, drowning out the incessant patter of the spray against the plastic surrounding his head. He sucked in a breath, desperately wanting to yell out to Abby. But the shower curtain wedged against his mouth. Darkness fringed his vision.

I can't breathe. I can't save her.

Chapter Twenty-Four

"Ethan?" Abby called again and paused just inside the foyer. Cold air flowed in behind her, washing over her back. Even with a security system, it seemed unlikely he would just leave the house unlocked. She closed the door and glanced at the alarm console, the answer becoming clear. Unarmed. He must have left it open for her.

Shrugging out of her coat, she hung it on the rack and walked toward the kitchen. As she passed the couch, she noted a dark stain covering one of the cushions, and the unique scent of sweet mint met her nose. Had he spilled something? Continuing to the kitchen, she peeked in but found it empty.

She glanced at her watch. Eleven-fifteen. He'd said he would be at home until noon.

The distinctive sound of running water reached her ears. Was he taking a shower? A floorboard creaked overhead followed by three thumps. It sounded as though someone might be repairing something. She headed up the stairs.

Tentatively, she entered the master bedroom. "Ethan?"

On the far side, the bath door stood ajar, sounds of the shower emanating through the crack. Perhaps he hadn't heard her.

"It's me." Crossing the room, she laid her palm against the door and nudged it open a little further. "Just wanted to let you know I was here."

When he didn't answer, she frowned. Opening the door wider, she peered inside.

"Ethan?"

The shower sprayed at full blast, and thin metal clasps hung at odd angles along the slightly canted shower rod. Abby moved deeper into the room, and her breath caught. In the bottom of the tub, he lay naked and crumpled, the shower curtain wrapped around his head and torso.

"Oh, my God!" She rushed to him, frantically swiveling the faucets off. "Ethan!"

Grasping the wet plastic, she struggled to unwind it from his body. Bright crimson poured along the creases and folds of the shower curtain. Her heart stuttered. Blood. So much blood. Her fingers worked the appalling mess, untwisting the plastic, until at last she shoved it up and over his head.

God, his lips were blue!

With a shaking hand, she checked for a pulse. Beneath her fingertips, she found a weak, erratic thumping. Relief swept through her.

Blood surged from the side of his head. Had he lost his balance, slipped, and banged his head?

Somewhere beyond, a door closed. Abby whipped her head around, her heart thrashing. Was someone else in the house?

She skulked out of the bathroom and silently closed the bedroom door. After turning the lock, she hurried to the phone on the bedside table, grabbed the handset, and hurried back to the bathroom. A second door securely locked behind her, she dialed 9-1-1.

She gave the address, described Ethan's injuries, and explained the attacker might still be in the house. The attendant assured her police and EMTs were on the way and to just sit tight.

"Help is coming," she told him. "You're going to be all right."

Crawling across the floor, she grabbed towels from beneath the sink and spread them over his damp body. She bit her lower lip, noting the myriad bruises that had already started to surface. Had the killer attempted to claim him as his next victim? She swallowed and laid a towel on his calves and feet.

Memories of his voice from her cell message phone played back in her mind. He'd apologized repeatedly, leaving several messages on her voice mail. She'd listened to each but had been too damned angry to respond. The last message had finally persuaded her. His voice had rung with true love's desperation. He'd wanted to talk, for them to get past the horrible secret he'd kept.

Guilt swarmed her, constricted her chest. God, what if she'd continued to be stubborn and hadn't come?

Unable to contemplate the thought, she squeezed her eyes closed. When she opened them, she gazed down at him.

"You're nothing like him," she whispered. With tentative fingers, she brushed back a damp lock of hair from his forehead. "You're honest and loving and true. I know that. If you'd been like him, I never would've fallen in love with you. You're a good man, Ethan Parker."

She grabbed a washcloth and dabbed the gash on the side of his head. "I don't...." She swallowed, and a well of tears spilled over her cheeks. "I don't know what I would've done if I'd lost you. I should've been here."

"Police!" a voice rang out downstairs.

Abby's heart leapt. Help had arrived. She pushed up onto unsteady legs and unlocked the bathroom door. "Up here!"

Heavy boots pounded up the stairs. After a moment, someone rapped on the bedroom door. "Abigail Montgomery?"

She hurried across the room. "Yes."

"Red River Police," the male voice said. "Please open the door."

With a shaky hand, she twisted the lock and allowed an officer to enter.

Gun drawn, the older officer swept the room and, deeming it

clear, turned to her. "Where is he?"

"In there," she said, gesturing toward the bathroom. Trailing after him, she paused in the doorway. "He's lost some blood, but he's still alive."

A second officer entered the bedroom. When Abby pivoted toward her, the woman holstered her gun and offered a grim smile. Crossing the room, the officer looked at her partner, who knelt on the bathroom floor and said, "Clear."

"Good." The male officer grabbed the mic attached to his shirt. "All clear. We got him. Upstairs master bath. Send up the EMTs. He's pretty beat up." Then he focused on Abby and said, "I'm Officer Hanson. That's Officer Moore."

She glanced at the woman, who dipped her head and said, "Ma'am."

"We've worked with Detective Parker for a lotta years," Hanson said. "He's a good man. We'll take care of him. Don't you worry."

Hope fluttered in Abby's chest. Ethan would be all right.

℥

The first thing Ethan registered was the cold. It seemed his whole body had been immersed in ice, and he quaked uncontrollably. Secondly, his head throbbed like a sonofabitch. Jackhammers couldn't do worse damage. The third was Abby's voice. So soft and caring, so concerned, her tone eased some of the anxiety that had crawled its way through his frozen veins.

She sobbed, the timbre of her words quavering. Why was she crying? What the hell was going on?

She hollered out, and a second later, her gentle touch vanished.

Shouts, male and female, accosted his head, making him wince. Where had Abby gone? Finally able to crack open his eyes, realization hit him like the snap of a bullwhip. He lay sprawled in his bathtub where he'd been attacked.

He struggled to get up, but his shaking hand slid on the

damp porcelain, and he dropped back into the tub. Damn it. "Abby! Abby, are you okay?"

"She's fine, Detective." Officer Hanson laid his hand on Ethan's shoulder. "Officer Moore is with her right over there in your bedroom."

Relief poured through him.

"You need to lie quiet till the paramedics get up here," Hanson said. "You're hurt pretty bad."

He squinted against the bright bathroom lights, his head throbbing as though it'd been pounded with a hammer. He tried to sit up again, but a grinding pain tore through his side. And damn, he just couldn't seem to catch his breath. Had he broken a rib or something? He glanced down and groaned. "Christ, Hanson, help me out of here. I'm in my fucking birthday suit here."

Abby pushed through the door before Hanson could reply. She knelt at the side of the bathtub and took his hand. "Oh, God, I was so afraid for you. I listened to your messages and came over to talk to you. The front door was unlocked, so I came in. I couldn't find you, so I came up here. When I saw you...dear Lord, Ethan. I thought I'd lost you." A shiver coursed through her, and her lips stretched into thin, pale line. "Then I heard the front door slam, realized someone had been here, and called 9-1-1. I'm so sorry. I never should have walked out on you. I know you didn't mean to hurt me...."

He chuckled, sending a spasm of pain up his neck and through his head. He cringed against the pain. Squeezing her hand, he urged her closer. "Shhh, honey, you're talking so fast I can't keep up. Are you okay? He didn't hurt you?"

She shook her head. "No, I'm fine. I didn't even see him."

"Okay, folks, need to make way. The paramedics just pulled up outside," Officer Hanson informed them. When the room cleared, he offered Ethan a hand, helping him from the tub. "Let's get you cleaned up and dressed."

The next fifteen minutes flashed by. The paramedics, trying to do their job, attempted to put a neck brace on him and lay him on a stretcher, but he wouldn't have any of it. Yeah, his head felt eight times bigger than normal and like a baseball bat grand-slammed it with every heartbeat, but other than that, he was fine—or would be once he could be alone with Abby.

She sat next to him on the edge of his bed while he received yet another lecture from the paramedic about the dangers of head wounds, concussions, the injury to his throat from being strangled, and how he needed to go to the Emergency Department and spend the night in the hospital for observation. Ethan let the guy talk but wanted no part of it. He'd survived worse than a knock on the head.

"Listen, I'm not going anywhere. Do what you have to do to fix me up here," he said, squinting at the paramedic. Damn, did someone change the light bulbs in his bedroom? It felt like daggers were being jabbed into his eyes. "I'll be fine."

The paramedic mumbled something under his breath. The word "idiot" rang clear enough, but he ignored the man. He was just doing his job, and if Ethan had been in the other guy's shoes, he would've called himself an idiot, too.

It had been beyond stupid not to reset the alarm or lock the door behind himself. He glanced toward the bathroom door and scowled. Big macho detective, he was. Nearly killed in the shower. Stark naked. It would be a while before he lived this one down.

"I'll take over here." Gary Black entered the room and nodded to him. "They tell me you're being stubborn about going to the hospital." He donned gloves and bent to inspect Ethan's head.

As the medical examiner prodded his scalp, Ethan flinched. "Hey, take it easy there. I'm still alive, unlike all the dead bodies you're so fond of poking."

Gary raised an eyebrow but said nothing.

"And as far as the hospital, I'm not being stubborn. I'm fine." He stared the ME in the eye and would've raised an eyebrow himself if it didn't hurt so damn much. "What the hell are you doing here anyway? Don't you only come when there's a corpse?"

Gary met Ethan's gaze. "Don't be snippy, and you're not fine. You've had a major trauma to your head. I'm here because I heard the call come across the scanner and thought there was an off chance I could help. Looks like I was right. Did you lose consciousness?"

"Yeah, but it couldn't have been that long. The last thing I remember is Abby calling my name from downstairs. And then she was talking to me in the bathroom." He shifted his focus to her. "How long did it take you from when you entered the house until you found me?"

Abby glanced from him to Gary. "Two, three minutes tops. I looked around for you downstairs and then came up. When I spoke to you, you didn't move. I didn't know you'd heard me."

He squeezed her hand, the memory of her voice drawing him back from the abyss replaying in his mind. "I heard you. I just couldn't move."

Gary cleaned Ethan's head wounds using saline and gauze from the paramedic's bag. "Are you feeling nauseous at all?"

A little, but he figured it had more to do with not eating all day than any head injury. "No, not really. Nothing some food wouldn't cure anyway."

"Mmm hmm. Look, I'm not going to argue with you. You could use about ten to fifteen staples in the two gashes you've got on your head. If these guys have a disposable staple kit in their rig, I can close the wounds up for you," Gary said.

Wonderful, more pain. He nodded once. "Sounds good."

Gary motioned to the two-man crew of the rescue squad. "I'll run down the list of symptoms you need to watch out for with you and your lady friend and let it go at that." His brow furrowed, a V creasing between his eyes. "But I want your word, Ethan. Any sign of a worse injury, and I want your ass in the Emergency Department. Got it?"

"I got it. You have my word."

Gary addressed Abby. "I assume you will be staying with him today and throughout the night?"

Next to him, she gasped almost silently, but he heard it. They had yet to talk, to get the ugly business of his lies behind them. He risked a glance in her direction, hope dancing in his chest. She had shown up, after all. But would she be willing to stay and help him out? He found himself holding his breath, waiting for her answer.

When she met his gaze, he found warmth and caring swirling in her eyes, and he sighed.

"Um, yes," she said and cleared her throat. "Of course I will be here."

"All right then, let's move this downstairs." Gary pointed his finger toward the ceiling and made circular motions. "The rest of the CSU team needs to get in here and process the bedroom and bathroom. I can staple that thick head of yours in the living room if that's okay with you."

He gathered the supplies he would need. Ethan shuffled to the door, with Abby offering herself as a crutch for him to lean on. Gary lagged behind in the bedroom, so Ethan paused in the hallway.

Taking her in his arms, he pulled her tight against him. For this quick moment in time, he savored the feel of her wrapped around him, the warmth and rightness of it. When he pulled back, he gazed at her, silently studying the hidden strength that ran deep within her. He'd almost lost her once. He wouldn't make the mistake again.

Chapter Twenty-Five

*F*rom his uneasy twilight of sleep, Ethan heard the front door shut. He opened his eyes. Confused to find himself on the couch, he attempted to sit up. Pain shot from his rib cage straight through the top of his head. Immediately easing back onto the pillow, he waited for the room to stop spinning.

Memories of the attack flooded his mind. He still couldn't believe he'd been assaulted in his own home, yet his aching body didn't lie. Moving more slowly this time, he sat up and scanned the living room. As he processed the day's earlier events, he remembered Gary stapling the gash in his head and giving him some painkillers.

Abby.

She'd agreed to stay with him. Had she changed her mind and left while he slept? Shifting toward a sound, Ethan gazed into her beautiful blue eyes as she padded toward him. He could get lost in them so easily. "I thought you might've gone."

She smiled at him, and his concerns dissipated. She might just forgive him after all. "Lie back. You're supposed to be taking it easy." She adjusted the pillow under his head and moved in front of him to fiddle with the afghan that covered him. "I told you I would stay; I meant it. The last of the CSU just left. They said you were all set, and they wouldn't need to come back."

He stared at her and sighed. The amount of comfort it

brought him, just to know she was still there looking after him, boggled his mind. He'd never needed anyone like this before. Now, he couldn't imagine his life without her. "How long was I sleeping?"

She knelt on the floor in front of him. Reaching out, she brushed a lock of hair from his eyes. "Four hours. Grant stopped by to check on you, but I sent him away. And your Chief Hague was here, but he talked to Gary and said for you to call him in the morning." Her gaze flitted to his head injury. "Gary left more pain pills for you. Do you need some now?"

Ethan captured her hand in his and brought it to his mouth, placing a heartfelt kiss on the smooth skin of her open palm. "What I need, is your forgiveness."

He sat up and pulled her next to him on the couch. Facing her, he took her hands in his and held on tight. "What I did by not telling you the truth about my half-brother is indefensible. I broke an unspoken trust between us. But I swear to you, I never meant to hurt you. I wanted to tell you so many times, but I didn't know how. It was selfish of me, I know. But I was afraid you would hate me for what my brother did. And the closer we got, the less I was willing to risk that."

Ethan stared into the depths of her eyes. His explanation had been a string of feeble words at best. How could he ever express how truly sorry he was, how important she'd become to him in such a short time?

She started to speak, but he stopped her by brushing his thumb across her supple lips. His pathetic apology would never be enough. But he had to try.

"I...damn...I will never know the pain...." He cleared his throat. "I, uh, aw hell, Abby. I would do anything to take away the pain he caused you. I detest the thought that he hurt you. I could kill him for that." Taking a ragged breath, he drew strength from the warmth of her touch, and said, "God, I can't bear the thought that I caused you even more pain by not telling you the truth. Heaven help me. I don't want to lose you. I'm so, so sorry."

Eyes glistening, she moved in slowly, her gaze locked with

his. When her lips hovered just over his, she whispered, "I love you, Ethan. You're forgiven."

Exhaling on a groan, he wrapped his arms around her and pulled her tight into him, ignoring the pain in his ribs. He buried his face in the crook of her neck and savored the warmth, the scent that comprised the woman he loved.

"Ah, God, Abby," he mumbled against her silken skin. Relief poured through him, leaving him lightheaded. His hands slid over her, one across her back, the other around her waist. It might have only been a day, but it felt like years since he'd held her in his arms. He moved his mouth to her ear and murmured, "I won't ever abuse your trust again, sweetheart. I promise you that."

She angled her head and kissed him. Ethan drew his tongue across her lips and begged for entrance. Once Granted, he dove in like a desperate, starved man. His tongue tangled with hers, fought for dominance, but she met his fervor and surpassed it.

He moaned. Heat rushed through his veins. Damn, but he thought he might internally combust.

Twisting toward him, she ground her body against his. Her taut nipples strained against the thin fabric of her blouse and grazed across his chest. Oh, how he ached to taste her sweet skin. Hands at the hem of her shirt, he prepared to help her out of it, but when she raked her hands through his hair, she jerked back, a horrified expression on her face.

"Oh, God, Ethan! Your head. We can't be doing this."

He chuckled. "We belong to each other. Let me show you how much."

She stood, held out her hand. "Not here. At least let me get you somewhere more comfortable. Come on, let's go upstairs."

Pausing to make certain the front door remained secure and the alarm system activated, he took solace in the fact that the bastard wouldn't get a second chance at him or the woman he loved. With their safety ensured, he turned his focus on the woman next to him and let her lead him up the stairs to his bedroom.

CS

Abby guided Ethan to the side of the bed and stopped in front of him, bending to switch on the bedside lamp. Straightening, she met his lust-filled gaze in the muted light. The sight of his overt hunger for her sent her heart racing. Silently, she removed his T-shirt, tossed it to the floor, and brought her attention to his well-sculpted chest and abdomen. Gracious, he was beautiful. She slid her palms over his skin from the waist up, roving over the hard sinew and muscle of his stomach, through the sparse chest hair, and up to his broad, strong shoulders.

She moved closer and let her mouth travel the same route her hands had. Taking time to gently kiss the fully formed bruises over his ribs, she ended her journey at his small, pebbled nipples, greedily laving each one with her tongue. Rewarded with a shiver and groan from him, she grew bolder. Stepping back, she grasped his sweats at the waist and shoved them over his hips.

On shaky legs, he stepped out of the pants and kicked them aside.

Dear Lord, she loved this man. His soulful apology had melted her heart, but frankly, she'd already decided to forgive him after listening to his last voice mail. Once she'd calmed down, she realized how telling her something like that would be difficult.

What his brother had done to her was in the past, and had nothing to do with the man standing before her. Forgiving him had been easy.

Especially after finding him unconscious in the bathroom.

When faced with the fact that she could have lost him forever, it was a no-brainer. Pride held no factor over love. Not for her anyway.

She knelt in front of him, inhaling his heady male scent. She'd never gone down on a man before, but she wanted to experience everything with him, to give him the same pleasure he'd given her. But before she got the chance, he reached for her, pulling her up to him.

Wide-eyed and suddenly unsure, she faltered. "I thought you would like that."

"Oh, sweetheart, I would," he said in a husky voice. "But right now, I don't think I'd last. I want you. We've got all night. I need to feel your skin against mine, to know you're really here with me and not just a dream my lonely heart conjured up." He sat on the bed, slid to the center. His heated gaze raked her from head to toe. "Undress for me."

Heart pounding, Abby did as he asked. She drew her shirt over her head, tossing it with the other discarded clothing. Moving her hands to the front clasp of her bra, she eagerly freed her breasts from their confinement.

The audible gasp from Ethan brought a smile to her lips.

"Hurry."

She understood his need because her body ached to have him, too. Making quick work of her jeans and underwear, she joined him on the bed, crawling up his body to straddle his lap.

His hands slipped over her hips, along her waist, and up to fondle her breasts. "Do you know how beautiful you are?"

Heat rushed to her face. "I know you make me feel that way."

"How else do I make you feel, Abby? Do you want me as bad as I want you?" He lowered one hand between them, and she writhed on his inquisitive fingers.

With his other hand, he reached over to the bedside stand, opened the drawer, and grabbed a foil packet. "As promised."

She took the condom from him and opened it. "I don't need protection from you, Ethan, but if you insist." She placed the rubber at the head of his erection and rolled it down, giggling when he squirmed and groaned.

"Damn, I don't know how much more I can bear." He grabbed her hips and pulled her to him. "Take me, Abby. Now."

Without hesitation, she raised herself over him and oh, so slowly sank down onto him until she'd seated herself firmly against his pelvis. A delicious shiver skittered along her limbs, and she bit her lower lip and moaned.

"Oh, God, sweetheart. You feel so damned good." He grasped her hips and arched against her.

The sensation started a coil tightening deep within her body. Oh, they were so good together. She could savor him, body and soul, for all eternity. Abby rode him, keeping time with his passion-filled thrusts.

But soon that pace wasn't enough. She needed more. Faster. Harder.

Head thrown back, she ground into Ethan, ecstasy overcoming her. She moved with him, frantic to reach the point of no return. Blood pounded in her ears, her breath coming in short gasps as she called out his name.

"That's it, sweetheart. Oh, yes!"

He slammed against her sweat-slickened skin, and then the world tilted, delicious spasms erupting deep inside her. Vivid hues burst behind her eyelids, and she tumbled over the edge into oblivion. Two more thrusts and he stilled, groaning her name on a breath of air.

Slowly, they drifted back to reality. Ethan pulled her down on top of him, holding her while his breathing returned to its normal rhythm. He showered tender kisses over her face and neck and murmured sexy words in her ear. They remained entwined for a long time before he rose from the bed and sauntered into the bathroom.

When he returned to the bed, he scooped her up in front of him and wrapped his strong arms around her. "You are amazing, you know that? I'm fairly sure I don't deserve you, but you should know, I'll fight to the death before I ever lose you again."

Happier than she'd ever been, she traced circles on his arm and snuggled in deeper. "You'll never have to. I'm yours."

Chapter Twenty-Six

The smell of bacon frying coaxed Ethan from sleep. He opened his eyes to find the bright shine of the early morning sun filtering in through the curtains and no way to erase the smile from his face. Hell, why would he ever want to? It was a new day, a new beginning, and he'd spend it with Abby by his side.

After a second round of lovemaking last night, they'd gone down to the kitchen where she'd warmed up chicken noodle soup and made him hot cocoa. She'd fussed over his head, changed the dressing, and tried to get him to take the pain medication. She didn't realize all he needed to ease the throbbing in his head and ribs was to look at her beautiful face. The life and sparkle in her eyes wiped away any ache that remained from the attack. She did more for him than any drug ever would.

He rolled over, sank his face into her pillow, and inhaled deeply. Her flowery scent still lingered. Memories of holding her soft and naked in his arms, knowing she was his, rushed into his mind. He didn't need pain meds to sleep. Abby was the best drug he knew.

Ethan rose and sauntered into the bathroom. He paused, momentarily cautious of the room. He was a strong man, and not much had scared him in his thirty-six years, but the attack in the shower had been straight out of Psycho. It would be a few days before he felt comfortable in his own bathroom, and that pissed him off.

He twisted on the cold water, cupped his hands, and splashed his face, the crisp, icy fluid doing its job to wake him the rest of the way. Easing back the gauze, he peered in the mirror. Damn, he looked like hell. The gash in his head had swollen and become dark purple. The staples Gary had used to close the wound glinted beneath the lights.

"Shit. I look like Frankenstein's monster," he grumbled and pressed the medical tape back against his skin, securing the bandage.

Grabbing his toothbrush, he cleaned his teeth with ruthless abandon, his frustration getting the better of him. When he straightened after rinsing his mouth, he glanced in the mirror and told himself the injury would heal. And looking at it didn't have to be all bad. It was the event that brought Abby and him together again.

Happy to have found a silver lining, he pulled on a fresh pair of sweats and headed downstairs to the inviting smells of breakfast. On entering the kitchen, he found her at the stove, expertly folding an omelet onto a plate.

"Hey there, gorgeous." He sidled up behind her and kissed the back of her neck. "Damn, that looks good."

"Oh, Ethan." She spun in his arms. "I wanted to surprise you with breakfast in bed."

He pulled her against him. "Then you should have stayed there."

"You are bad." She smacked him on the shoulder then stood on her toes, covering his mouth with hers for a long, sultry kiss. "Go sit at the table. It's all ready."

He headed to the fridge instead. "What do you want to drink?"

She placed the two omelets on the table and returned to the stove, retrieving the bacon and home fries. "Orange juice, please."

"Two OJs coming up." He grabbed the glasses from the cabinet, filled them, and set them on the table in front of the two plates. "Damn, I didn't know I had the makings for all this. You're good."

She joined him at the table. "It's no big deal. Some eggs, ham, and cheese. You had bacon, potatoes, and onion, and presto. Breakfast."

He dug into the food with gusto. "We're supposed to get a whopper of a snowstorm this afternoon. What say we rent some movies and cuddle on the couch all day?"

"I'd like that." A sexy smile curved her luscious lips. "I've already called work and told them I needed a few days off. They were very understanding."

His cell rang, and Abby snagged it from the counter. "Probably your chief checking in on you. He said he'd call."

He took the phone. "Parker here."

"Ethan?" a female voice came over the line. "Is that you?"

He grinned. "Ever?"

"Yeah," his sister said. "Must be the connection. You sound weirder than normal."

"Must be." He laughed. "So, where are you? What hell hole did they ship you off to in order to get that sheepskin certifying you as a real live archeologist?"

"No place exotic, sad to say. I'm just outside of Moab, Utah."

"Digging in the dirt." He took a swallow of juice. "How much longer till you're finished?"

"It's the last semester, big brother." She sighed. "Then I'm back home to Vermont for a while, or at least till I find a job."

"Good to know."

"But on a serious note, I was really calling to check up on you. Been getting some strange vibes, and I know you don't believe in any of that, but I thought I'd check on you anyway."

Ethan closed his eyes. Damn. Well, she'd certainly nailed this one on the head. But he wasn't about to tell her that. "Nope," he lied. "Not a thing. Wrong as Ever."

"Hey, you. Watch the jokes," she said and giggled. "I got a

shovel, and there are plenty of holes out here that you'd fit nicely in. Cover you right up. No one would find you...Ever."

"I hear you."

"Good."

She paused while someone nearby spoke to her. The words might have been indistinguishable, but the timbre was definitely male. Ethan kicked into protective mode.

"Hey, who ya talking to? You out there stringing some guy along?"

"What, you going all police detective on me? Sheesh! It never ends." She laughed.

"Never will."

"You're my brother. And by definition that means you're to keep your sniffer out of my love life."

"Fine," he grumbled. But he'd already worked a plan in his head on how to get a list of everyone on the dig.

"Well, gotta go, big brother. You take care of yourself. Love you."

"Love you, too," Ethan said and ended the call. When he looked up, he found Abby staring at him, one exquisite eyebrow arched.

"And who was that, might I ask?"

"Why?" He grinned, enjoying her reaction to the call. "Jealous?"

"No." She gulped her juice, emptied the glass. "So?"

He forked a healthy bite of omelet into his mouth, the flavor bringing a moan. No way he could torture her after tasting that. The woman could cook.

"There's a photo up on my dresser in the bedroom."

"The one of you with your mom and dad before they died?"

He nodded. "The girl next to me is my sister, Ever. And that's also who was on the phone. She's about to finish grad school, working on a project or thesis or whatever the hell the university requires."

"Your sister?" A smile played on Abby's lips. "When is she coming home? Can I meet her?"

He raised his brows in mock horror. "Oh, I don't know. The two of you together? Nothing but trouble. Might even burn down the town. Can't have that. No, I'll have to keep you two apart for sure."

Abby laughed, the sound music dancing on the air. She rose, carried her dishes to the sink, and turned back toward him. "I can't wait to meet her, ask about all the secrets of when you two were kids. Should be interesting." Then her brow knitted, and she grimaced as though the last swallow of juice had soured in her mouth. "What about, uh, your...."

"Brother?" He reached out, snagged her hand, and squeezed it. No more secrets between them. He would tell her everything. "He'd gone to live with his dad by the time Ever came along. I guess a new baby made him feel unwanted or something." He shrugged and met her gaze. "He wasn't always a delinquent. When we were kids, he was okay. But...."

"When he went to live with his dad?" she whispered.

"Yeah." Ethan swallowed, remembering the changes in his half-brother. "The guy was bad news, into all kinds of stuff. Drugs. Armed robbery. Took Michael along for the ride." He looked out the window. Damn, things had gotten so...fucked up.

She sighed. "I'm sorry."

Ethan shook his head. "Not your fault. It just happened. Not much anybody could do about it." He risked a glance at her, afraid she would remember his own recent transgression and walk out on him. "I'm the one who's sorry, Abby."

She moved closer and dropped a kiss on his good cheek. "As long as I've got you, everything is wonderful. But for now, I need to run home, get some clean clothes and shower. Why don't I pick up the movies on my way back?"

His fingers tightened around his glass. He hated the thought of her leaving. Would she think it too fast if he asked her to move in with him? Jesus! Of course she would. "Sounds good, but I was hoping you'd save the shower for here."

Now he sounded desperate. Hell, maybe he was. The idea of a shower alone in the place where he'd come within inches of being killed didn't appeal all that much to him. Having her naked, wet body next to him would be an excellent distraction.

Her face brightened. "I can do that. Do you mind if I bring my toothbrush?"

He laughed out loud. "Sweetheart, I would like nothing better. You can even bring a pink washcloth."

"You're my kind of man, Ethan Parker."

He inhaled the remainder of his omelet and helped her clean up. Doing the dishes had never been so much fun. God, he was becoming so domesticated. And he loved it.

He loved her.

Having her meet Ever would be the highlight of his life. He was so proud of each of them, and loved them both dearly. With his grandparents long passed, Abby and Ever were the only people he held in his heart.

After deciding on movies—two action-packed and two chick-flicks—she shrugged on her coat.

"I won't be long," she said then kissed him. She opened the door, and a swirl of icy air rushed in. "You just take it easy. And I have my cell phone if you need me."

When she'd closed the door behind her, Ethan strode to the window and watched her maneuver down the snow-covered driveway. He glanced at the dark, gray sky, heavy with another round of snow. Hopefully, it would hold off until she returned.

Letting the curtain fall back into place, he pivoted from the window. Silence met him. How had he managed to live alone for so long?

In the kitchen, his cell phone went off again. Thinking it might be Abby calling to say that she missed him already brought a grin to his face. God, she hadn't been gone five minutes, and he craved her voice. He rushed to answer the cell. "Parker."

"Hey," Will's voice boomed through the phone. "I thought for sure I'd hear from you yesterday after I sent that fax through. Looks like your gut paid off this time."

Ethan froze. How could he have forgotten the fax? "Shit, Will. I had some trouble here yesterday and got a good knock on my head. I forgot all about it. Hang on, I'm running up the stairs now."

"Don't rush on my account. You okay?"

He jogged up the stairs. "Yeah, the psychotic bastard tried to take me out in the shower. Turns out I have a harder head than he thought."

"Hell, I could've told him that. You're a tough sonofabitch to kill. Just ask those insurgents in Pakistan who tried their damnedest to do it." Will chuckled. "Seriously, though, in the shower? Damn, this guy isn't fooling around."

"No, he's not." Ethan entered the spare room, went straight to the fax machine, and pulled the papers from the tray. "So, anyway, the fax is here. Give me a minute to read through it, and I'll call you back. By the way, thanks for the memory jog."

"Anytime, pal. I'll be here."

He disconnected, sank into the desk chair, and read the report.

Martin Montgomery. Age fifty-eight. Found dead in an abandoned hunting shack in the woods approximately five miles from his residence in Elm Ridge, New Hampshire.

Ethan's blood froze, and the room tilted as he read further.

The victim was tied to a bed with duct tape in the cabin. The vic's eyes were removed, castration was performed, and the word BASTARD was carved across the chest. All events occurred prior to demise. Death occurred when the femoral and carotid arteries were cut. Cause of death: exsanguination.

His heart hammered against his sternum, and his hands shook. This was the practically the same damn M.O. as his perp. The same! Why hadn't Grant mentioned this? Surely he knew the details of his uncle's murder. Holy shit!

There was only one reason he would leave this out of the investigation—it would make him look guilty. What other possible reason could there be? Ethan thought back on his partner's behavior. The mood swings, the open resentment, the anger he'd displayed toward him.

Panicked, he grabbed his cell phone. He had to call Abby and warn her. He dialed her cell and rushed to his bedroom.

Damn it. Voice mail. He tried her house phone. While the line connected and the ringing on the other end grated against his eardrum, he grabbed jeans, a T-shirt, and sweatshirt out of his dresser.

"Hello?"

"Abby? Oh, thank God I got you." Ethan kicked out of his sweats and pulled on his jeans with his free hand. "Is Grant home?"

"I'm not sure. Let me go look."

"No!" he yelled into the phone. Taking a breath, he forced a calm, reassuring tone. "Listen, sweetheart. I want you to get out of there right now. Come straight back here, and I'll explain everything."

"Ethan, what is going on?"

"Baby, please just do what I ask." He wanted her out of there and back with him pronto.

"If it's that dangerous, I should warn him. He shouldn't be left here alone if you are so worried. Let me go tell him, and then I'll leave right away."

"Abby, wait." He didn't want to tell her on the phone, but she'd left him no choice. "It's Grant I'm worried about."

"What? That's ridiculous. I understand you're still upset with him. So am I. But he's no danger to either one of us."

Ethan pulled the T-shirt over his head, snatched his sweatshirt off the bed, and jogged to the stairs. "Do you remember any of the details of your uncle's death?"

"No. I was young at the time. Grant told me all I needed to know was he'd been murdered. He said the police assured him it'd been random, and we had nothing to worry about. Why?"

Fully dressed except for his feet, he paced the living room floor. He wanted her to come to him but was afraid to tell her too much. It might be better if he just went and got her. "Honey, did he know how your uncle died?"

"Of course. He found him." She cleared her throat. "What's going on? You're scaring me."

"Stay right where you are. I'm going to come get you." Ethan stepped into his boots, not bothering to tie them. "Stay on the phone with me 'til I get there."

"No...your head, you can't leave. If it's that important to you, I'll—"

The phone went silent.

"Abby?"

No response.

His grip tightened on his cell. "Abby!"

Heart thrashing, Ethan tugged on his jacket, set his alarm, and sprinted out the door. Bitterly cold wind swept around him. He jumped into his truck and thumbed the redial on his cell. Revving the engine, he slammed the shifter into reverse and backed up. He yanked the wheel, and the front of the truck slid over the slush-covered concrete, ending with the nose pointing down the driveway. Snow swirled through the air, the flakes fluttering over the windshield.

Her voice mail picked up. He clicked off, redialed again.

"Hi, this is Abby—"

"Fuck!"

Cramming the shifter into drive, he stomped on the gas pedal. The engine roared, and the rear tires spun, sending the truck fishtailing down the driveway. God, he needed to get to her.

It was time to call the one person he trusted with his life. He dialed Will.

"Donovan."

"Will, it's Ethan. My gut is talking again, and it's not good." He jammed his foot on the accelerator, sliding across the snowy road and into the other lane. Finessing the brakes and steering wheel, he maneuvered back to the proper lane.

"Yeah, I figured as much when I read that report. My first question was why your partner didn't mention his uncle's C.O.D. It's the same way all your victims were found."

He sped around a slow-moving sedan then swerved onto a secondary street.

"Exactly! Listen, his sister Abby might be in danger. I called her at her house. Tried to get her to leave. But the phone went dead. I'm pulling in her drive now." He jammed on the brakes. The slick road sent the truck into a spin, and he careened into the ditch. But instead of backing out, he accelerated and plowed across the yard. Thank God for four-wheel-drive. "Was there any indication in the report that the police were suspicious of her brother?"

Ethan rammed the Tahoe's shifter into park and leapt from the truck, not bothering to shut it off. Sprinting up the walk, he bolted up the stairs and onto the porch. With his hand raised to knock, he noticed the front door stood slightly ajar. Pulling his gun from his jacket pocket, he eased inside the house.

Silence. He held his breath, swallowed. Shit, maybe they were both hurt or in trouble.

Will continued to talk. "Nothing concrete regarding the brother. He was questioned and ruled out. He was only eighteen and had been at the movies with a girl at the time the uncle had been killed. The girl verified his story."

He clenched his jaw. It didn't make sense. "Then why the hell would he leave something like this out of the investigation? He had to know we'd look into his and Abby's past eventually."

He edged down the hallway, listening for any sounds that would tell him her location. When he rounded the corner into the kitchen, a movement to his right caught his attention. He jerked around, but before he could raise his Glock and squeeze the trigger, something crashed against his wrist. Blistering pain shot up his arm and, unable to keep his grip, the gun flew from his hand. Damn, it felt like a sledgehammer had crushed the bones in his arm. A yell ripped from his mouth.

"Ethan?" Will shouted into the phone.

"Ethan!" Abby screamed from somewhere nearby.

He spun in the direction of her voice, only to discover the butt of a rifle rushing toward his face. Shit. This was going to hurt like hell.

With a resounding crack, immense pain radiated throughout his head, and a blinding light flashed before his eyes. His knees buckled, and everything went black.

Chapter Twenty-Seven

Musty mold and dust filled Ethan's nose. God, what a horrid smell. That, along with the excruciating pain pulsating through his face, sent his stomach rolling. He swallowed so he wouldn't gag. Vomiting at this moment would not be a good thing— especially since duct tape sealed his mouth, and he'd more than likely choke to death.

He kept his eyes closed, forced himself to lie still and take a moment to get his bearings. A wisp of cold air flowed over him. Icy tendrils shrouded his bare feet and caressed his nude chest. Well, it appeared his socks, shoes, and shirt had been removed. Thank God he still had his jeans on.

He lay on a mattress or bed, and after several small tugs, he realized his arms had been tied over his head and his legs secured at the bottom, leaving him spread-eagled. A desperate mix of anger and fear shot through him. *Fuck!*

Remaining quiet, he peered around the semi-darkened area through his lashes but didn't recognize the room. However, he could tell it hadn't been used in a while. Spider webs hung from the corners of the walls, and dust had settled over the one dresser at the foot of the bed.

The door creaked, and Ethan forced his breathing into a normal, calm rhythm. The overhead light flicked on.

"You may as well open your eyes," a familiar voice said. "I know you're awake."

He complied and locked gazes with his captor.

Grant Montgomery smirked. Crossing to Ethan, he laid a rolled-up cloth bag on the nightstand next to the bed.

Sonofabitch. Ethan gritted his teeth. He hadn't wanted to believe it, but his gut had screamed otherwise. Hell, the evidence had screamed otherwise. He glared at Grant, taking in the bastard's every movement. The asshole had done it all. His own partner had turned out to be a psychopathic killer.

"What, you're not surprised it's me?" He unwrapped the cloth revealing various knives, tools, and sharpening stones. He straightened the implements, his fingers brushing over them with apparent reverence. A sly grin on his face, he glanced at Ethan. "It sure took you long enough to catch on. The big, bad Detective Ethan Parker, working right alongside the man responsible for ridding this town of its filth. You're a fucking joke, Detective."

He eyed the wicked contents in the bag. His hand itched to snatch one of the razor-sharp knives, slice through his bonds, and then jam it between two of Grant's ribs. But the twisted duct tape that restrained him wouldn't allow it. The tool bag rested on the stand next to the bed, close enough for him to see each blade glint in the light but woefully out of his reach. So, he remained still while inside he seethed. Fury coiled snakelike in his gut, waiting for the moment he could rip the sonofabitch's head off.

A groan came from the far side of the room, and Ethan turned his head. Tucked in the shadowy corner with her arms bound together in front of her and one slender ankle handcuffed to the chair, sat Abby, gagged with the same duct tape that covered his own mouth.

His breath caught. Pulling at his restraints, he tried frantically to break free while he called her name. But the tape across his mouth muffled his words, and he realized his attempts to rescue her were futile. Slamming his head back against the mattress, he met Grant's gaze and held it. How could he do this to her? She was his sister for God's sake. Ethan stared at him, willed him to do the right thing.

Laughing, Grant leaned over and whispered in Ethan's ear. "I have such plans for you. Surprises, too. Oh, wait 'til you see my best surprise."

He straightened, grabbed a corner of the duct tape, and violently ripped it off Ethan's mouth. Trickles of warmth oozed from Ethan's mouth and sides of his face. He licked his lips, tasted blood.

"Go ahead, Detective, have your say," he said in that same hoarse whisper. "But what I really want is to hear your screams when I carve my final word in your chest."

Ethan jerked his head in Abby's direction. "Are you okay?"

She nodded, but the tears that streaked down her cheeks told a different story.

He swallowed his desperation and forced himself to calm down. If he wanted a hope in hell to get them both out of there alive, he needed his wits about him.

Turning back to his captor, he weighed his words carefully. "Look, Grant, nothing's been done here today that can't be taken back. Just wait a moment. Think about what you're doing."

"Oh, Ethan, I know exactly what I'm doing. I'm getting my sister back." He sauntered over to her and knelt in front of her. Gently, he removed the tape from her mouth. "It didn't have to be like this, you know. Why couldn't you have just been satisfied with me? Our lives were great. You depended on me, needed me. Then you had to go and get it in your head that you wanted more." He leaned toward her, "Why, Abby? You. Had. Me!"

Tears streamed down her face, but she met her brother's gaze head-on. She sat straight in the chair, her tied hands in her lap, and her head held high. "I don't understand, Grant. Tell me this is all some big misunderstanding. Tell me you didn't kill those men. They were friends. That's all. Just friends."

He reached up, took her bound hands in his own. "Everything I've done has been for you. I've protected you for so long, Abby. It's my job above all else. You don't understand how

245

dangerous life can be. You don't realize how many monsters are out there, waiting for an innocent woman like you to prey on. I thought after your rape, you knew all this. But apparently you've forgotten."

She shook her head. "How could you think killing my friends was protecting me? I get that you think you have to look after me. It's been the two of us since Uncle Marty died, but I'm a grown woman now. It's time for me to move on. But that doesn't mean I would ever stop loving you."

He bowed his head. "I know. I love you, too."

A dark, oily chill oozed down Ethan's spine. Grant's words intimated more than a sibling relationship. Obsession wove deep within his tone.

He laid his head on Abby's lap. "I couldn't have endured protecting you for all those years if I didn't love you so much." Lifting his head, he met her gaze. "Did you know Mom and Dad thought I'd be jealous of you when they brought you home? I wasn't, though. I loved you from the minute I saw you. I knew then I could never let anyone hurt you, and I didn't."

She appeared to be calming her brother. She wasn't falling apart but staying strong, trying to talk her brother down. Maybe they'd make it out of here alive after all.

"What do you mean you protected me, Grant? What are you talking about?"

Standing, he paced the room in front of his sister. "Uncle Marty. That's what I'm talking about." He spun back to face her. "You didn't know it, but Uncle Marty used to pay me visits at night. In the beginning, he'd just lay down with me and hug me to him. Then he'd have me...touch him, had me rub him inside his underwear while he moaned and groaned and rocked his hips. As I got older, he made me use my mouth on him, until even that wasn't enough."

Ethan couldn't believe what he was hearing. But it all made sense in a sick sort of way. The man had never stood a chance as a kid when the pervert uncle got custody. Grant must have been so betrayed.

"I tried to get him to stop, but he told me if I didn't please him, that he would have you do it." He knelt back in front of her, his hands latching on to her legs "I couldn't let that happen. I couldn't let him soil you. So I let him have what he wanted, and God help me, Abby, but I liked it. I liked the power I had over him. Knowing I could bring him to his knees or have him at my mercy. Even if I was the one bent over the bed, he needed me. Do you know what a high that is?" He frowned. "But he went too far. He promised not to ever touch you, but one night I caught him going into your room. It was the last time he ever drew breath."

Tears streamed down her face. "You never told me. I could have helped you."

"So why, Abby?"

"Why what?" She looked down at her brother, confusion threading across her features.

Grant raised his head. "Why him?" he growled. "He's not good enough for you."

"But I love him. I told you that."

He shoved away from her. When he turned, Ethan saw the madness in his eyes, and another chill rent his spine, this one icy and laden with fear. Grant stalked the room, his movements that of a cornered beast.

"Love him?" he ranted. "God, Abby. He's a prick. Trash. Dog shit is more respectable than him. And I can't for the life of me figure out how he scammed his way into your pants. Just the thought of it...the images in my mind...." He grabbed the side of his head and growled. After a moment, he looked up at her, a deadly calm masking his features. "It's fucking disgusting."

"Grant—"

"Shut up!" he roared. Curling his fingers, he brought his fist to his lips and stared at her while he calmed himself again. His nostrils flared with each deep, angry breath. After a moment, he said, "Just shut up. Please. Everything will be fine very soon."

Abby stared at her brother. How could he be responsible for all those deaths? Her gaze flicked to the nightstand where he'd unrolled the bag with all those knives. Her stomach heaved.

She squeezed her eyes closed. *Please let me wake up. Please let me wake up. Please—*

"Look at me," he commanded.

She looked up at him, at the brother she'd believed she'd known.

He stood before her, palms pressed together, the tips of his index fingers poised against his bottom lip. "It will all be okay. Trust me."

She pressed her lips together, afraid to speak, afraid anything she said might send him off on a rampage. This wasn't the brother she'd grown up with, the sweet, funny guy who'd watched over her since their parents' deaths.

Pulling a key from his front pocket, Grant knelt on one knee and opened the handcuff that kept her shackled to the chair. "I just want you to know I'm sorry, Abs."

"Just let her go," Ethan said from the bed. "It's me you want. I'm the one that had hot, sweaty sex with—"

"Shut up!" Grant snapped. "Just shut the fuck up."

"But she didn't do anything," he continued. "I pushed myself on her, tricked her into believing I was a good guy. But you figured out the truth."

Grant gazed into her eyes, and the resolve she saw there, the chillingly calm hopefulness on his face caused her heart to stutter.

"Yes," he said, his voice rough. "I did."

"Then let her go," Ethan persisted. "This is between you and me."

His lips stretched into a thin line. His attention firmly on his sister, he squeezed her hands and said in a quiet voice, "I'm sorry, Abby. Truly I am. But I have to do this."

"Do what?" she whispered. Terror gripped her lungs.

"Things will be better once it's all over. You'll be better." He gave her a small smile. "We'll both be better."

"What do you—?"

He grabbed her upper arm and yanked her from the chair.

"Stop it, Grant. Just stop."

When he lifted her over his shoulder, she realized he wasn't going to let her go, and panic seared through her. He planned to murder them both for their betrayal.

"Put her down, you bastard!" Ethan yelled.

As her brother carried her to the door, she caught sight of Ethan on the bed, jerking against the duct tape that held him captive.

"Abby!" His eyes flared with fear and fury. "Just hold on. I'll come get you. I swear I will." His face aglow with urgency, he yanked the twisted rope of tape taut while he reached toward the bag of knives. But it lay well beyond his fingertips. With a growl, he yelled, "Let her go, you bastard. You hurt her, I will kill you. I swear I will."

Grant exited the room, Ethan's threats following after them. After an abrupt turn, her brother mounted the stairs, the steps creaking beneath their weight.

"Put me down." She slammed her bound hands against his back and tried to kick her legs, but he'd clamped his arm firmly over her thighs. Tears burned her eyes, and she sobbed. "Please, Grant. Just put me down. I'm your sister. Why are you doing this?"

"Because I love you, Abby. I need you back." At the upstairs landing, he turned down the hallway. "You're my life, Abs. Always have been. I'm doing this for you. For us."

"I don't know what the hell you're talking about," she wailed, continuing to club her hands against his back.

"Don't worry." He lowered her to the floor, held the ropes on her wrist firm so she couldn't run. "This shouldn't take long. Just know I'm sorry. And I promise I'll take care of you when it's over."

She shook her head. "Don't do this." A sob ripped from her throat. "Please. I'll stay with you. Forever. I promise."

His mouth twisted into a grim smile. "You're all I have left, Abs."

Retrieving a key from a nail next to the door, he used it to release the lock and replaced it on the hook. He disengaged two deadbolts, the heavy metal cores slamming free of their strike plates. With his hand on the doorknob, he paused.

"This is for your own good."

"What, Grant? What are you going to do to me?" Desperation tore through her, and she clawed at his shirt. Would he take her in that room and kill her? "Please don't do this. Please."

He cupped the sides of her face with his hands, and his brow furrowed. "Look. I'm doing this so we can be together."

Fear constricted her throat.

Twisting the knob, he pushed the door open and backed her into the room. "Just remember how much I love you."

With a forceful hand, he spun her around.

When her gaze landed on the man standing across the room, her mouth went dry and her stomach clenched. Oh, God. She tried to back away, but Grant held her in place. Her body shook with terror, and her knees buckled. Heart pounding, she gulped ragged breaths.

Abby's own personal nightmare from seven years earlier swaggered toward her, the scent of peppermints rancid in the air. "Well, hello there, sweet cheeks."

Chapter Twenty-Eight

*W*ith a shove from behind, Abby stumbled into Mikey. His arms clamped down hard around her and drew her tight against his chest, muffling the scream of terror that ripped from her mouth. She gasped for breath, but his shirt smothered her face, and she couldn't breathe.

Oh, God! His hands. That smell of peppermint. She turned her face from side to side, trying to get air, but he held her arms so tight she couldn't move them. Twisting and bucking, she shoved and kicked at him, rocking her body in a desperate attempt to escape.

He leaned his head down and spoke into her ear. "Damn, girl, you know how to get me excited. Keep moving like that, and I'll do you right here in front of your brother." He spun her around to face her brother.

"Don't do this to me, Grant," she wailed. Her heart clattered. "Please, I'll do anything."

He said nothing, looked away.

"First things first," her captor drawled. "We need to work out the details, don't we, boss?"

With his gaze still cast away from the two of them, Grant said, "I don't need to know the details. Just do whatever you did before. And no screwing around this time like you did with the phone, trying to warn your brother."

"Oh, I'll be screwing all right. But not with a phone." Mikey rubbed his hand down Abby's arm. "And, what did you expect anyway? When a guy's tied up and held hostage, he might want to call for some assistance. How the hell was I to know you wanted *me* to help *you*? You had me trussed up like a damned pig for Sunday dinner."

She jerked her shoulder, tried to wrench free from his iron grip. But he just pulled her even closer, his hot, fetid breath on her cheek. The scent of peppermint swirled around her, and the room spun. "No, no, no, no," she sobbed.

Grant shifted from one foot to the other, glaring at Mikey. "Yeah, whatever. Just get the damn job done. I want my sister back. The one who needed me." He met Abby's gaze. "I really am sorry it had to come to this, Abs. But, I promise, you'll thank me down the road. You will."

Opening the door, he turned to leave.

"Hey, big guy," Mikey said. "What about the money you promised me?"

"It's downstairs. Twenty thousand, the amount we discussed. It should be plenty to get you started far away from here."

"That's what I'm talking about. Not the fifty I tried to get out of my tightwad bro, but it's twenty G's, baby. Just like old times." He slid his tongue up the side of Abby's face and laughed. "You and me are gonna have us a fine time. Yes, we are."

She thrashed against him, tried to elbow him in the ribs, but it was useless. His tight grip on her was unyielding. She could barely breathe let alone break free.

Her gaze fell on her brother. How could he leave her to a maniac? Sorrow tore through her chest. She'd loved him, trusted him her entire life. How could he pay this animal to...to...? "Grant, please, you can't let this happen. It won't make me need you. I will never be able to forgive you. Never."

"I'm sorry, Abby. It'll all be okay, you'll see." His hand on the doorknob, he looked back at her. "I'll be here for you when he's done."

The door shut, and the sound of the dead bolts sliding home may as well have been the sound of death. Terror wound its icy tendrils through her body and dragged a desperate scream from the depths of her soul.

Mikey's hand clamped over her mouth, effectively silencing her. "Damn, woman," he hissed into her ear. "Would you shut up a minute?"

Shocked into petrified submission, she quieted, and the clunk of Grant's boots as he descended the stairs reached her ears. A tremor resonated from her core until her entire body shook. Oh, dear God, if her brother had left her to this horror, what would he do to Ethan?

Mikey turned her to face her. "Hold still," he said in a raspy whisper. Grabbing her hands, he began to untie them.

"What are you doing?"

"Look, I didn't sign up for this shit." He tugged at the knot, his focus on her bindings. "I did my time and planned to go my own way. Next thing I know, I woke up in this room, shackled to the bed." With a last tug, he tossed the rope to the floor. He grimaced and ran a hand through his unruly hair. "What I did seven years ago, well, let's just say I was in a bad place back then. Pissed off at the whole damned world, thought I knew it all. Hell, I was so high on ecstasy and coke I don't remember most of that night."

Lord, she so did not want to be having this conversation. Not with him. But talking was better than...the other. Shaking uncontrollably, she hugged herself and whispered, "Why are you telling me this?"

"I fucked up that night. I hurt you." Mikey met her gaze straight on for the first time. "I don't expect you to ever forgive me. Hell, I'm not askin' for forgiveness, but seven years locked up gives a person a lot of time to think. I'm not the shit-ass little pissant I used to be. Despite what my little bro believes, what I let him believe, I ain't that guy. Shit, I just wanted to move on and live my life in peace." He jerked his thumb toward the door. "But your brother? He's more fucked up than I'll ever be. We're gonna have to work together if we want to get out of here alive."

Abby wanted to believe him, wanted to believe that she and Ethan might somehow survive the night. But it was too much to hope for.

"Grant's going to kill you," she said, her voice quavering.

"You think I don't know that?" he shot back and glared at her. "I've been called a lot of things, but in case you haven't noticed, sweetheart, your brother is a psychopath."

She winced. Yeah, she'd noticed. So, who did she trust? The animal who raped her seven years ago and left her for dead, or her own flesh and blood, who'd mutilated and murdered five men? She rubbed her arms in an attempt to ward of the bone-deep chill that plagued her. Averting her gaze, she looked toward the window and noticed the heavy, steel bars for the first time. God, she'd never look at her parents' cabin the same way again—if she lived.

So, her brother had imprisoned Mikey as well. Did that mean she should trust this supposed goodness he seemed to have found?

"So what's all the talk of money? Is he paying you to...?"

"Yes," he said. His brow furrowed. "But I ain't actually gonna do it. I told you I changed. I'm just playing along, tying to find a way out of this nightmare just like you. Hell, when I found myself here and Grant finally showed himself, he started going on and on about how I needed to fix you, turn you back into the needy little girl you'd been." He shrugged, and a look of disgust filled his face. "Apparently I messed you up pretty good. Again, I'm not making excuses for myself." He shook his head, his eyes filled with guilt. He dragged his gaze to hers, met her stare. "I'm sorry. Okay?"

Tears pricked Abby's eyes. Oh, God. He meant it.

"Anyway." He ran a hand through his hair and looked away, breaking the moment. "I know he has no intention of letting me leave here alive, but I plan to do everything I can to make sure I do. That plan includes you. So like it or not, we gotta work together here."

"Ethan is downstairs. Grant has him tied to the bed. I think he's going to do to him what he did to those other men. You have to help him."

"Sonofabitch!" he snarled, his brows drawing low over his eyes. "We have to hurry then. Maybe this time I'll get to be the hero. Won't that be a kick in the ass for E?"

"What are you going to do?"

"Earn my twenty grand."

She jolted, and when he stalked toward her, she stumbled back and fell on the bed. But instead of attacking her, he crossed over to a wooden chair sitting in the corner, grabbed it, and spun back around to face her. With a loud growl, he heaved the chair across the room then turned to her. "Scream!"

She needed no further prompting, letting lose a pent-up shriek. And when Mikey pivoted, grabbed the bedside lamp, and hurled it, the light grazing by her head, Abby screamed for all she was worth.

∛

Ethan struggled against the ropes that held him captive on the bed, but they didn't give any slack. His gaze shot toward the door for the thousandth time. Grant had taken Abby upstairs, and he had no idea what the sick bastard was doing to her. If rage alone could free him, he'd have been loose long ago and after that piece of shit.

The door swung open, and Grant stood in the opening.

Ethan's whole body tensed, yanking his restraints taut. He glared at the bastard and growled, "Come on, you sonofabitch. You afraid of a fair fight? Let me up, and I'll kick your psychotic ass." Sweat dripped down his face and his muscles ached, but he wanted nothing more than to get his hands on Grant. "Where is Abby, you sick fuck? What have you done with her?"

He laughed. "You know what, tough guy? If it wasn't for your interference, we wouldn't be here tonight."

He sauntered over to the satchel of tools he'd laid out on the table and ran his fingers over each knife and gadget with a lover's caress. "Abby and I would be home talking about my day over supper. You would be doing whatever it is you do in your pathetic life, and we could have all been happy. But you had to go and stick your nose into something that was none of your business. She was happy with just me until *you* came along."

"Apparently not, dumbass, or you wouldn't have started killing all her friends."

Without a word, Grant pivoted and slammed his fist into Ethan's ribcage, the power of the blow forcing an involuntary gasp from him. Taking a second punch to the gut, a shot of pain radiated through to his back and caused him to cough and fight for every breath.

"You're pretty cocky for someone in your shoes." He glanced down at Ethan's bare feet and laughed. "Or lack thereof."

Gaining control of his breath, Ethan shoved the pain to another part of his brain. He needed to focus, to keep Grant distracted until he could figure a way to get Abby and himself out of here.

"Listen, I can understand how you felt when your parents died. Mine died when I was ten. But what your uncle did to you was unfathomable."

Grant returned to perusing his instruments of torture. "My parents' deaths just made it easier for Uncle Marty. He'd been using me since I was four or five. My parents never knew." He raised his head, stared at the wall. "Well, I assume they didn't. Once my sister came along, she got all their attention. But she deserved it. She was such a beautiful baby. I knew it was my duty to protect her."

The horror of what Grant had been through sent Ethan's stomach roiling. "You must have hated him."

He blinked, his reverie broken, and turned his attention back to his tool bag. "Who? My uncle? No, I didn't hate him. But he crossed a line when he threatened Abby." He glanced over at Ethan. "Kind of like you have. Uncle Marty knew it, too. He knew as soon as he threatened her he was dead. I have to say, though, of all the kills, his was the one I took the greatest pleasure in. Until yours, that is."

Ethan gritted his teeth. He couldn't stand to listen to him any longer. He pulled on his bonds, but again made no progress. No matter how hard he tugged, the twisted duct tape didn't stretch a millimeter. Might as well have been nylon rope. "Damn it. Where the fuck is Abby?"

Grant rolled his eyes toward the ceiling and smiled. "She's being taken care of. Don't you want to know what's going to happen to you?"

"I don't give a fuck about me. Just let her go."

Grant raised a finger to his mouth and pointed upward. The sound of furniture crashing to the floor followed by Abby's screams rained down, and a cold chill washed over Ethan.

"What are you doing to her?" he demanded. His gaze rolled toward the ceiling. "Stop!"

"I'm not doing a thing to her. That's your brother's job." Grant laughed.

"Mikey?" The room spun. Nothing made sense. "What the fuck does Mikey have to do with this?"

"He's reminding her why she needs me and only me in her life. He's repeating her past. Is that brilliant or what?" He closed his eyes, and his mouth curved into a satisfied smile.

"Brilliant?" he shot back. "You're going to have to kill me. How the hell do you plan to explain that?"

Another crash resounded through the floor, drawing Ethan's focus. Feet stomped. Screams and curses filtered down from the room above. My God, what was Mikey doing to her?

Grant breathed deeply then sighed. Opening his eyes, he moved to stand directly over Ethan. Staring down, he frowned and said in a sing-song voice, "Aw, Poor Ethan and Abby. They came up here to get away for the weekend. But when my dear, sweet sister didn't answer my call, I came looking for you—after all, I know there's a murderer out there and was worried."

Something heavy slammed against the floor upstairs, interrupting Grant. They both lifted their faces toward the ceiling. Another scream, and then all became chillingly quiet above them. Ethan's gut clenched, and his breath jammed in his throat. Oh, shit. No, not....

"Huh," Grant said, his gaze returning to him. He smirked, satisfaction glittering in his eyes, and his voice changed to a lecture tone.

"I knew something was wrong, Chief Hague. But I was too late. By the time I arrived, I found my partner murdered and Abby on the floor, unconscious. I drew my gun, and while checking my sister's vitals, the perp rushed me. I had no choice but to shoot the evil bastard responsible for so many deaths." He snorted. "Nice and tidy. Too bad your own brother killed you."

"You won't get away with this, you bastard," Ethan spat. "Besides, there's a flaw to your story."

Grant raised an eyebrow. "That so?"

"Yeah." He grinned and so desperately wanted to punch the asshole in the mouth. "Mikey was in jail until this last Friday. Two murders took place before he ever got out."

Grant waved a hand, dismissing Ethan's words. "As lead investigator into the heinous murder to my partner's untimely death, I can make the evidence look like anything I want it to. Everyone will be focused on the fact that the cop-killer is dead. They'll all be relieved, and I'll be the hero." He snorted, jerking his thumb toward the door. "And the stupid bastard actually thinks he's getting paid to fix my sister. You know, I almost shot the sonofabitch before he ever made it to trial last time. Who'd have thought I'd need his services again? Ain't life funny?"

Ethan lost it. He tore against the restraints, bucked and kicked like a madman. Overwhelming frustration erupted in a cry of rage.

Across the room, Grant sat in the chair his sister had once occupied. Pressing his palms together, he brought his index fingers to his lips. Above, Abby's scream broke the silence. More thumps on the floor, and then came the shrill, repetitive screeching of mattress springs.

Grant let out a whoop of victory.

Chapter Twenty-Nine

*U*pstairs, Abby cowered on the corner of the bed, paralyzed by the sight of Michael Greene jumping up and down on the mattress. With each jostle, her stomach clenched, coiling tighter and tighter until she thought she might vomit. God, the moment was surreal. Never in her most terrifying nightmare could she have dreamt this up. Yet here he was—the embodiment of all she believed evil and also her only hope for survival. How sickeningly ironic.

Hot tears coursed down her face, and she swallowed the acid that pushed into her throat. Only the image of Ethan firmly planted in her mind saved her from a total meltdown. When the bouncing finally ended, she glanced up at the man hovering over her. Sweat rolled down the sides of his face and stained his dark green T-shirt. His long hair, damp and stringy, partially occluded his face. Mikey shoved it back, exposing a pair of dark brown eyes filled with determination.

He jumped off the bed and stood in front of her. "Gimme your hands."

Keeping her gaze locked on him, Abby held her hands out, and he retied the rope around her wrists. The scent of peppermint swirled beneath her nose, and she trembled. God, how she wanted to run. But she rooted her feet to the floor, forced herself to stand still. Everything she did to ensure the success of their ruse got her that much closer to Ethan.

"Now, when the time comes, just yank this right here, and the ropes'll loosen and you can get free." He tucked the end of the rope between her wrists. The hard candy in his mouth clicked against his teeth while he worked. "But remember to do all the other stuff we talked about first."

She nodded, unable to find words for the bizarre moment. Conspiring with the man who ruined her life? Lord above, please let this plan work.

Mikey stared at her, shook his head, and mumbled, "Not right."

Oh, please don't let him change his mind. She didn't want to think about what Grant might be doing to Ethan. She just wanted to get to him and stop her brother.

Without notice, his hand snaked out and ruffled her hair. She jerked back at the contact, her heart scrabbling with fear.

"Sorry, but...uh...you don't look like a woman who's been...." His gaze flicked to the bed and back. "Well, you know. We gotta fix that."

He reached over, ripped the sleeve of her sweater, and she yelped in surprise. She stared at the tear, the once tightly woven fibers now hanging loose and frayed. Unfixable. Abby glanced up, noticed Mikey's furrowed brow, and he shrugged. His hand came toward her again, and she stumbled back.

"Stop. I can handle this part." She twisted away from him and unbuttoned her shirt. When she buttoned it back up, she deliberately missed a few holes. Finished, she turned back, gave him a hard stare, and uttered words she'd never thought she'd willingly say. "You're going to have to hit me."

His mouth dropped open. "Oh, I don't think so. I told you, I've changed. I ain't hitting a woman."

God, was she really having this conversation? "It's going to look funny after all that banging around and furniture breaking, if I'm not marked up in a couple places."

"I said no." Mikey shoved his hands in his pockets. "Ain't no way in hell I'm hitting you."

"Well, you have to." She stared toward the door, imagined her brother entering and finding her unharmed. What would he do to Ethan then? "If Grant doesn't see—"

"Look," he said, removing one hand from his pocket and slicing the air. "If he says anything, I'll just tell him I didn't want to mess up that pretty little face of yours. That's all. It's the truth. He'll buy it."

"But how can you be sure?"

"Just look at you." He gestured toward her. "The tears, the mussed hair, your clothes. Shit, your brother's so far out there, he'll see what he wants to anyway. Won't matter about the bruises."

Relief rushed through Abby. She hadn't liked the idea when she'd come up with it, but for Ethan, she would've endured it.

"Not to mention that my brother's probably already gonna kill me just for being in here with you," he muttered. "I already got one damn psychopath on my ass. I don't need another."

"Yeah, things are kind of different when you're not jacked up on drugs, huh?" She gasped, surprised she'd said that out loud.

He glared at her, pivoted toward the door, and raised his hand.

"Wait," she said.

His shoulders sagged, and he spun toward her. "What now?"

"I know my part in the plan," she murmured. "I just wanted to—"

"Don't thank me," he growled. "I don't want any thanks. Just sit there on the edge of the bed and look like something horrible happened."

"No." She balled her hands, her fingernails digging into her palms. "Well, yes, thank you for...." God, this was harder than she'd thought. "Helping Ethan and me. But what I wanted was for you to...to...."

"Spit it out, darlin'. We're on a schedule here."

"Yes," she said in a breathy gasp. "Spit it out. Please. The mint. In your mouth."

He tilted his head, narrowed his eyes. Parting his lips, he exposed the peppermint captured between his front teeth. "This?"

She averted her eyes, studied the rag rug beneath her feet. She clenched her hands and started to shake. How could she continue to let a piece of candy rule her life after all these years? She dragged her gaze back to Mikey's face. "Yes."

The candy disappeared back into his mouth, and he cocked an eyebrow. "What's the big deal? It's a mint."

She took a deep breath and held his gaze. "It's a strong scent. One that's stayed with me for the last seven years." At the look of confusion on his face, she continued. "You had one in your mouth that night. Your face was right in mine. I couldn't get away...from you or the stench of that candy."

"Ah, yeah. Ethan mentioned that something about that."

She lowered her gaze, studied the floor. "I still have anxiety attacks when I get an unexpected whiff or even see the damn things. Irrational, I know, but there it is."

"Yeah, yeah." He spat the mint into his hand and glanced around the room. Navigating the broken furniture littered across the floor, he crossed to the bed, bent over, and dropped the candy into the partially open nightstand. He slapped his palm against the wood face, slamming the splintered drawer closed with a sharp bang.

Abby sighed, the tremors coursing through her subsiding.

"Someday you need to get over all that. I have." Straightening, he looked over at her, his expression masked. "Can we get on with it now?"

Gritting her teeth she eased down onto the corner of the bed and glared at him. *Fucking asshole.*

Mikey strode to the door and banged his fist against it three times. Moments later, sounds of the heavy bolts being thrown back vibrated the air. She lowered her chin to her chest, hunched her shoulders, and attempted to make herself small. When the door opened, she cringed.

"Got the job done," he said, his voice gruff. "Now where's my damn money?"

Grant strode to Abby and stopped on the rug, his shoes just within her limited view. When his fingers brushed her hair, she jerked away and whimpered. He leaned over, his head near hers, and she trembled.

"It's okay, Abs. I'm here for you," he whispered.

Mikey cleared his throat. "Ready whenever you are, boss."

Grant straightened. "It's downstairs."

"Fine." He strode across the room, grabbed her arm, and lifted her over his shoulder. "Lead the way."

Abby moaned, prayed she wouldn't vomit down his back. When they'd first discussed the part about how best to get her downstairs, he'd told her if he carried her, it would be easier to hide the fact that she hadn't been injured. She'd agreed, believing it prudent to keep Grant from getting too close. However, now that she hung upside down over Mikey's shoulder, she found the act more challenging than she'd first believed. She swallowed a rush of bile and forced herself to go limp. Thank God he'd gotten rid of that peppermint, otherwise, she would've hurled for sure.

Grant inhaled sharply. "Don't—"

"Hurt her?" Mikey snapped then snorted. "That train done left the station, boss. Don'tcha think?"

"I meant—"

"I know what you meant," he said, cutting her brother off again. Mikey slapped his palm against her thigh, and she yelped. "Mighty fine fuck, but her ass is getting a bit heavy. So, if you don't mind...."

"Yeah." A subtle tightness in Grant's voice belied the anger that simmered just below his businesslike façade. "Right."

Mikey hauled Abby downstairs. Between the strands of her long hair, she caught sight of her brother's shoes on the treads as he followed them. At the bottom, Mikey carried her to the bar that separated the living area from the kitchen. A single torch lamp illuminated the area, and the deep shadows of the early winter evening crawled over every surface, stealing the vibrant hues that adorned the room.

With unexpected care, he lowered her onto a stool at the kitchen bar. He brushed aside the curtain of hair that covered her face. Mouth grim, he stared down at her then flicked his gaze to the left.

Ever so slightly, Abby turned her head and spotted the knife block at the edge of the counter. The heavy walnut container sat less than an arm's length from her. Meeting Mikey's gaze, she blinked twice to let him know she understood.

"Well, there ya go, princess," he said and pivoted toward Grant. "She's just like you wanted her. So, time to pay up."

With Mikey creating a screen between her and Grant, she reached toward the block and snatched a long, narrow fillet knife. She edged the blade up her sweater sleeve, the steel cool against her skin, and cradled the handle in her palm. Biting her lower lip, she prayed their plan would work.

Mikey's head angled toward the downstairs bedroom door. "Whatcha got in there?"

"Just the last step to putting Abby back the way she was."

He glanced over his shoulder then back to the door. "Aw. You've got Ethan in there, don't you? I knew he had a thing for your sister."

Grant shifted his weight. "He's been a huge factor in her newfound desire for...something more."

"I hear you." Mikey chuckled. "Been a pain in my ass for years. Bastard helped prosecute me. With blood being thicker and all, you'd think he would've corrupted some evidence or something to help get me off. But I guess he don't see the value in family. Not like you do. Seems you and your sis got it all figured out."

"That we do."

"Hey," Mikey drawled. "What are your plans for him?"

Her brother paused as though weighing his words and said, "Slice him up. Make it so she can't look at him without revulsion."

"Hot damn!" Mikey slapped his hands together. "Now that's

something I gotta see. I'd like to slice an ear or cut off a toe for all the shit he's caused me. Tell me I'm not too late."

Grant laughed, and her stomach flipped. She squeezed her eyes closed, dread curling in her chest. *Please let Ethan be safe.*

"As a matter of fact, I was just about to get started."

At Grant's words, an icy shiver of relief coursed through Abby. Ethan was safe. For now.

"Well, I'll tell you what, boss," Mikey drawled. "You let me have a turn at him, and I'll give you back half your payment."

"Ten thousand to help cut up Ethan?"

"Hell, just for the satisfaction of watching that asshole squirm and scream, I'd give you the whole twenty Gs. 'Cept I need some money for relocation proposes. You know, to set up shop."

Grant laughed. "Deal."

Mikey reached out and shook his hand. Abby stared in horror, the sight of two devils sealing a contract all but sent her over the edge. If she hadn't known one of them planned to rescue the love of her life, she might've fainted right then.

"One sec," Mikey said and rounded toward her.

She cringed and braced for the inevitable. Grabbing her arm, he lifted her over his shoulder again, and she moaned. She clenched her jaw, determined to do whatever necessary to get to Ethan.

Mikey swung back toward Grant and said, "Wouldn't want your sister to miss the show."

"No, we wouldn't," her brother said.

The sound of the bedroom door creaking open filled Abby's ears. She held her breath and prayed everything would work the way Mikey had promised.

As he carried her toward the room where Ethan lay captive on the bed, she knew her time had become limited. Taking great care, she removed the knife she'd hidden up her sweater sleeve. Inch by inch it slid free. However, the combination of hanging upside down along with Mikey's jaunty stride disoriented her.

The blade slipped.

Shit! Terror streaked through her, and she fumbled for the only weapon of defense she and Mikey had. Catching it on the very ends her fingertips, she clutched the handle as though it were a priceless treasure.

Tears welled in her eyes, and she blinked them back. Too close.

Abby pulled up the tail of his sweaty T-shirt, and slipped the knife through the two belt loops on the back of his jeans.

Chapter Thirty

*E*than worked feverishly at his restraints. The muscles in his arms, legs, and abdomen burned from his constant struggles, but nothing helped. All he'd succeeded in doing was weakening himself, not the ties that bound him to the bed. He wouldn't give up, though. One way or the other he would get Abby and himself out of there.

He tried to block his mind from what might have happened upstairs. The noise had stopped, and now, an unsettling silence commenced. Was his brother really up there with Abby, or had Grant told him that to keep him off balance? And if it wasn't Mikey, then who the hell had made all that noise? He growled and jerked at his bonds. Shit, anybody could be up there with her. He didn't know. But if it was his half-brother, Ethan was afraid of what he might do to her.

At one of his first visits after his half-brother's incarceration, Mikey had sworn he'd changed. That he wasn't the same angry man who'd gotten himself into trouble. But that had been early on, and their interactions had tapered off. The last visit before his release his half-brother had reverted to his old ways, trying to push every button Ethan had.

Anger pulsed through him. Damn it, he'd wanted so much to believe his brother had dried out, redeemed himself. That it truly had been anger and drugs fueling Mikey's trouble with the law. But after the sounds he'd heard from the room above, he had no idea what to believe anymore.

He ground his teeth and growled, unable to wrap his mind around the possibility of his brother being in cahoots with a murderer. Mikey wasn't a killer. Was he?

The sound of voices reached him from outside the room. He ceased struggling, strained to hear the words being spoken, but between the blood pulsing in his ears and the harsh rasping of his breath, he couldn't understand the murmurs.

The door flew open with a bang. Mikey entered with Abby slung over his shoulder.

Oh, shit. It was him. He'd been upstairs with her the entire time. Through all of it. The crashing. The banging. The screaming.

The bed springs squeaking.

Bile gorged Ethan's throat.

Oh, God.

Mikey raised his head, and their gazes met, locked. Ethan searched his brother's face, hoping to find something, anything that would tell him his deepest fears hadn't just been realized.

Mikey stared back at him. Silently, he mouthed, *she's okay,* and rolled his eyes toward Abby. Ethan flinched with comprehension. His heartbeat kicked up a notch. Good God, could he really be on their side?

He crossed the room and lowered her into the chair she'd previously occupied. Her shirt was torn and mis-buttoned, eyes swollen and red, and her hair a tangled mess. Ethan sought her gaze, catching the brief flash of intense determination and a quick blink of her lids. Then her eyes glazed, and she stared at the floor.

His mind raced. Had he really seen signs from both of them that they were working together? He sent up a silent prayer.

The sound of the door slamming brought Ethan's gaze to Grant, where he stood with his hand still pressed against the paneled oak slab. He stared at his sister with an intense—and if

Ethan wasn't mistaken—confused expression on his face.

He glanced at Abby, who remained immobile and appeared subdued. His heart stuttered. Could Grant see through her act? Did he plan to hurt her further? Ethan couldn't let that happen. He yanked arms and legs against his restraints as far as the tape would allow.

"You sonofabitch. I'll fucking kill you for this. Do you hear me? I'll fucking kill you!"

Grant turned his attention to him and laughed. "I don't think you're in any position to follow through on your meaningless threats, partner." He sauntered over to the bed. Whipping out his hand, he clamped down on Ethan's crotch with a viselike grip. "Besides, you don't have the balls. Well, you won't in a few minutes anyway."

The sadistic bastard squeezed harder and twisted, sending more pain than he'd ever experienced spiraling up his spine and into his abdomen. A surge of nausea consumed him, and black spots danced before his eyes. The bitter acidic contents of his stomach gushed into his mouth, and he gagged.

With enormous effort, he gathered the remaining foul saliva in his mouth and spat it into Grant's face. Through gritted teeth, he ground out, "Fuck you."

Grant released him, wiped his face, and then rounded on Ethan with three viscous blows to the gut. The attack overcame his self-control, and he turned his head, puking over the side of the narrow bed while gasping for air. The pain seizing his body rendered him lightheaded. He shook his head, the sound of Abby screaming his name a distant echo.

His stomach emptied, and he lolled his head in her direction, but Mikey had moved in front of her, blocking his view.

"Hey, boss man," Mikey said, his brows drawn in concern. "Thought you were gonna let me have a turn at him. You keep that up, there won't be nothing left."

Grant pivoted to eye Mikey. "You just stay over there right now. There will be time for you later." He leaned over the satchel of knives and picked out the surgical blade. As he straightened, a sadistic grin warped his face, and he spun back to Mikey. "On second thought, bring Abby over here. I want her to watch this."

"No," Ethan said and coughed, spitting the remnants of bile from his mouth. "You leave her out of this."

Grant laughed. "No. She needs to see the final word in my message to her, so she'll never forget."

"Hey, big man," Michael said from the other side of the bed. He held her next to him. "You didn't say nothing about no message. You been leaving notes or something?"

"Words," Grant said, his voice resonating with satisfaction. "Each man that drew my sister away from me earned a word cut into his chest."

Mikey's eyebrows shot up. "That so? This I gotta see." He yanked her closer to the bed. "What we carving here, boss?"

Grant narrowed his eyes, the corner of his mouth twitching. "The message so far is 'You Are Mine For.'"

"Well, don't leave me in suspense, man. What's the rest of it?"

He looked at Abby, he eyes softening. "Ever. You are mine forever."

She quivered, and rage engulfed Ethan.

"Sonofabitch!" He glared at Grant. "I promise you, I will get free, and I will send you straight to hell where you belong."

"Sure you will." He smirked. "Now, hold still. This might sting a bit."

Ethan had known it would come this. Had known the moment Grant rolled open that damn butcher's bag that he'd intended to cut him. Adrenaline dumped into his system, making his heart pound and shoving the pain and nausea aside.

The evil bastard lowered the blade, resting it high on Ethan's pectoral. The blade glinted in the overhead light.

Ethan tensed, bracing for what would come next. However, when the knife pierced his flesh and slipped down into his chest, he realized he'd been nowhere near prepared for the intensity. He squeezed his eyes shut and bit down on the scream that welled in his throat. An excruciating burn danced along his nerve endings, molten fire splitting his skin apart.

Oh, God. Slowly. So fucking slowly, Grant drew the knife down Ethan's chest in a straight line.

Icy sweat beaded on his forehead, dripped down his face. He gritted his teeth and tried to block out the sound of Abby's screams. "Ethan! Oh, my God!"

Unable to hold back any longer, he released a strangled yell. The burning eased up, but he knew the torture was far from finished. When he opened his eyes, he stared down at the wound in his chest. A line of crimson welled atop his skin, thick droplets coursing off the edges.

Grant repositioned the knife, preparing to carve the next line.

Ice filled Abby's veins at the sight of blood flowing from where Grant had cut Ethan. Her brother had done this—all of this—because of her. She had to stop him. She had to save Ethan.

With a sharp squeeze to her arm, Mikey released her. He strode around the foot of the bed, his hand retrieving the knife she'd slipped through his belt loops. "Wait a minute there, boss. Let me get some of that action."

Grant hesitated, and Mikey pulled out the knife. His arm swung around, his aim for her brother's ribs, but Grant swiveled at the last second. His eyes widened.

"Bastard!" he roared. Bright crimson bloomed on the side of his shirt.

Abby's breath caught. Oh, God. Mikey had missed. The blade had only sliced through her brother's side.

Grant swung around, aiming his knife toward Mikey's stomach. But with a sharp swipe of his arm, he blocked the jab and sent the blade flying from her brother's hand. Mikey came at him again, arcing underhand, but he dodged and kicked. Caught off-guard, Mikey sprawled, managing to latch on to Grant's calf, dragging them both to the floor.

Abby didn't hesitate. Grasping the end of the rope between her teeth, she yanked her hands and loosened the knot constricting her wrists. She jerked against her binding until she freed one hand and then the other. Heart pounding, she glanced up and found Ethan's gaze locked on her, hope creasing his brow.

She leapt onto the bed and reached toward the bag on the bedside table. Mother have mercy, so many knives. Had Grant used them all?

She shoved the thought aside, and grabbed a serrated blade and sawed through the rope of duct tape that held one of Ethan's hands above his head. Giving the knife to him so he could cut his other binding, she grabbed another from the bag. Spinning around, she crawled to the foot of the bed and went to work on freeing his feet.

On the floor beside her, Mikey and Grant struggled to gain control of the kitchen knife. Her brother had somehow managed to apprehend the blade from Mikey and, straddling his opponent, her brother shoved the point down toward Mikey's face.

Mikey growled and shoved back. "You ain't gonna win this one, boss," he ground out. "Ain't no way."

Grant released a strained laugh. "We'll see about that."

Abby released Ethan's foot and scrambled to release the other. She sucked in air, one harsh, short breath after another. *Gotta hurry, or he'll get Ethan.*

From the corner of her eye, she caught movement. Ethan had finished freeing his arms and sat up. Swiveling toward the men fighting on the floor, he rammed his heel into her brother's side. The pair rolled, this time with Mikey ending on top.

Abby sawed the duct tape with quick strokes, the blade gnawing at the tightly twisted braid. Just before she'd finished, Ethan jerked his leg and broke the last of the binding. She scurried from the bed, giving him the room he needed to maneuver. But as she spun around, her heart stuttered.

Grant's knuckles smashed into Mikey's gaunt jaw, the sickening *smack* resounding through the room. The guy fell back, and her brother scooted free. The two men hastened to their feet in preparation for another round, but Grant reached behind to his waistband and pulled a small pistol from his back holster.

The name Glock rang in Abby's mind. She remembered her brother saying that the subcompact might appear small, but it packed a deadly punch. The perfect backup weapon.

Mikey squeezed the knife handle then released it, letting it drop to the floor with a clatter. He held up his hands. "Aw now, boss, that just ain't playing fair."

A tight smile appeared on her brother's mouth, and he shuffled to the side, keeping both Mikey and Ethan in his sights. "Sure it is. Especially when it means I'm about to get rid of the biggest pain in my ass." He swung the gun toward Ethan.

"No!" Abby screamed.

Mikey lunged. Grant squeezed the trigger. The report from the pistol erupted a sharp, explosive crack.

"Sonofa...." He glanced down at his chest and staggered back.

Ethan caught his half-brother, toppled back on the bed with him. "Mikey."

She jerked into action. Pivoting toward the twin bed behind her, she grabbed the pillow and ripped the case from it. "Here," she said and handed the musty material to Ethan.

Blood leaked from the hole in Mikey's chest. The crimson flow streaked down his green shirt, staining it black. Concern flooded Ethan's face while he wadded the pillowcase and pressed it to the wound.

The gun fired again.

Abby jolted and cringed at the edge of the bed, her ears ringing from the volatile report. She glanced at Grant, whose gaze remained fixed on Mikey. Staring down, she found a second stain growing on his shirt, this one just above his hip. *Oh, my God.*

"Mikey!" Ethan yelled and clutched his brother.

A twisted and pain-filled grin spread across the dying man's face. He looked up at his brother, his eyes glazed with agony. His grip tightened on Ethan's arm, and he said, "See you around, E."

"No, wait!" Ethan barked.

His hand relaxed and slipped from his brother's arm to fall limply to the bed.

"Mikey!"

Abby lifted her fingers to her lips to stifle a sob. The monster that had devastated her life and haunted her dreams for the last seven years lay lifeless on the narrow bed. But for her, Mikey's death brought no comfort. And to watch her brother pull the trigger? She bit her lip.

A growl erupted from Ethan and, in a swift stroke, he hurled the knife he'd used to free himself toward Grant. The blade stuck him in the shoulder, and he staggered back. Leaping from the bed, Ethan slammed into her brother, both of them crashing against the wall. The impact must have loosened his grip on the pistol because it flew from his hand and skittered across the floor.

She trembled as she watched the two men fight.

Grant shoved Ethan back, and with a snarl, yanked the knife from his shoulder. Blood coated the end of the blade, and her brother held his arm against his side, favoring it. Clutching the handle, he pointed the knife at him.

"I'm done with you, partner."

"Yeah?" Ethan said and shuffled to the side as though searching for a better angle of attack. "I was going to say the same to you."

Grant laughed then lunged, the knife slicing Ethan's abdomen.

A thin line of blood welled from the cut, and Abby's stomach twisted. Edging to the foot of the bed, she crouched and scanned the floor for the gun, while keeping her attention on the fight.

Ethan hissed through gritted teeth, the sound drawing her attention. "But I am going to keep my promise." He maneuvered left as though testing Grant's agility. "I'm going to send you straight to Hell." Feinting right, he shifted left and lunged for the knife.

Her brother grabbed Ethan's arm and yanked, twisting it behind his back. Crossing his other arm over his partner's chest, he positioned the knife against Ethan's neck.

"We'll see who gets to Hell first," Grant rasped.

Frantic, Abby glanced down and spotted the pistol beneath the edge of the bed. Fingers curling around cold metal, she grasped the weapon and jumped to her feet. Hands tight on the Glock's handgrip, she aimed the business end toward her brother.

Grant's eyes widened. "Abby, what are you doing?"

"Pull the trigger, Abby," Ethan said.

"Shut up!" He pressed the knife into Ethan's skin, and blood trickled over the blade.

Her heart skipped a beat. Her hands shook, the muzzle of the gun wavering in the air.

Ethan's gaze remained locked on her, his eyes shining with a mix of hope and love. "I know it's hard, sweetie, but—"

"I said...." Grant dragged the knife further, and blood spilled down Ethan's neck, discoloring his shirt.

Panic seized Abby, and an anguished wail pushed up from the depths of her soul. She squeezed the trigger.

Chapter Thirty-One

The explosive pop of the gun reverberated through the small room, roaring in Ethan's ears. Grant jerked, his body stiffening. The knife dug deeper into his neck, and he gritted his teeth against the fiery pain. Shit, even shot, the bastard intended to take him with him.

A moment later, Grant's vigorous hold relaxed. Knees buckling, he sagged against Ethan, and dragged the knife across his exposed body. The honed blade lanced open his neck, chest, and side before slipping from Grant's grip and clattering to the floor.

Ethan bit back a scream. Rivulets of warm blood streamed over his skin. *Oh, shit, that hurt like hell.*

Staggering under the heavy burden of Grant's body, Ethan lowered him to the floor and kicked the knife away. He stared down at his partner, seeing the gash in his neck and the deep scarlet fluid that leaked from the hole.

Grant's breathing stuttered, his chest wracking sporadically as he fought to get air. He gazed up with anxious eyes, and his mouth worked, emitting whispery sounds amidst wet gurgles.

He wasn't dead yet, but he didn't have long. Blood poured from the wound, and with the rhythmic surge of red, it appeared the bullet had nicked his carotid artery. Seconds remained.

Ethan glanced over at Abby. She stood poised in the same position. Both hands remained on the gun, the barrel pointed in his direction. Her eyes wide, unblinking, her hands shaking.

"Abby, honey, it's over," he said and went to her. Placing his hand on her shoulder, he gently ran his palm down her arm to where her fingers strangled the pistol's grip. When he grasped the Glock, she relinquished the gun to him, and he shoved it in his waistband.

Cupping her face with his hands, he forced her to look at him. "It's over."

Her gaze locked with his, and the dam broke. Her lips quivered, and her eyes welled with tears. She threw her arms around him as sobs shook her body. Ethan held her tight and whispered words of comfort in her ear, the fragility of their embrace not lost on him. If she hadn't pulled that trigger, no doubt he'd be dead right now. But what she'd done would have emotional consequences for her. He peered over at Grant, knowing if he was still alive, she needed to say her piece.

"Honey, he doesn't have long."

She pulled back to look up at him. "He's not dead?"

"Not yet. But soon. He can't hurt you anymore."

She drew back, and he saw where his blood had drenched the front of her sweater. But she didn't appear to notice. Stepping from his embrace, she stumbled over to her brother and fell to her knees at his side. Reaching down, she took his hand.

Grant opened his eyes and stared up at her. He opened his mouth, but no words came out. Tears poured down her face.

Ethan's heart broke for her. He knelt behind her and laid his hand on her shoulder.

She brought her brother's hand up to her heart. "I'm so sorry for what you went through. I wish you knew how much I truly love you."

His eyes closed then opened again, his anguished gaze set on Abby.

"I forgive you."

He inhaled a raspy breath and released a sigh, his eyelids fluttering. The last of Grant Montgomery's energy appeared to ebb as his brow smoothed, and his grip on her hand slackened.

He was gone.

Ethan pulled her up, drew her away from her brother's body. The small effort caused his head to spin, and he swayed. Abby's attention shifted from her brother back to him.

"Oh! All this blood, the cuts."

She hauled him over to the other bed and forced him to sit, which took little effort on her part since he suddenly found it very difficult to stay upright.

"I'm fine. Just a little dizzy is all."

She grabbed a sheet and ripped a strip free. Ethan reached out and placed his hand on hers.

"Abby."

She paused and looked at him, her eyes so large, so full of sadness that his heart ached for her. For her pain. For having a sick, monstrous brother. For having to pull the damned trigger. God, for everything.

"Come sit."

"I need to get that bleeding stopped."

"No." He pulled her down beside him and twisted to face her, clenching his jaw against the pain. "I need to make sure you're okay. My brother, he didn't...he didn't hurt you, did he?"

She peered down at her ripped clothes. "No, this time he was as much a victim in all this as we were. He never laid a hand on me. He saved our lives."

He glanced over at Mikey's prone, unmoving body and a stab of pain lanced in his chest. They'd never had a normal sibling relationship. He'd always believed there would be more time, and now time had run out.

Abby squeezed his hand. "You know, above all else, I think Mikey wanted your respect. He loved you."

"Someday, you're gonna have to tell me what you two talked about." He looked at her and frowned. "It must have been so hard for you, being locked in that room with him."

She shook her head, tears streaming over her cheeks. "Not as hard as wondering what was happening to you. How can you ever forgive me for what my brother has done? What he did to you, to those other men. God, Ethan, those men were my friends."

He cupped her face in his hands and swiped away the tears. "Oh, honey, there's nothing to forgive. Grant did those things, not you. Something went wrong inside him a long time ago, and there's nothing you or anyone else could've done to change that."

She nodded, but the tears kept coming. "Look at you," she said between sobs. "He hurt you so much, and I couldn't stop him."

"But you did stop him." He pulled her close, holding her tight. "You saved my life."

"I need to stop the bleeding, Ethan," she mumbled against his chest.

He set her back just far enough to look her in the eyes. "And I need to tell you how much I love you."

"Oh, you fool. I know that."

Without warning, the front door crashed open. He jolted and reached for the Glock at the back of his waistband. But when Will Donovan rushed into the cabin with gun drawn, followed by Chief Hague and Officer Moore, his shoulders sagged with relief. The cavalry had arrived.

"In here," Ethan called. "The fun's all over. What the hell took you so long?"

Will yelled an all clear over his shoulder, holstered his gun, and strode into the bedroom, stopping short. He grimaced. "Jesus, man. You look like one of the Japanese Steakhouse guys went all crazy on your ass." Pivoting, he shouted out the door, "Officer Hanson, get those paramedics in here, now!"

He tried to force a smile, but his face had become numb and seemed disconnected from his body. And when he stared at his friend from Quantico, he realized the edges of his vision had darkened. *Crap, I've come this far. Don't let me pass out now.* Swallowing, he managed some words. "Will, this is Abby, the love of my life."

"Hi, Abby, nice to meet you. Sorry it has to be under these circumstances." His gaze dipped to her sweater. "You're covered in blood. Where are you hurt?"

"Oh, no, it's not mine. It's all Ethan's."

"Hey, we've got a pulse over here with Ethan's brother," Chief Hague shouted.

Ethan jumped up off the bed, but a wave of lightheadedness engulfed him, and his knees buckled. He would have hit the floor had Will and Abby not grabbed him and helped him back to the bed.

"Where in the hell are those paramedics?" Will yelled.

"I'm fine," he said. The darkening edges of his vision increased. "Help my brother."

"Oh no, pal, you're not fine. You're hanging on by a thread. And I don't feel like donating blood here in this shack."

No sooner had the words left Will's mouth than two paramedics rushed into the cabin. Ethan tried to squeeze Abby's hand, but he couldn't. Damn it. His fingers had numbed. He looked toward Will. "I guess you won't...have to make...."

"Ethan?" Her voice floated to him from somewhere far away.

"That...."

"Ethan!" Will grabbed Ethan's shoulder, gave him a shake. "Medic!"

"Donation."

"I'll do whatever's needed," Will said. "Stay with me, buddy."

Everything grew darker. Shit. *Cuts too deep. Too much blood. I'm not going to....* He blinked, forced his eyes to focus on Abby, but his vision had dimmed. Dark shadows encroached on her beautiful face. He had to tell her one last time.

"I...love...."

Chapter Thirty-Two

*E*than woke to the rhythmic sound of electronic beeping—the same sound a garbage truck emits when backing up. Beyond that, voices murmured, the words unintelligible. Little by little, he pieced together his surroundings. And thankfully, he wasn't in the back of a dump truck. However, he did lie on a mattress that could've easily doubled for a door, and his nose burned with the sharp scent of antiseptic.

Abby! His hand jerked, needing to feel the warmth of her touch.

But he couldn't find her. Curling his fingers against the starched sheet, he remembered the knife. The gun. The blade slicing through his skin. Damn, he must've passed out at the cabin from blood loss, and they'd brought him to the hospital. How long had he been unconscious?

He pried his eyes open, the act more difficult than it should have been. What kind of drugs had they pumped into him? Forcing his head to turn toward the voices, he squinted, attempting to determine who spoke. As his vision cleared, he realized the murmurs came from Abby and Will, who stood in the corner of the room whispering to each other.

Seeing her healthy and whole brought a rush of relief through him. *Thank God she's all right.* Ethan opened his mouth to speak, but only a croak came out. Christ, his tongue was stuck to the roof of his mouth.

She glanced in his direction and, obviously realizing he'd awakened, rushed across the room to the side of his bed. "Oh, Ethan, you're awake." She grabbed a cup with a straw in it and brought it to his mouth.

Water had never tasted so good.

"Hey, beautiful." With the water lubricating his mouth and throat the words came out much easier. "Don't go getting too comfortable with that guy over there. He can sweet talk candy from a baby. I don't want to have to kick his ass."

Will laughed and strode toward his bed. "I'm not too worried about you kicking anyone's ass for a while, big guy." He put his arm around Abby. "But, you have nothing to worry about here. I pulled out every line I've ever used—the no-fail, get-the-girl-every-time, Donovan come-ons—and she still insists she only has eyes for you." He squeezed her shoulder and dropped his arm back to his side. "There's no accounting for taste."

She shook her head. "Don't you listen to him. He did no such thing." She sat in the chair next to his bed and took his hand. "I can see why you consider him such a good friend. He hasn't left this hospital the entire time."

Ethan relaxed even more at her touch, the warmth of her fingers twined with his grounding him. He hated hospitals and couldn't wait to get out of this one. A couple more hours and he would demand to be discharged.

"What, a half hour of his time and he's already a saint in your book?" He scowled at Will, but couldn't hide the smile on his face. "I'm keeping my eye on you."

"Uh, Ethan." Abby tightened her hold on his hand. "You've been here two days."

For a moment the room spun. He tried to sit up, but grinding pain in his arm stopped him. "Two days? What the hell are you talking about?"

"You lost a lot of blood at the cabin and went unconscious." She paused to give him another sip of water. "They called it a class three hemorrhage, which means you were down around forty percent of your normal blood volume. You had to have a transfusion." She glanced over at Will. "Will and Officer Moore donated."

"And don't think I'm not going to add that to the ever growing list of things you owe me," Will said and pointed toward the bandages that swathed Ethan's bicep. "You also needed surgery on that arm to repair a couple severed tendons."

She ran her fingers through the hair by his ear. "They kept you sedated most of the first twenty-four hours. You woke a couple times in the night, but they said you wouldn't remember."

"I tried getting your girl to go lie down in another room, but she wouldn't leave you." Will gestured across the room. "We ended up sleeping in the chairs here. I'm just glad I could be here for you two."

His stomach clenched as he tried to wrap his mind around everything. He'd come damn close to buying the farm—twice. Abby had pulled the trigger that had ended the whole ordeal, but if Michael hadn't jumped in front of Grant's gun....

Oh, shit. He looked at the woman he loved and his best friend. "Mikey?"

Her brow furrowed, and she glanced at Will.

"I'm sorry, pal," Will said. His mouth thinned into a grimace, and he shook his head. "He didn't make it. He coded on the way to the hospital, and they weren't able to resuscitate him." He shoved his hands in his pockets. "I really am sorry. But from what she told me, he came through in the end. Maybe he could've been the man you'd always hoped for."

"Yeah, maybe." Ethan swallowed, looked toward the window. "Guess I'll never know."

"He saved our lives." She stood, leaned over him, and kissed his cheek. "I may never be able to forgive what he did to me, but he proved he wasn't that man anymore, you know." She smoothed back his hair from his forehead. "I have to go make a quick call to Chief Hague. I promised to contact him as soon as you woke. The whole station has been waiting for word. Be right back."

The door closed behind her with a sharp click. Will sat in the chair next to Ethan's bed.

"That's one hell of a woman you've got there."

"I know." He glanced at his friend. "Tell me, how has she been handling Grant's death?"

"Like a trooper. She gave her statement but hasn't talked about it since. I tried to get her to discuss it, but frankly all her energy has been focused on you." He ran a hand over his chin. "She's strong, but she's going to need to get it out soon."

Ethan nodded. "Thank you. For everything. For finding us, for staying with her. I meant what I said, I owe you, big time."

"Don't worry, I'll find a way for you to repay me." He laughed.

When Abby returned, Will stood and strode to the door. He pulled it partially open and said, "Listen, you two. I'm gonna go find a hotel and sleep for a day. I'll check back in with you tomorrow."

"Wait." Ethan said. "Go to my house. Abby can give you the key and security code. No sense in paying for a room."

"Okay," he said and released the door. "I'll take you up on that."

She retrieved the key and code from her purse and handed them to Will.

"When do you have to head back to Quantico?" Ethan said. "I thought you had an open case."

"I've got a day or two." Will's eyebrows drew down, and he clenched his jaw. He gave Ethan a hard stare. "Frankly, I need the break to clear my head. This guy I'm up against is a bad one. He's got me at a loss as to where to turn next." He shook his head, opening the door again.

"You want to talk about it?"

Will paused for a moment. "Yeah, I might, but not tonight." He glanced at Abby then back to Ethan. "Right now, you and your girl need some time, and I need some sleep. I'll check in with you tomorrow. Later."

The door clicked shut behind him, and Abby crossed to Ethan's bed. "That's a good man. I'll be forever grateful to him for everything he's done for us."

She fussed with the sheets and blankets that covered him. She smoothed them, but when she lifted her hand, it trembled. He reached out and grasped her fingers. Her shoulders hunched, and she released a long, shaky sigh.

"I was so scared for you," she whispered. "I thought I'd lost you."

Fatigue washed over him, a wave that threatened to leach what little energy he had left.

"Never," he said in a gravelly voice. "We went through a lot in that damn cabin and came through it in one piece." He glanced at the numerous stitches and bandages that plastered his body. "Mostly. You will never lose me." He slid as far over in the bed as he could and patted the bed with his good arm. He wanted nothing more than to hold the woman he loved. "Come lie down with me. I need to feel you next to me."

She crawled onto the bed and curled up against to him, resting her cheek on his chest. Wrapping his good arm around her, he kissed the top of her head and savored the warmth of her body. They would have to talk about all that had happened, but right now they needed time together. Time to be close. To relish the warmth of their embrace. To appreciate the depth of their love.

Chapter Thirty-Three

*E*than stood next to his SUV and breathed in the crisp cold air. He'd been out of the hospital four hours and still couldn't get enough fresh air. Skirting around the front of the truck, he opened the door for Abby and offered her his good arm to help her out.

While elated at being out of the hospital, today wasn't one of joy. They'd decided to have Grant and Mikey's services together. In light of what happened, they'd forgone the church services and settled on the inurnments at the Red River Cemetery.

Richard Kingston, the funeral director, had met with them in the hospital and discussed what they wanted for their brothers. Neither man had ever been overly religious. Whatever beliefs Mikey had, he'd kept to himself. And Grant? Well, Abby still wasn't talking about him. So, in the end, they'd decided a simple burial with a few words by the funeral director would be a sufficient end to this chapter of their lives.

Ethan would have always wondered what Michael could have done for himself if he'd been given that second chance. But after deep reflection while lying in the hospital, he chose to believe what Will and Abby had told him—Mikey had proven himself. But Ethan would forever grieve the potential his brother had held in his sights.

He had phoned Ever, but his sister hadn't been as forgiving. After a short conversation, she told him she would've come for Ethan's sake, but she couldn't get away from the dig she was on. When he hung up, he'd known she'd been honest with him. Unlike his deceased brother, Ever had never let him down. If she could've stood by his side at the gravesite, she would have.

With a sad smile on her lips, Abby took Ethan's arm and traversed the freshly shoveled path to the area where their brothers would be buried. Icy slush crunched beneath their feet. He squeezed her hand, offering what condolence he could. All these years, she'd had no idea her brother had been a psychotic killer, and today she would bury him.

As they crested the rise, she paused and glanced up at him, her eyes brimming with sadness. "It looks like they managed to...."

"Yes," he said. He saw that the two mounds of frozen soil next to the graves had each been covered with a bright green swathe of artificial grass, the color a brilliant contrast against the surrounding snow. "The grave digger is a friend. I explained the situation, and he offered to prepare everything, so we wouldn't have to postpone till warmer weather."

She squeezed his hand, her gaze turning toward the twin sites. With a nod, she said, "I really appreciate that. Make sure he knows."

"I will."

He pulled her closer. He didn't know exactly when Abby would break, but it would happen soon. He urged her forward, but voices from behind caused them to turn.

"Oh," She gasped, and she covered her mouth with her hand.

Tremors of surprise coursed through Ethan. Roughly thirty people treaded up the path toward them. Will Donovan headed the group, with Chief Hague, Officers Moore and Hanson, Gary, Steve, and the rest of the Red River Police Department on his heels. Behind them, many of Abby's co-workers from the hospital strode up the hill, and among them, he caught sight of

Joann Barker, the leader of Abby's therapy group.

She tightened her grip on his arm. "What are they all doing here?"

"My guess is they're here to support us."

"But the things my brother did...." Tears formed in her eyes. "How could anyone want to mourn his passing?"

He pulled her into his arms and held her tight. "They're our friends. They're showing us they believe in us, and right or wrong, they understand our loss. That's what friends do."

At the gravesite, Ethan's and Abby's friends surrounded them one by one until a ring formed around them. With everyone in place, Mr. Kingston said a few words about death and loss and those left behind to handle the burden. He asked if anyone wanted to speak, and Will stepped up.

"Ethan, Abby. The people gathered today are here for many reasons. Friendship, community, forgiveness, healing, and love. The fact that you two are standing here today is a true testament to the word love." Will glanced down at the caskets as though gathering his thoughts. When he raised his head, he said, "Ethan, your brother loved you and ultimately gave up his life for you. Abby, in his own way, Grant loved you. And, while no one can ever begin to understand what drove him to do the things he did, he was still your brother, and you lost him." He gestured toward the circle of friends around them. "We all just want you to know that we can help shoulder your burdens. Every one of us will stand up and say we are proud to call you two friends. We just wanted you to know that."

A tear slid over Abby's cheek, and she whispered, "Thank you."

Ethan swallowed, tightening his hold on her, and found himself unable to utter a word. Instead, he gave his friend a nod, knowing Will would know his appreciation.

Mr. Kingston asked if anyone else wanted to speak. When no one did, he nodded and asked that they all recite the 23rd Psalm. In unison, all spoke:

The Lord is my shepherd; I shall not be in want.
He makes me lie down in green pastures;
he leads me beside quiet waters, he restores my soul.
He guides me in paths of righteousness for his name's sake.
Even though I walk through the valley of the shadow of death,
I will fear no evil, for you are with me.
Your rod and your staff, they comfort me.
You prepare a table before me in the presence of my enemies.
You anoint my head with oil; my cup overflows.
Surely goodness and love will follow me all the days of my life,
and I will dwell in the house of the Lord
Forever.

Mr. Kingston concluded the service, and Abby and Ethan met with everyone in the parking lot, shaking their hands, hugging them, and thanking each person for coming.

When only Will remained, he came to Abby, embraced her, and said, "You take care of my friend here. He needs all the help he can get, and if you ever figure out you're too good for him, you have my number." He kissed her on the cheek and stepped over to Ethan.

"My arm might be all messed up, but I can still kick your ass." He grinned and gave Will a one-arm bear hug, pounding several hearty pats on his back. "By the way, I already know she's too good for me, but I'm not giving her up. Go find your own woman."

"If only," Will said.

"Seriously, man. Thanks for coming, and what you said meant a lot to us. Can you stick around for a few days?"

"No, I should've been out of here hours ago." His eyes darkened. Running a hand over his jaw, he said, "They've found another body, so I've got to get back. Apparently, this guy left a message for me. If I'm not back by tomorrow, another girl dies. I just can't get a handle on this one, Ethan. For some reason, it's personal for him, and I have no clue yet as to why." Will jammed his hands in his pockets.

"You'll get him. I've no doubts. If you need someone to bounce ideas off of, give me a call."

"Count on it." Will hugged them both again, gave an extra peck to Abby's cheek, and left.

Exhausted from the day's events, Ethan sighed and faced her. "Well, what say, woman? Home?"

She squeezed his hand, the shadows beneath her eyes a testament to all she'd been through. When her gaze met his, a soft smile filled with love curved her lips. "Oh, yes!"

ᘓ

Once back home, he set logs and started the fire while Abby curled up on the couch and watched. She hadn't spoken on the drive home, and he'd decided now was as good a time as any to discuss the horror they'd endured. With the fire roaring, he sat on the couch next to her and pulled her onto his lap.

"Okay, talk."

Her eyebrows knitted. "What do you mean?"

"Grant. You haven't talked about what happened." Gently, he brushed a lock of hair behind her ear. "You need to. *We* need to."

Abby stiffened, pulled away from him. "What is there to say? I'll never understand why he did what he did. I guess if I got all psychological, I could trace it back to our uncle, but—"

"That's not what I'm talking about. You haven't talked about having to pull that trigger."

"Oh, Jesus, Ethan. What am I supposed to say?" She crossed her arms, hugging herself, and stared him straight in the eyes. "It was you or him. I chose you."

He met her gaze. She'd said exactly what he'd expected her to say, and now he had to ask the question he feared most. "Are you sorry you did that?"

"I'm sorry I had to make that choice," she said without hesitation. "But I'll never be sorry for the choice I made. My brother had become something evil. He was no longer the man I knew and loved. You, on the other hand, are the man I love. If I had to do it again, I would do it the same way every time." She moved her hands to her lap, and stared down while she picked at her thumbnail. "Does it hurt? Yes. Do I ache for the brother I lost, the one I used to know? Yes. Yet, I still wouldn't change my actions." Raising her head, she gazed at him with clear eyes, her expression open and honest. "I love you."

Ethan's heart thumped double-time, banging against his sternum. He hadn't been prepared for all that. He'd been prepared for tears and damning fate and maybe even her blaming him. But she was strong, stronger than he'd ever imagined she could be.

"And I love you. More than any words could ever explain. You've seen me at my worst, my most vulnerable moment, and it should shame me. But it only makes me feel closer to you." He reached out, cupped her face, and locked his gaze on hers to make sure she heard every word he said. "I love you, Abby Montgomery. I want to grow old with you, share every moment of my life with you, raise children and watch them raise their own. I need you with me...forever." Taking a breath, he spoke the words his soul longed to pose. "Will you marry me?"

She jolted, her eyes widening, and then she laughed. Laughed! "You know, Will told me you would say anything to try to get me in bed."

He stared at her, speechless.

"Oh, Ethan." She leaned toward him and pressed her lips against his.

The familiar heat that only her touch could ignite wound its way through his veins, and before he knew it, he'd taken over the kiss. Pressing his body closer, he leaned her back onto the cushions, his hands sliding down to her waist.

Wait a minute.

He broke off the kiss. "Hey, I just asked you to marry me, and you laughed at me."

"Will told me to." She grinned and gave him a quick kiss. "Of course I'll marry you. You're my life."

"I am going to kick his ass," he growled. "How the hell did he know I was even going to ask you to marry me?"

"Do you really want to talk about Will?" Abby asked and unbuttoned her shirt, the creamy flesh beneath capturing his attention. Flicking the front clasp of her bra open, she revealed her luscious breasts, her nipples already erect. She arched toward him, her body seeming to strain for his touch. "Wouldn't you rather start on those babies you were talking about?"

Damn, he loved this woman. "Will who?"

~ABOUT THE AUTHORS~

Though born and raised in the south, L.J. Garland has lived on both the east and west coasts. She adores traveling, the latest adventures added to her Bucket List: Machu Pichu and Australia's Rainforest and Great Barrier Reef.

Married to her best friend for over twenty years, she spends her time home schooling three rambunctious boys, editing in the epub industry, and writing stories that she hopes catches her readers' imaginations as much as the characters and plotlines captivate her. In her spare time (what there is of it LOL), she has a multitude of hobbies, including building archery equipment from scratch and creating stained glass. She has a passion for anything that goes *Boom!*...from fireworks to high-powered combat rifles...it's all good. She and her husband are both rated helicopter pilots and spent their 10th anniversary flying cross-country from east to west coast...an adventure she highly recommends.

A member of RWA, she has several published books, and is hard at work, brainstorming and writing her next romance story.

You can visit L.J. at:
www.lj-garland.com

Born in Wichita Falls, Texas, at the age of two Debbie Gould and her mother moved to New Jersey, spending many happy years on her grandparents' horse farm. You'll sometimes find this setting as a backdrop in her work.

As a teenager, she and her mother found a new home in Vermont, where she currently resides. With a daughter in the Air Force (along with Debbie's six-year-old grandson), and two sons working for the family Well Drilling business, Debbie Gould now shuffles her time between a husband, full time job as a nurse and her writing career.

About seven years ago, while looking at over three hundred treasured books lining her shelves, she realized there was a multitude of stories of her own clamoring for release. Since then, she's seriously persevered in keeping the keyboard in constant motion.

With three published books, Debbie is now working with a partner, L.J. Garland. Together, they have finished one manuscript, *Sins Of the Mind*.

Debbie has been a member of KOD, FTHRW, ELEMENTS and RWA Online.

You can visit Debbie at:
http://authordebbiegould.com

Or Debbie and Laura at:
www.garland-and-gould@blogspot.com

Dead or Alive

Rhykar Evierse has been on the Most Wanted list for years. His attempts to expose the evil deeds of Vast Innovations' founder, Mertan Graiton, has landed him on the wrong end of the law—and on the wrong end of a sexy bounty hunter's pistol. Now, Rhykar's wanted for a murder he didn't commit. Desperate to clear his name, he contacts the one woman who can save him. He hopes she'll give him one night to prove himself.

When Selea Val'keer receives Rhykar's call for help, anger and lust rip through her. How can she be attracted to a criminal? Unable to resist, she accepts his invitation to meet through Madame Evangeline's 1Night Stand service. But what will she do when she sees him again—kiss him or shoot him?

Second Chance by Debbie Gould

Lieutenant Colin Beckett, US Air Force special ops, lost his wife in childbirth while off on a mission. Two years later, he's still trying to come to grips with the guilt that tortures him. And to complicate matters, he finds himself undeniably attracted to his wife's sister, Emily. Struggling with his desire, he tells himself he doesn't deserve a second chance with such an amazing woman.

Emily wants Colin in her life and her bed. Enlisting the help of Colin's teammates and Madame Eve's 1Night Stand dating service, she plans to prove to Colin he can have everything he lost once again.

Will their one night lead to the happy ending she longs for or the loneliness he thinks he deserves?